Nark

By the Same Author

Hack

Snap

John Burns

Nark

MACMILLAN

First published 1999 by Macmillan
an imprint of Macmillan Publishers Ltd
25 Eccleston Place, London SW1W 9NF
Basingstoke and Oxford.
Associated companies throughout the world
www.macmillan.co.uk

ISBN 0 333 74620 1

1 3 5 7 9 8 6 4 2

A CIP catalogue record for this book is available from
the British Library.

Phototypeset by Intype London Ltd
Printed and bound in Great Britain by
Mackays of Chatham plc, Chatham, Kent

To John – who breathed life into Cindy

Acknowledgement

Anyone interested in the dirty business of washing money is strongly recommended to read Jeffrey Robinson's terrific book, *The Laundrymen*, published by Simon & Schuster, 1994.

Chapter One

First off I got frisked. Head to heel. That was just in case I had a Scud missile tucked down my socks. I didn't.

Next they cast a sour eye over my Press card snapshot to see whether I was somebody else. I wasn't.

Then they ruffled through my pockets, but I expect that was just out of plain nosiness. Nothing iffy there either.

Finally they grunted. That meant okay, I could pass.

Sometimes you have to be innocent of an awful lot of things before they let you into an English court of law.

I elbowed through the ruck of uniforms to the double-decker Press box. It was already more than full. But Jena from the *Standard* squeezed up to make room for me. We both enjoyed that.

Everybody had been through the same security sieve on the way in. We didn't complain. It was that sort of trial. We settled back to await the grand opening of the long-awaited Zeller Maine safe deposit case. There was a certain air of expectancy, for we all knew there was some tasty stuff on the menu. A supergrass, no less.

They made us wait for him. They like to do that. We hung around till the fifth day of the trial before they wheeled on their star witness. We sat up and took an interest. We were expecting some blue-jawed, bottle-scarred villain with dodgy eyes. That's the E-Fit of your usual criminal supergrass. Also, we'd already been tipped off by the Crime Squad that they had a big fish on the line. Their cliché, not ours.

So there was a sudden 'oof' of excitement from the Press benches when *she* took the stand. Nobody had expected that.

The mystery woman up there in the French navy suit looked like many things. The one thing she didn't look like was a big fish. She had rusty hair and a palish face. From where I was sitting you couldn't tell the colour of her eyes, but they seemed to match up with the rest of her which was pretty okay. She swivelled her head this way and that, taking in the whole court scene without curiosity. Her gaze lingered for a while on the seven Sarf Londoners cluttering up the dock. That too was not what we've come to expect. Normally supergrasses lock their eyes on the judge, the lady barristers' legs, the wall, anywhere but on the men they're about to grass up.

We sat chewing our pens waiting for them to kick off. They were in no hurry. She didn't seem to mind. I spent the interlude taking her in. We all did. She didn't mind that either. Her head was slightly cocked to one side, waiting for the questions to come. Her mouth, which was on the wide side, was not quite closed. She had her shoulders back but she wasn't stiff. She was still in the sunlit uplands of her thirties. She turned her head full on and gave us a very cool, very level stare. I reciprocated. It might just have been my imagination, but I think her mouth turned up at the edges ever so slightly. She turned away from us again and waited for them to get on with it.

After a minute the clerk dug himself out from underneath a raft of papers and began rattling off the easy questions.

Yes, said the woman in the stand: she was Maureen Amanda Frew, aged thirty-two, of Cymbeline Walk, Godstone. Yes, she agreed, she was the wife of one Barry Dowling Frew. Then she changed her mind and said she was the *estranged* wife of the above. She floated a smile across at us when she said that. We started scribbling.

The Prosecution lead cantilevered himself upright and started on the meaty stuff. He asked, 'Erm, Missus Frew, would you please describe to the court how it transpired that you came to become involved in the handling of the moneys and the other valuables stolen in the course of the Zeller Maine safe deposit robbery on the seventeenth of May of last year.'

Maybe the prosecutor was getting paid by the word.

It took Maureen Frew only a nanosecond to decode the question. Then she got describing.

Two days later she was still describing. In the meantime most of the reporters had filled six notebooks and were in the last throes of writer's cramp. I just wrote down the important bits. Basically they added up to this. She and her husband, the absent

Barry Frew, had helped launder five million in cash and stuff. Furthermore, she could identify the seven men opposite as having done this, that and the other. At this point the seven chipped in with witticisms such as 'You're dead meat, Mo' and 'There's a bullet with your name on it.' I have deleted the expletives. In the cheap seats the villains' kith and kin joined in the fun, causing the judge to play a drum solo with his gavel.

Maureen Frew got a shade frosty around here, but all the while she had two mean and lumpy police minders stationed on either side. They pulled in their bellies, flexed their muscles and narrowed their eyes. She got motoring again.

The Defence did the usual job of calling her a liar, a thief and a general bad lot. You could see she felt the same way about them. She did a lot of smiling, though on the second day of the cross-examination her lips suddenly tightened up.

That happened after a woman brief for Edward Purce, the wheelman in the robbery, said sweetly, 'You are quite sure that Mister Purce was involved?'

Maureen Frew said she was.

'Yet,' said her inquisitor, oozing smiles, 'you have never met him. Is that not correct?'

Supergrass Maureen went super silent.

'Indeed,' said the brief, her beam lighting up the court, 'you have never met *any* of the accused. Is that not also correct?'

Maureen Frew's lips quivered but nothing came out.

'So,' – significant pause – 'how can you claim to know them?'

The brief pushed back a blade of black hair and waited. And waited. Maureen's eyes tightened up in a frown.

'Erm,' she said.

'Yes?'

Her gaze roamed around the courtroom. It fetched up on the face of the prosecutor. He glared up at her. Still nothing. The prosecutor rifled through his papers. Inspiration came at last.

'Because I paid them,' said Mo.

After which she went into a long spiel about how she had given each of them various baubles and twenty grand as a taster of their slice of the loot. She asked the judge if she could consult her notes. The judge, always keen to encourage a pretty witness, said okay. Maureen consulted and came back with the exact dates the payments were made and which banks they were paid into.

For the life of me, I couldn't see the issue here. We'd already had all the payout details on Day One of her evidence. And before that, the Old Bill had thrilled us with how they parted the seven defendants from sundry chunks of jewellery and bank deposit books.

At any rate the woman brief stopped smiling and went and sat down again. She'd earned her crust for the day.

Nobody else had anything useful to say, so they wheeled Mo Frew around and marched her off. Her legs were worth a mention. We all shuffled out for a smoke break while the Prosecution cobbled its closing speech together. I won't bore you with the details. Nor need we bother with the Defence and the judge's summing up. He doesn't half like the sound of his voice, that man.

I missed most of it because I was across the road in Horniman's, drinking drink and filing copy to Babette, the only one of our copytakers who is not aurally challenged. Twenty minutes later when I was lighting into my third Gordons the rest of the Press pack steamed up and rattled off their stuff. And when that was all done, we got down to tackling the main issue of the day: the great end-of-trial sweepstake.

All this involves is guessing when the verdict will be delivered. We *never* gamble on whether the jury will find 'em guilty or otherwise. Only a crazy man would do that. Instead we chip a tenner into the kitty and pick a time and a day. There were fourteen of us playing, so the pot stood at a hundred and forty quid.

The general mood was the jury would give voice the following afternoon, that is Wednesday. My money was for late on Friday. This was no idle hunch. I'd been keeping a sharp eye on the jurors, in particular a tasty brunette and the Jack-the-Lad type to her left. Every now and then they exchanged cutesy little glances which had nothing to do with the evidence before them, but everything to do with the evening ahead of them, cooped up in a hotel. I guessed they were both married elsewhere but they'd like to spin it out to the very last throw. That meant the weekend when they'd have to go home to their regular partners. Call me cynical, but have *you* never wondered how it is that all the monster trials always end on Friday?

Coming up three-thirty, we sent a runner over to the court and he returned with the glad tidings that the judge had sent the jury off for the night. And he reported that the Old Bill too were banking on a Friday verdict. No doubt they'd also been watching the antics of the juror and the jurette. We returned to our glasses.

Some while later my conscience kicked in and I gave News Desk a check call. No, they didn't want to talk to me either. I asked what the big story was for the morrow. They were still working on that one. But the likely lead was all about the bad egg twin sister of a TV soap star found in the gutter. The bad egg sister that is, not the one who opens supermarkets.

I asked News Desk what sort of show I could expect on the supergrass story. They hedged and edged. That meant I'd be lucky if I got a page lead buried way back in the paper. I wasn't bitter. I know the rules of tabloid newspapers: if it's about somebody who appears on TV, it's news. If it concerns someone else, it might just get a paragraph between all those great news stories.

Chapter Two

Just gone three on Wednesday afternoon I kissed goodbye to my tenner. The jury snaked back into their box, causing a headlong stampede from Horniman's. We charged into court huffing and puffing. I gave the jury the once-over. Ten of them were looking mightily pleased with themselves. Two of their number were less than tickled. You know who I'm talking about.

It was a straight guilty call. On all counts. Which gave the judge another chance to air his finely tuned baritone. Behind us in the stalls, the South London Seven's nearest and dearest gnashed their teeth, bewailed, bemoaned and generally behaved like they were on the Jerry Springer Show.

Mister Justice Courtney Larkin pretended not to hear. He weighed off the gang for a total of 132 years, which in real time meant about four years apiece.

He also took time out to congratulate the Old Bill and 'those who have contributed in no small measure to the unmasking of this sinister conspiracy'. That meant Maureen Amanda Frew. It was all wasted because Mo was nowhere around.

I left the agency reporters to pick up feedback from the villains' aggrieved next of kin. With our deadlines,

I don't have time to hang about for that. Anyway I could make up better quotes myself.

I legged it out onto Tooley Street and straight into Balls Brothers where I had a quick sharpener before piecing it all together in my head. I got through to Winifred on Copy. Care in the Community is all very well, but sticking somebody like Winifred on Copy is just taking the mick.

I pushed the story right to the edge, but not so much that anyone would notice. Roughly speaking this is how I played it:

MO the Grass was in hiding last night with SEVEN death sentences hanging over her.

Gang leaders vowed bloody revenge after her evidence caged the men who looted £5 million in the Zeller Maine robbery.

I got this far before Winifred chimed in. 'Is there much more of this?'

Yes there is. Reams and reams of it. I took a pull on my Bensons and cracked on.

But the ruthless masterminds of the daring raid are still on the run.

And they are determined to track down and murder the stunning redhead who broke the underworld's code of silence.

Friends of the seven crooks jailed by Mo Frew's testimony have also sworn to even the score.

A senior police officer said: 'She will spend the rest of her life looking over her shoulder.'

Winifred heaved her bosoms and let loose a sigh. That meant she was bored. I don't know about you, but I thought it was a ripping yarn.

I ignored her and ploughed on. Some twenty minutes later it was all through. Winifred clicked off and got back to her knitting. I checked in with News Desk. This time they were willing to talk to me. Angela Whipple, my fragrant News Editor, said, 'I'm going through it now. Looks like you've missed a few things.'

I examined my fingernails. 'Such as?'

'You haven't said where the five million is.'

That was largely because neither I nor the assembled hordes of Scotland Yard had the faintest idea where it might be hiding itself. But you can't explain that sort of thing to a News Editor. It takes too long. Therefore I just lied.

'They got it offshore as soon as Mo switched sides. The betting is it's been laundered through shell companies in the Turks and Caicos islands.'

I'd already lost her. 'The where?'

'The West Indies.'

Angie had heard of them. 'Oh. Well you'd better give us a line on that, and what the police are doing to recover the money.'

Yes, Angie.

I said, 'Anything else?'

She didn't think so but I had to check back in twenty minutes.

So that was the newser done and dusted. I'd already filed the backgrounders two weeks before the trial started. For the uninitiated, the newser is the up-to-the-very-minute story. The backgrounders, which you can also call waffle, are long chunks on the various players. I'd filed a stack on Maureen Frew, no mean feat, considering I knew slightly less than nothing about her. I'd also pasted together a profile on Mr Big himself, Dave Stretch. That was mostly crafted from crumbs dropped by the Crime Squad. There was a yard of equally imaginative tosh because we – like all the other red tops – were going mega on this one. Maybe all our editors had kept their lolly in Zeller Maine. I'd like to think so anyway.

I stuck it out in Balls Brothers for another longish hour, giving Angela Whipple the occasional trill to check that all was hunky-dory. It wasn't. She had spotted another major omission in my crackling crisp copy: I had not revealed the current whereabouts of Maureen Frew.

Sometimes you wonder what these Desk people are on.

Anyways, the calls finally tailed off. Her last broadcast was: 'Nice job, Max. Now go off and enjoy yourself.'

I did.

It was late, way, way too late in the evening and I was feeling no pain. I was in Hamptons, a drinkerie which likes to pretend it's a kosher wine bar. It is nothing of the sort. It's a festering cesspit piled to the rafters with ambulance-chasing lawyers and tabloid reporters. That's the only good thing that can be said of Hamptons: nobody holds the moral high ground, so the rack-it-up lawyers and the make-it-up hacks get along okay.

By day I'm a crime reporter, no, let's not be coy here, I'm the Chief Crime Correspondent of your favourite tabloid. By night I'm the same thing only I drink more.

On the night under review I was at my well-worn corner of the fake marble bar, tilting a glass or two with Susannah who is one of the perks of our trade.

Susannah is a hack too, though not a staffer. She mostly freelances as a reporter around the Fleet Street red tops except when times are rough and she has to bite the bullet and put in a shift at the *Observer* or one of the other comics.

Susannah has big blue double-glazed eyes which seem to get bigger and bluer the more you drink, or maybe it's the more she drinks. She also has the rest of the gear to go with the eyes and she likes to let you know it. At any rate, there comes a stage in the evening when you start forgetting there's another woman out there who would slit your gizzard if she knew you were knocking it back with Susannah.

This was the stage I'd hit.

Susannah leaned a smidgeon closer and let her hair flop into my face. It smelled of flowers and cigarettes. She said, 'I like you, Max. You make me laugh.'

I had one half-sober brain cell still awake. It said, 'Uh-oh.'

Susannah didn't hear it. She just laced her china fingers through mine and did that thing with her eyes.

It was around here I realized she was a stiff gin or seven ahead of me in the drinking stakes. She's usually like that. I also remembered she had just junked her wimp boyfriend. I suppose the decent thing to do was to whistle up a taxi and pour what was left of her into it. I wasn't feeling decent. I called for another matching pair of Gordons. Susannah tucked into her ration, all the while keeping me locked in her blue glaze. Then she started turning my hand over and looking at it like she was Madame Zingazangazoo, ace fortune-teller.

'That's your love line,' she said, tracking a high-gloss fingernail from the heel of my palm to the foot-hills of my index finger.

I said, 'And what does it say?'

Susannah put on a purry voice. 'It tells me—'

Alas I will never know. At that very moment Tommy, my alleged mate from the *Express*, bellied up and dropped a fistful of meal receipts on the bar between us.

He said, 'Are these any use to you?'

Lust went clean out the window and fingers were rapidly disengaged as Susannah and I scrabbled for the spoils. I won hands down. She ended up with two bills. I had six or seven.

'You're a rat,' she said. Only her word had seven letters in it. I relented and gave her one of my bills. Well, it was from a restaurant in Saffron Walden dated last Friday and I already had a legit bill for the day. Besides, there was no way I could con the office into thinking I'd gone to Saffron Walden when I'd spent Friday down Southwark Crown Court on the Maureen Frew case.

Susannah was singularly unimpressed by my generosity.

She said, 'How am I supposed to charge this up to expenses?'

Frankly that was her problem, but I'm a helpful

soul. 'Just tell them you were entertaining a contact for info on crooked antique dealers.'

'Antique dealers? Why them?'

Honestly, sometimes you have to explain every little thing. I said patiently, 'Because Saffron Walden is Lovejoy territory. Remember the lovable rogue on the TV series?'

Tommy said, 'Yeh. Ian McKellen, wasn't it?'

We ignored him. Susannah was still acting peeved. 'You forget I'm a freelance. I can't stick in a bill unless I have a story to back it up.'

I lit a Bensons. 'Write one then.'

The big blue eyes boggled. 'Write one? You mean make it up?'

As if she'd never invented a quote before.

I said, 'Just stick together a story which looks *nearly* good enough to print.'

Susannah said, 'What happens if they do print it?'

'Make it vague enough so that no one can track it down or catch you out.'

She sat back and thought about that one.

Tommy chipped in. 'Better still, make it good enough to run, get it in the paper.'

Susannah and I turned to stare at him. The same lunatic idea was chasing through our heads. Subbing it down to two words, it was: why not? After all, half the stuff you get to read while you're munching your Frosto Superpops is pure invention anyways, especially the political and showbiz tosh.

Susannah echoed, 'Make it good enough to run.'

I was otherwise engaged lining up a bottle of roguish house red for Tommy. But I was thinking.

Usually when you verbal someone or dream up a senior police source you do it in the context of a real story: all you're doing is tickling the thing up. But Tommy's wizard wheeze meant the whole story had to be sheer Mickey Mouse.

Susannah had run up against the same fence. She said, 'So what's the story about?'

Tommy who had already been revving up his tonsils elsewhere weighed in with a plot to flood Britain with illegal immigrants by shipping them over in antique wardrobes.

'Be serious,' said Susannah.

Tommy retired hurt.

I suggested a variation, whereby the crooks stuffed kilos of coke down the back of Louis Soixante-neuf *chaises longues*.

She didn't like that one either. So I forgot her and started swopping the latest Fleet Street slanders with Tommy. We were midway through a yarn about the newly-fired circulation manager at the *Mirror* and a man who was not his wife when Susannah piped up, 'I've got it.'

I made her wait until I'd told Tommy every gory detail before I let her spill out her hot little heart. She said, 'It's all to do with art forgeries. There's some master forger somewhere and he's churning out all these Constables and things.'

'Michelangelos,' Tommy supplied, still not quite with us.

I said, 'And who's your contact?'

'Contact?'

I prodded the Saffron Walden bill with my finger. 'That's what all this is supposed to be about.'

Ooops. She'd overlooked that bit. She suggested, 'A copper?'

No. Not a copper. Scotland Yard has its own Fine Art squad and they just might ask embarrassing questions about who this copper was.

I said, 'Make him a dealer. That way you don't have to pin him down to any specific area. He could even be foreign.'

Susannah said, 'Why he? What's wrong with him being a woman?'

I said, 'Because women don't buy drinks.'

She took the hint and shouted for emergency gin refills. I sploshed out the tonics because I'm good at that.

Susannah said, 'Anyway, *my* contact is a woman. What do you think I should call her?'

She turfed out Joan Smith (from Tommy) and Paula Peroni (from me).

'Why Peroni?' she asked.

Because that's the name of a frothy little lager they cook up in Italy, I explained. And that set us all thinking. We gazed across the bar for enlightenment.

'I can't call her Cindy Budweiser,' Susannah said. She seemed to have settled the first name anyway.

So we ran the gamut. Cindy Gordon, Cindy Haig, Cindy Ballantine, Cindy Daniels, Cindy Smirnov. Tommy had tired of the game. 'Just call her Cinderella.'

'That's it,' said Susannah.

'What? Cinderella?' from us.

She said, 'Don't be stupid. Cindy *Reilly*.'

'Oh.'

After that we fell to inventing an age (thirty), marital status (single) and job (freelance art valuer). Apart from the art valuer line, Cindy Reilly had an awful lot in common with Susannah.

She meanwhile had developed a cool and calculating look around the eyes. 'And what do you two give me if I get this story in one of the papers?'

I thought we'd already been through that. She got a buckshee sixty quid restaurant bill from Saffron Walden. But she wanted more. Much more. In the end it came down to a bottle of Hamptons pretend champagne from each of us.

A stray brainwave nudged me. 'And if I mention somebody called Cindy Reilly in any story I write, I get a bottle too.'

'And me too,' said Tommy.

Susannah beat us down to a large gin apiece. I summoned up another round to seal the deal with due solemnity. We drank to the health and good fortune of our brainchild.

And thus at 10.55 on Wednesday 14 June Cindy Reilly was conceived and born. Hers turned out to be a tragically short life.

But it was fun while it lasted.

Chapter Three

Roughly about the same time that I was getting airborne, Maureen Frew was heading that way too. The big difference was it took a plane to get her flying.

I wasn't there to see her off, but later I got to talk to all who were. So what follows is a reconstruction of the actual event. Maybe I've egged it up a bit, but here's the general picture.

They sneaked Mo out in the thick end of the night when no one was looking because that's the way they do these things. She was not alone. On her left was Clovis, the main minder. To her right was Kay, the minor minder. And bringing up the rear was Stan Defoe, whose only claim to fame was that he was keeping the sheets warm now that Maureen's husband had gone AWOL.

The foursome trekked straight across the departure lounge at RAF Brize Norton, their eyes fixed dead ahead. Maureen was dressed down for the occasion in a plain black business suit. She couldn't do anything about her rusty hair so she copped a fair sprinkling of leers from the passing lechers.

Clovis led them to a sawn-off room which served as the VIP lounge. They were the only people there.

Kay played mum at the courtesy bar. She rubbed her hands and put on her brightest smile. 'Right, then. What's everybody having?'

Maureen gave the bar a cool appraisal. 'Orange juice – providing it's fresh orange.'

Stan Defoe pushed the boat out. 'I'll have a Bacardi and Coke. A double.' Anything free, he was first in line.

Clovis just shook his head no.

Even here, with half the British Army clogging up the terminal, they were taking no chances. Both Clovis and Kay had guns. Both had a still alertness about them. If she was feeling edgy, Maureen wasn't showing it. She sat in one of the easy chairs, her nose stuck in a woman's glossy, like she was at her local hair salon.

The most lively member of the quartet was Kay, a spiky blonde with wideawake eyes. She had big round granny glasses, more for show than anything else. They made her eyes bigger and her face small and perky. You would have paid her a lot of attention if Maureen hadn't been there. Kay was decked out in a floppy grey sweatshirt and jeans. She took up position in the chair next to Maureen's, stretched out her legs and tucked one ankle over the other. She didn't look much like an armed policewoman.

They had a couple of hours to waste before they got out. Stan Defoe was good at killing time. He stood by the steel-framed window and watched the crimson and purple bleed from the sky. After that it got dark and there was only the runway lights and the occasional tailplane to gawp at.

He had the build of a middleweight, encased in a navy mohair job. The lemon shirt looked like it too had cost him a few bob. His eyes were hidden behind Carlos the Jackal specs. He hadn't shaved since the morning and his chin was already blue. He stood with his back to the others, just staring out the window and sometimes sipping his Bacardi.

Clovis watched Stan Defoe out of the side of his eyes. He didn't say anything, but he was thinking what Barry Frew would do to Maureen's boyfriend, given the skin of a chance. Defoe didn't seem bothered. He turned round to face the others. Kay saw his glass was empty. She said, 'Another drink?'

'Why not?' Defoe stuck out the glass. There was a brief flash of teeth in the square face. Kay poured him a triple.

Clovis didn't like Defoe. But then Clovis had been born with a deep contempt for his fellow man. Anything he had seen along the way had only confirmed his prejudices. He was already bored. Defoe felt just the same. They'd been cooped up together in the safe house for almost a month now and he didn't much like Clovis either.

Criminal Intelligence had sucked Maureen dry of all the good stuff and she wasn't into small talk. Stan left most of the yakking up to her, for she was the star of the show. But sometimes he would rabbit to Kay. He never said anything of consequence.

Clovis stood a couple of yards off to one side, looking out through the glass panel in the door towards the rows of hard orange seats in the departure lounge. He was thin, somewhere in his mid-forties, with a long jaw hanging off his ears and hard little black stones for eyes. They were always wary, but never nervous. He wore a dark brownish grey suit with a muddy green shirt and a skinny tie. Clovis liked to be anonymous in an ugly sort of way.

Stan Defoe came over to join him. 'So how much will all this cost?'

He already knew the answer.

Clovis said, 'Half a million, and then some.'

Stan said, 'You got your money's worth.'

That one didn't even deserve an answer. Clovis turned away.

In the VIP lounge the night trickled past. The mood was about as lively as in a crematorium chapel. Whatever everyone was thinking, they didn't feel like sharing it. Especially not Clovis. He was working out the percentages of getting Maureen on her own. The calculations were complicated by the fact that he and Kay had been enjoying themselves in the safe house. Kay was not the sort of girl to let you off easily.

A faraway chime sounded, signalling that the Akrotiri flight was now boarding. Maureen resurfaced. 'Is that us?'

Without looking round Clovis said, 'Yeh.'

Kay chipped in, 'Well, let's go then.'

Clovis turned to face her. 'Go get a book or something. It's a long flight.'

'What are we waiting for?'

Clovis pulled the tickets out of his pocket. Maureen was down on the manifest as a medic with the Nursing Corps. She was travelling as a Dr D. Lawn. As in grass. Somebody in the Crime Squad probably thought that was funny.

The chime chipped in again. Clovis stayed precisely where he was.

Kay said, 'Shouldn't we make a move?'

'We wait.'

They waited until a crocodile of soldiers filtering through the gate was down to its last two or three men. Only then, and without hurrying, Clovis started walking. He led the other three back through the departure hall. Out of habit he stuck close to the wall.

When they reached the gate everyone else had gone through. The WAAF checking the manifest clicked her teeth in irritation. Clovis stared coldly at her. 'Something wrong with your dentures?'

The WAAF opened her mouth to say something snotty. Clovis was looking her hard in the eye. She changed her mind.

Now they were on the tarmac and walking to the plane. It was a clapped-out, bashed-about knackered old Hercules. He'd expected as much. They walked under its bloated tail to the single flight of steps leading up into its belly. Clovis was still in the front, with Maureen tucked in behind him. Stan brought up the rear. His shoes clanked on the steel of the steps.

At the top of the ramp Clovis swung left up inside the plane. Maureen didn't even pause for a last look back at England. She lowered herself into what the RAF call an aircraft seat, a plain canvas sling backing onto the dimly lit fuselage.

Clovis said to Defoe, 'You'll need these.' He handed him a plastic sachet holding what looked like two dayglo-yellow filter-tips.

Defoe cocked an eyebrow. 'Why?'

'To stick in your ears. This thing isn't pressurized.'

'What else do I need to know?'

'No food, no drinks, no in-flight movie. And if you need a pee, that's where you do it.'

He aimed a finger at a transparent plastic bag hanging against the fuselage.

Defoe said, 'You're taking the piss.'

Clovis said, 'No, *that* takes the piss.' And for the first time that night he smiled.

The Hercules lumbered down the runway, a great ungainly brute of a thing. The roar from its turbo-props vibrated throughout its unlovely frame and the passengers swayed in their canvas slings. And then somehow it was airborne, swimming lazily above the silent fields of Oxfordshire.

Maureen Frew had her eyes closed, her lips slightly parted. Kay was flicking through her discarded magazine.

Stan Defoe said, 'So now I'm an exile.'

But Clovis had his ear-plugs in and nobody heard him.

Chapter Four

The morning after is a bummer of an idea. It's right up there with hair gel and Liebfraumilch. Though maybe if you're really stuck you could get used to Liebfraumilch. You never get used to the morning after.

This particular a.m. was giving me the usual gyp. I wakened with extreme care and cautiously put myself back together again. I faked a smile into the bathroom mirror and dolloped on an extra layer of shaving foam.

There was nothing for breakfast in my fridge, apart from something called wheat germ, a half-empty tub of yoghurt, and a hunk of low-fat cheese, all of which belonged to Rosie. I'll explain Rosie when we both feel up to it. Anyways, I wasn't hungry, so I just got busy with the tea bags. After three cups of Waitrose's finest I got down to the dirty job of reading the papers. And if you don't think that's a dirty job, you just try raking through fourteen acres of newsprint without ending up looking like a coal miner.

I read our own great organ first, just to make sure that the subs had spelled my name right. Yep, there it was on the splash and over a couple of inside pages. They'd lifted a chunk from my main newser and run it as a sidebar story under the head: BLONDE GUN

GIRL SET TO BLOW MO. Its basic thrust was that a mystery hitwoman, of the platinum persuasion, had been offered a hundred thousand pound contract to blow Maureen Frew's red head off. And if you think I'm making that up, let me tell you we crime hacks had to pour lashings of drink into one of the Robbery Squad officers until he agreed that just might be true. So there.

All the tabloid reporters ran with more or less the same stuff. Except for Clive at the *Mirror*, who described the hitgirl as 'a raven-haired killer, branded the Black Widow'. Clive gets carried away sometimes.

Our reports also ran a brief reprise of the Zeller Maine safe deposit job, partly to pad out the story but mostly because our editors truly believe the average reader has the memory bank of a goldfish with Alzheimer's. Basically it was a straight-up-and-downer raid. Apart from the size of the whack it wasn't worth talking about. You get more excitement when somebody turfs a brick through a shop window. But just for the benefit of any goldfish out there, this is how it went down. A year ago, on the Saturday morning of the spring bank holiday weekend, a security guard at the Zeller Maine blockhouse in Cheapside nipped out the back door for a crafty smoke. Before he even got his fags out, another bloke, dressed just like him, stuck a gun in his ear and threatened serious mischief. The real guard played it sensible and did what he was told to do. So the guard, the fake guard and an assorted mob of geezers in balaclavas shuffled through the back door. En route they knocked out the closed circuit camera at the door before proceeding to a small room on the ground floor where there was absolutely nothing of value or interest, especially no spy camera.

So far, so humdrum. But here's where the robbers got creative. They made the security guard call up his mates to tell them he'd just found a right little raver and her boss cavorting buck naked in the room. The others thundered up to see the fun, whereupon the gang relieved them of their keys and trussed them up. For the next four hours the baddies called the place their own until they'd emptied all the little piggy banks. After which, they scarpered.

And that, in a dozen or so lines is the whole story; a story which it took us fifty zillion words to cover. But then a safe deposit job is always good for copy because you can speculate your head off about what was in the vaults and nobody can say you're wrong. Among the more imaginative contributions was a shipment of heroin, belonging to the Russian Mafia, and a pile of naughty photos of somebody famous, belonging to a blackmailer.

The Old Bill were baffled. But there's nothing new in that so we had to make up stories that they were on the trail of various sinister Mr Bigs. They never even rang us up to say thanks.

That's where the story languished for many a month, while the Law went around giving every known lowlife a bad time. Still nothing. Then one morning a redhead accompanied by a hawkish lawyer checked herself into the Zeller Maine Robbery Squad at Cannon Row nick. 'I'm Maureen Frew,' she said.

'So?' they said.

'My husband is Barry Frew.'

'Who he?'

Maureen crossed her legs, straightened her skirt, and said, 'Well, let's talk about Dave Stretch instead.'

When they heard that name the assorted detectives stopped scratching their brains and sat up: they'd had Stretch in the frame early on, because he had a bit of form. But they'd nothing really to connect him. Not until now.

They didn't interrupt as she spilled it all out. Stretch was the mastermind. Her hubby, Barry Frew, was the main moneyman on the Zeller Maine job. She knew that because she, dutiful wife that she was, helped him do it. Their contribution was to launder the spoils – she put the figure at five million-plus. Though to the big-eared Robbery boys that sounded a shade modest. Anyway, Maureen told them that everything went as planned, but for one minor hiccup. Her husband had legged it with some little rascal, forgetting to pay Maureen her bit. And when she tried to put the squeeze on his friends, they offered to head-cap her. So here she was, out to get even, providing the Law gave her an airline ticket to the ends of the earth and a whole new identity. Oh, and she wanted the same deal for her new-found boyfriend, Stan Defoe, who had nothing to do with anything.

The Old Bill stashed both of them in a safe house and let Maureen rattle away to her heart's content. Along the way she also told them that the other baddies were X, Y, Z, etc. So early next morning the detectives jumped into their cars and went banging on doors all over South London. In the end they collared seven of the gang, including the real security guard. Now why does that not surprise you? But Dave Stretch and Barry Frew were nowhere to be found. And the money was stashed in countries the police had never even heard of.

That brings us right up to yesterday afternoon, when the seven blaggers were shipped off to Belmarsh, Durham, the Scrubs and any other nick you can think of. And off Maureen went to God knows where.

So that's the story everyone regurgitated, apart from slight embellishments. A broadsheet, which will remain nameless, but just for the hell of it we'll call the *Guardian*, reported that the Zeller Maine security guard was 'confronted by a man brandishing a gnu'.

The *Independent* threw open a whole features page to who and what was Maureen Frew. There was a stonking great headline, GRASS ROOTS, and under that about a thousand words of copy. This is how it started:

HER former school pals at Bertherton Secondary remember her for one paradoxical reason: there was nothing memorable about Maureen Frew.

No, I didn't understand that either. But I got the scissors out and snipped the page for future reference, for you never know when these things might come in handy. I folded the cutting and neatly filed it away in my briefcase.

So much for the day's dirty work. I went and showered the carbon out of my pores and got myself kitted out in a low-key two-piece. By now I was almost human again. I was also running late.

But even as I opened the door, the wall phone gave a nervous br-rringg. I had one foot out, the other all set to follow. My curiosity reeled me back in.

'Hello?' I said, laying particular emphasis on the question mark.

'You missed a great party last night.'

Rosie.

I thought we'd agreed not to get round to her until later. I said, 'I did?'

She said, 'You should have been there; where were you anyway?'

As if she didn't know already. I said, 'I was hauled in to help out on the Nazi gold story.'

She said, 'No you weren't. You were down in Hamptons again.'

See – I told you.

This was not going anywhere I wanted it to go. I put on a bright and biffy voice. 'Anyway, what's the plans for tonight? Do I come and see you or vice versa?'

She said, 'What do you have in mind?'

Here is one of life's golden rules: you will never beat women at the ask-a-question game. They invented it.

I said, 'We could always rent a video and sit around watching it with a glass in hand.'

Rosie has a nose as fine as porcelain, with nostrils to match. But she can snort like a tuba. 'Can't you think of anything to do that doesn't involve drink?'

Not a lot.

I said, 'All right, whatever you're doing, count me in.'

She went quietish. 'Well, Hannah and Matt are having a dinner party . . .'

I said, 'Apart from a dinner party.'

She fired back, 'I'll talk to you when you've got over your hangover.'

And the phone went ker-plunk. That meant I had a fight on my hands, or at the very least a small ice age, during which she would pout and frown and at the end of which I'd agree to sit across the table at some Godawful dinner party where people yakked on about nothing worth yakking about. The good news was that afterwards she'd make it up to me.

And so, eventually, to work. As I breezed into the newsroom, I saw Angela Whipple was absent from her slot on News Desk. No doubt she was off sucking her Biro in morning conference. In her absence, the whole show was in the incapable hands of her deputy, Nige. He tossed me a sideways glance and then made a big deal out of staring at the wall clock. Nige is everything Angie is not. He's nasty, ugly and stupid. He'll probably go far. I ignored him, squeezed a plastic cup of tea from the machine and headed off for my distant corner.

There is a sort of vague rule in newspapers: if you've just finished a long, long job, such as the supergrass trial, they let you take it easy for a day. More, if you're lucky. Therefore today I was anticipating nothing more strenuous than lunch with my mates. I dragged the phone towards me and began ringing around.

I was on my third or so call when Nige materialized off my left shoulder, a piece of paper in his mitt. He *always* has a piece of paper in his mitt. Maybe it's his pet.

I put down the phone. Nige said, 'I've got a goodie for you.'

This was a blatant lie. Nige never has a goodie for anybody. I gave a less than enthusiastic grunt.

He pretended not to notice. 'I'm just giving you an early warning shout. The *Star* have a big one on the go for Monday. We'll probably want you to catch up on it over the weekend.'

Terrific.

I said, 'What is it?'

'We haven't got all the details, but you know Vincent Sohn?'

Intimately. I always spend my afternoons watching some floppy-wristed TV cook bashing his pots about.

Nige said, 'He's supposed to be having it off with a kid.'

I had to ask. 'Is that a male kid, a female kid or just the usual billy goat variety?'

Not even a flicker. 'He's got himself tangled up with some underage girl. We don't have a name for her yet but we hope to hear this afternoon.'

I said, 'Why me?'

'Why you what?'

You have to explain everything to Desk people. I said, 'Nige, I cover crime. Vincent Sohn isn't exactly a master criminal. Isn't this one for news, or maybe showbiz?'

He pulled executive rank. 'Sex with a minor is crime.'

Oh all right, if you put it like that.

I said, 'So what do you want me to do?'

'We'll need a spoiler on the *Star* story. If we can't

get to Sohn or the girl, maybe you'll be able to track down a relative or an ex-girlfriend or something.'

That was a very big maybe. But I didn't kick.

Nige said, 'We'll probably know more in an hour or so. I'll brief you then.'

I said, 'Where are we getting this from?'

Nige put a long finger against his long nose. 'Can't say, old boy. Need to know basis only.' And off he sloped back to Desk trying to look smart.

Need to know. I had a good old growl. What he meant was that I was outside the loop and not privileged enough to be told our source. He must think I'm as thick as he is. I already guessed where our info came from. Somebody on the *Star*, somebody in the Desk Mafia, had called in the tip.

We are locked in mortal combat with the *Star*. So why would someone there spill the beans to us? The answer is sordid but simple. Sacking is an occupational hazard for all Desk executives. They have the life expectancy of the average ace kamikaze pilot. When they get the chop, they look around for some other fool to give them a job. It helps if the other fool owes them a favour. So when someone on the *Star* leaked the Vincent Sohn story, he or she was simply building up insurance. The chances were the mole had also tipped off the *Mirror*, the *Sun* and everyone else, for Desk people need all the insurance they can get.

I keyed myself in to our library machine and turned up all we had on Sohn. So far his lovelife hadn't been all that wonderful. His one and only wife had done a runner with his chief bottle-washer or somebody. But Sohn still had Zoo, his ritzy rake-off restaurant round the back of Shepherd's Market. It was a smoke-free zone. I was beginning to see why his missus gave him the heave. In between fiddling his customers, Sohn had found time to rattle off a best-seller on the nosh dished up at his restaurant. And guess what he called it? That's right, *Feeding Time at the Zoo*. Somehow I managed not to split my sides. That's just about all there was in our files, except for stuff like his age (anything from thirty-six to forty-four), his birthplace (Stavanger), and his TV show. It didn't say anything about how he kept his year-round tan or why he owned a moustache.

I switched off the library machine. I was already bored with Vincent Sohn. Besides, it was nudging lunchtime and my tonsils were clamouring for a work-out. I stopped by News Desk and told them I was heading out for a quick one. Angie, back in her rightful place, knows just how long my quick ones can last, but she just said, 'Okay, as long as you've got your mobile with you.'

I teamed up with a motley assortment of crime hacks at the Blackfriar's. It's not my favourite pub, but it's handy, should our respective News Editors suddenly feel the urge to whip us back to Docklands. It is also part of the real world. I settled in with a Gordons and promptly forgot everything I'd ever known about Vincent Bloody Sohn. It was easy because everyone else was in swashbuckling form, having nothing better to do than drink the day dry. Thus we continued for the best part of an hour until my mobile chattered into life. Suddenly Vincent B. Sohn sprung to mind.

'Yes,' I barked into the mobile.

'Put that woman down, Chard. I've got a great wee story for you.'

I relaxed. It wasn't Desk. It was Mac. He's my very own tame Plod who tips me off whenever the Old Bill have a hot one on their hands.

I said, 'It's not a woman. It's your wife.'

Mac cackled. 'Me? A wife? That'd be a fine thing.'

This is horribly true. Mac is more interested in having some other bloke's wife than one of his own.

I said, 'Cut to the chase. What's the story?'

'You'd better get your skates on. This only happened about half an hour ago—'

'What—'

'—Hold your horses. Three fellas have just been shot in a car at Coldharbour Lane. What you lot call a drive-by killing. Two dead so far, and the other one's not too clever either.'

I jumped in. 'Drugs?'

'Looks that way, but there's something funny going on. The Intelligence boys are involved and there's a lot of people running around in here like headless chickens.'

Mac works in New Scotland Yard so I'd have imagined he'd regard that sort of thing as normal.

I said, 'Maybe they were coppers.'

'You're a sick man, Max Chard. They're not ours.'

'Whose are they then?'

'Give me an hour and I might know. I'll keep you filled in when I get to hear the rest of it.'

I said, 'I take it this is not an exclusive tip-off?'

Another cackle. 'What? At the money your paper pays? Do me a favour and pass it on to the rest of the lads. And don't forget to get me a credit on it.' He went away.

I turned to my partners in crime hackery and told all. Even the bit about crediting Mac with a tip-off fee. There then followed a brief but intense discussion. If you had been in the Blackfriar's that lunchtime you would have seen the Gentlemen of the Press at their most gentlemanly.

The deal was this: Mark on the *Sun*, Clive on the *Mirror* and Dhiran on the *Telegraph* would head back east and start hitting the phones. The rest of us would hammer down to Coldharbour Lane. And around four o'clock, we'd fill each other in.

We collared a couple of taxis and shot off south. En route I rang News Desk to tell them to wake up the Picture Desk and send a snapper. I got Nige who whinged and said: 'This means we've got to get somebody else to do the Vincent Sohn piece.'

You could tell by his tone he reckoned I'd done the killings just to get out of chasing Sohn.

It was easy to find the murder spot. Half the police cars in London were clogging up the approach roads. So far they hadn't dug out a Press liaison officer so they had to lie to us themselves. The closest we could get to the scene was about fifty yards off. The death car, shrouded in a tarpaulin, was being winched onto a transporter. Assorted Plods were down on their hands and knees drawing pretty chalk circles round shell casings.

I flashed my Press pass at a pink-cheeked inspector. 'What sort of car was it?'

'I can't tell you.'

I had another go.

'What colour, then?'

'I can't tell you.'

I said, 'Is colour blindness hereditary or does it come free with the job?'

He snarled and turned his back on us. But you get used to this. Instead I hunted around for some intelligent eyewitnesses. There were too many by far.

'It was a white van,' said the bloke from the doner kebab.

I pointed at the transporter. Even under the tarpaulin you could see it was a car, not a van.

'Nah, not *that* one: the one that did the shooting.'

Oh.

And how many men were in it?

'Three.'

'The white van?'

'Nah. The car.'

Let's start again. 'What sort of car?'

The other witnesses got in on the act. According to them it was variously a Merc, a Ford Scorpio, a Datsun, a Rover, and so forth. The one thing it wasn't was a Rolls or a Mini. They also agreed it was red. We were getting somewhere.

After about twenty minutes I thought I had it. The red car was coasting up to the lights with three men aboard, two up front, one in the back. They were all white. The white van, carrying two men, equally white, was drifting along on their tail. Suddenly it whisked out, pulled alongside them and stopped. The van door opened, out jumped a bloke with a shooter. Judging by the descriptions it was an Uzi or suchlike. He poked the gun through the driver's open window and let rip. Two seconds later he'd emptied the magazine and was hopping back into the van, and off it screeched in the general direction of Brixton. Neither the gunman nor his driver was masked. But the gunman had a baseball cap with its peak hiding his mug. And that's the whole thing.

There were a couple of perplexing items in there. Drive-by drug shootings don't normally occur until after dark. Item two: white drug dealers don't normally get shot in Brixton. I pushed my musings aside because a Press liaison bod had finally showed up. He had only two nuggets of information. The death car was an Audi and the third victim had been airlifted to St Thomas's hospital. We piled back into our cabs and returned to base. The other hacks, who had been doing the phone checks, had nothing much to share.

I sat down at my console and started cobbling together the story.

POLICE were last night braced for bloody gang warfare after three suspected drug barons were gunned down in broad daylight.

You can fill in the rest yourself. It was bubbling along nicely when my phone burbled. Mac. Mac hails originally from somewhere in Ulster. I say this just so that you understand why he speaks the way he does.

He said, 'Have you ever heard tell of Benny "Belly" Sloman?'

Strangely I hadn't.

Mac said, 'He was the front-seat passenger.'

I said, 'Let me make a guess. He's fat. He's a man known to the police. He flogs drugs for a living.'

'Hey, boy, two out of three isn't bad. You're coming along.'

I said, 'So what am I missing?'

'He was fat. He was a villain. But his racket wasn't drugs.'

'What was it?'

'Thieving, blagging, GBH, attempted murder, breaking and entering. The whole heap.'

'Except drugs.'

'Except drugs.'

There followed a silence at his end. I said, 'All right, out with it. What's the rest?'

'Ach, you know me. I always save the best till last. I told you he was a known blagger, right?'

Mac likes to string these things out. I lit a cigarette and waited.

'Well, just you guess who he did the blagging for?'

I guessed the Reverend Ian Paisley. Wrong guess.

'Dave Stretch.'

I blinked. 'What? Zeller Maine? *That* Dave Stretch?'

Yup. That one.

I was thinking it through but I couldn't tie up the ends. I said, 'Did Sloman grass too?'

'No. The whisper is that he was up to his neck in the Zeller Maine job, but there wasn't the evidence.'

That made even less sense. I said, 'I thought Maureen Frew narked up all of them.'

'Maybe she didn't have enough on Belly Sloman. Or the others.'

'What others?'

'The other two in the car, you eejit.'

'They were in the Dave Stretch mob too?'

'That's the word. Might have been that he wanted to cut them out of their share. I haven't got their names yet. But you can see why everybody's going ballistic in the Robbery Squad. Call you later.'

Click.

I stared at the screen in front of me. On it were a dozen sharp-edged paragraphs about a drugs war, not a single word of it true. I wiped the lot and started again. Or tried to. The trouble was I had no idea where to start. Nothing hung together. *If* the three were in on the Zeller Maine caper, why did Maureen Frew not grass them up? Maybe Mac was right. There just wasn't enough evidence on them for a *prima facie*. That left the big question unanswered: who popped them?

In the end I took the easy way out. I blamed Dave Stretch. Thus:

RUTHLESS gang boss Dave Stretch yesterday ordered the point-blank murder of his three top henchmen.

The trio were cut down in a drive-by shooting in broad daylight.

Underworld hard man Benny 'The Belly' Sloman and another gangster died in a hail of machinegun bullets.

Last night the third victim was desperately clinging to life in an intensive care unit.

All three were linked with the £5 million Zeller Maine robbery which Stretch masterminded.

And as armed police hunted the hitman, a senior officer said: 'It looks like he got greedy and had them topped so he didn't have to pay them their share.'

And much more in similar vein. Any nit-pickety lawyers out there might deem the above a vile and unwarranted slur on the good name of Dave Stretch. True. But I didn't care. The one thing I knew for sure was that he wouldn't pop up to sue us for libel.

When it was all done, I had to hang around for a while, just in case there were any further developments. Only one. Sometime around eight o'clock the third villain pegged out. By now I was in Hamptons and I reasoned maybe I should hang around some more. I was tucking into my second bottle when Rosie rang. A distinctly frosty Rosie. Where was I? What was I doing? Had I forgotten that we were supposed to be going to a dinner party?

Dear me, in the excitement of it all, it had clean slipped my mind. I billed and cooed my apologies but I don't think she was listening. Her final words were: 'It's too late now. I'll just have to go on my own.'

Curses.

Chapter Five

The Coldharbour Lane killings kept me on the go all the way through Friday, so it wasn't until Saturday morning that I got to see Rosie.

Or the other way around.

I woke up and there she was sitting on the edge of my duvet munching an apple. She's big on apples.

'Hello,' she said, and took a bite.

I lay flat as a steamrollered pancake and pondered. What sort of 'Hello' did she have in mind? Sometimes it's hard to tell with Rosie.

She said, 'Your coffee's getting cold.'

That sounded safe enough. I opened the other eye. She was wearing a diamond-white short-sleeved thing with a skirt to match. The skirt must have been at least three inches long. I sat up for a better look.

'Tennis,' she explained, just so I didn't start getting any crazy ideas.

'Did you win?'

'Nearly.'

I took a swig of lukewarm coffee. No sugar. I eyed her over the rim of the cup. White suits her, especially like now when she's sporting a tan. Rosie's got blue-black hair which usually cascades in curls and whirls all over the shop. But today she had it tied back with a chalky pink bandana, the same colour as the stripes on her trainers. From the neck up she looked like a bandit queen.

She finished her apple and gave me a bright toothsome smile. 'Breakfast?'

Rosie has a smoky voice that makes you think she's saying something else. 'Yes please.'

She leaned over and kissed me right in the middle of my forehead. She smelt of apples, which I don't suppose is all that surprising. I slapped the mug down on the bedside table and stuck out my manly arms to wrap her in a fond embrace, but she was way too fast for me.

She stood up, patted her microskirt and skipped off to the kitchen. I watched her legs till all I had left was the memory. Rosie and I have been sort of together some while so you'd think I'd be used to her by now. Not even slightly. Rosie has a habit of turning up unannounced while I'm still in my pit. This is what comes of my giving her a key. Somehow she's never got around to reciprocating. Yet her vile, hoity-toity, mincy-pincy, shaggy-bummed old cat, Blue, has got his very own door to her flat. Rosie doesn't seem to find anything odd about this.

I lay there looking like the English Patient and listening to her juggling the crockery. For some strange reason I felt happy with the world.

Later, as we sat around spooning boiled egg (me) and gunge (her) into our respective mouths, we talked through the day ahead. Or she did the talking. Rosie had it all mapped out. She has a 'friend', who calls himself Verdun, in honour of his great-grandpop who was killed thereabouts. Sad, I agree, but nowhere near as tragic as the fact he sired a son before he got himself shot. That son, in turn, had one of his own, and if you follow the line long enough you end up at Verdun.

Verdun and Rosie were once more than friends. But I'd rather not think too much about that. Anyway, when she eventually gave him the elbow they stayed pals. Though God knows why. Verdun, when he's not dishing up hamburgers, is an actor, which he pronounces with a capital A. He's not one of those familiar faces you spot on telly, bringing joy and sunshine to the masses. His stomping ground is downstage in fringe theatres where he mooches around in mascara looking consumptive. I suppose some people would say he is handsome.

His latest foray was in a play called *Dragon's Teeth*, presently showing at the Stonor in Hammersmith. Out of the goodness of his foul heart he had slipped Rosie a couple of freebie tickets for this evening's performance.

I asked Rosie what the play was about. No idea. But I was prepared to bet good money that it had nothing to do with dragons, or with their teeth. Also,I wasn't expecting any good jokes.

Rosie chattered on, ' . . . and afterwards he's invited us to the cast party. There'll be a whole bunch of people there and it sounds like it's going to be a lot of fun. So I need to do some shopping this afternoon because I got paint on my new lemon dress and it won't come off. You know, the lemon summer one I got from Kookai? I was planning on wearing that but yesterday I was mixing paint and Blue walked in it and then he jumped on the bed and I had the lemon dress left out to iron and . . .'

Somewhere around here I switched off. In case you're puzzling over that thing about the paint, I'd better explain. Rosie is an artist, or a designer, as she prefers. She churns out exotic patterns which end up on curtains and frocks and all sorts of stuff. Many of her doodles feature lizards and other weird creatures, frisking and frolicking and generally showing off. There's probably something deeply Freudian in there if you looked hard enough.

I think I yawned, for she darted me a flinty look. 'You're not listening.'

'Me? I heard every word. Blue tramped paint all over your dress.'

'That was *ages* ago. I was saying there's a christening party for Barnaby, you know, Zoë's baby tomorrow. What do you think I should get him?'

I said, 'Am I supposed to be going to that too?'

'I *told* you last week and you said okay. Why, had you something else in mind?'

Actually I did, but maybe this wasn't a good time to mention it. I didn't have to.

She looked at me with cool blue eyes. Rosie is fully aware of the power she has over me. It doesn't bother her much. If anything, she thinks it's funny.

I gave her a slow melting smile. Nothing doing.

She said, 'It's time I got going. I don't suppose you want to come with me?'

She supposed right. Instead I hung around the flat, watched at least fifteen minutes of cricket and then hauled myself off the pub for a Saturday wind-down. I bumped into a couple of Aussie mates and we fell to swopping jokes and tall tales. And so the hours wheeled past.

Before I knew it, it was kicking on seven o'clock. I fought free of the Ozzers and jumped a cab to Battersea. Rosie sprung open the door of her flat, wearing a silvery thing which looked like it came from the lingerie department.

'My new dress,' said she. 'Like it?'

Like it? I loved it. I wanted to nuzzle and caress it, to bury my nose in its soft dunes and to trace its every silken stitch.

Rosie straightarmed me. 'We're late already. If we don't hurry we'll miss half Verdun's play.'

Alas, we got there on time. The play was considerably worse than feared. Various bods ran around shouting and swearing at each other in a querulous sort of way. In Act Two Verdun's character died. That was the best bit. But we had to sit through another hour of yelling and quivering before they switched on the lights. Everybody, and there must have been at least twenty of us culture vultures in the audience, applauded the lighting guy.

And then came the party. The only drink on hand was cheap wine, red or white. Somehow the stuff tastes better when you drink it in Hamptons. Maybe it's because they use real glasses. The oaf Verdun saw us from afar and came poncing over to Rosie, arms outstretched.

'Ro-sieee!!!'

'Verrr-dunnn!!!'

His squeal was pitched a demi-semi-quaver or something above hers. There was a good five seconds of silence while they said it all over again with kisses.

After a while Verdun hoicked his grinning chops out of her curls. He was still smeared in warpaint. He saw me. '*Mark!* So good of you to come.'

'Great play, Ver*dumb*. You died a terrific death.'

We both had our teeth bared.

Rosie swung around and gave me a sharpish glance. I just shrugged.

Verdun grabbed her arm. 'Come on. There's some absolutely *lovely* people I want you to meet.'

And off pranced the drama queen with Rosie in tow. She threw me a distressed damsel look. Tough. She got herself into this mess so she could dig her own way out. I headed for the bar and a fresh plastic cup of sulphuric acid. Behind the bar, which was just a knocked-about old table, last seen pretending to be an altar in the play, was a girl called Pru. She was the one splashing out the plonk, therefore the only person in the place worth talking to. The fact that she was a peppy little thing with a tight tee shirt and no bra did not make her any the less interesting. We hit it off fine. I kept grinning, she kept filling up my cup and telling me all about herself. That's the one thing about these actor types. They have this pathological need to rabbit on about themselves. They're almost as bad as reporters.

Anyway, I'm a good listener so I just hoisted one eyebrow, laughed in all the right places and pushed my cup at her when the occasion demanded. From time to time other drinkers trundled up hollering for refills and she had to break off to calm them down. But she was soon back, continuing where she'd left off. From what Pru said about herself, I got the picture that she was way down the batting order in the theatre company, so I don't suppose she got much chance to talk about herself. She certainly wasn't letting me get away. Whenever she got to an important bit, her boobs jiggled about. There were a lot of important bits but I didn't mind.

After I'd thrown back about a litre of vinegar, Pru took a breather. I think that meant she'd run through her whole repertoire. She curved me her best audition smile. 'What about you? You're not in the Theatre?'

I reassured her on that score.

She chucked in some more stuff about herself and then she returned to me.

'So what do you do? Are you a friend of one of the Cast?'

Her smile had gone a shade shaky.

I said I sort of knew Verdun. The smile stayed shaky. Maybe she couldn't stand the berk either.

I said, 'But I don't know him very well. It's just he gave a friend of mine a couple of tickets.'

Her tee shirt heaved and the smile fattened out. She had bright blue eyes.

'And did you enjoy the Play?'

'Do I look like a masochist?'

She giggled, showing me her little white teeth. She folded her arms and puffed out her chest at me. 'You still haven't told me what you do.'

Over in the corner I could see Rosie amidst a clutch of luvvies. She had bright spots high up her cheeks and she was batting her eyelids, for Rosie is a wanton and shameless flirt. She shot me a quick glance, too fast to read.

I said to Pru, 'I'm a talent spotter for Page Three girls.'

She knew I wasn't but she went along with it.

'So what exactly do you look for?'

She straightened her pose and started acting pert all over.

I said, 'Personality. Yep, personality and a *great* pair of eyes.'

She didn't blink. She said, 'And how are *my* eyes?'

I might just have told her, but suddenly a smoky voice entered stage left. 'Hello, Max. Having a nice time?'

Rosie the serial flirt.

She knitted an arm tightly through mine. That just about said it all. I wagged my head sorrowfully at Pru. 'This is Rosie. Rosie's not allowed out on her own. It's time I got her home. Come along, Rosie.'

Pru's smile had faded to a pucker. But I threw her a big cheesy one before I wheeled Rosie about and led her off.

As we breezed out into the street she clicked her tongue and said, 'Honestly, I can't leave you on your own for five minutes.'

I didn't argue.

I'd never been to a christening party before, unless you count my own, which I don't remember too well. If I had I would have made pretty damn sure I didn't go anywhere near the thrash for the infant Barnaby. Judging by the racket he kicked up, Barnaby didn't think it was all that hot either. The rest of us stood around snorting Buck's Fizz and acting like we enjoyed it.

We got out of there sometime after four and went back to my flat because that's where all the Sunday papers were and I hadn't had time to bone up on them properly. There was a solid chunk on the Coldharbour Lane killings, but in the absence of any useful stuff from the Old Bill, it was mostly made up. I was leafing through one of the more gruesome heavies when an odd little item leapt out and made me chortle. This is what it said:

ANTIQUE dealers are facing a flood of skilfully-crafted fakes as unscrupulous Continental forgers seek to take advantage of the record sales prices being fetched in Britain's auction rooms.

Among the replicas detected before they have gone under the hammer are watercolours purporting to come from the late 19th Century English school.

Dealers are also reporting a burgeoning trade in fake antique furniture, often made out of old doors, or cannibalized from genuine pieces which have been damaged and would otherwise be worthless.

Freelance valuation expert Cindy Reilly warned: 'Buyers have to be on their guard and to question the provenance of antiques and paintings before they bid.

'To be candid, many of the English watercolourists were little more than daubers and their work is easily copied.

'But because there is an unprecedented demand for

such paintings, forgers can offload their fakes as quickly as they paint them.'

There was a good eight or nine paragraphs more, but Susannah is not the sharpest of writers so I'll spare you the rest. But you get the drift. Susannah had stuck Cindy Reilly's name into a news story, which meant I owed her a bottle of champers. I didn't mind. She deserved it. Anyways, I'd help her drink it.

But that was just the start. Within a week everybody was getting in on the game. Thus, a few days later, a Miss Cindy Reilly popped up in the *Sun*, though this time she was merely an eyewitness to a gas mains explosion in Carshalton. ('I thought it was a bomb.') Hard on the heels of that, a Mrs Cindy Reilly, a former nurse, aged sixty-one, was quoted elsewhere on the subject of joyriders in Wembley. ('The streets aren't safe for pensioners anymore.') Next, seven-year-old schoolgirl Cindy Reilly aired her views on the subject of pocket money. ('My Dad's mean.') I didn't see the sense in that one. There's no way you can knock up drink expenses for a seven-year-old kid.

Pretty soon it was getting to the stage where you couldn't read any news story without Cindy Reilly sticking her oar in. It was just getting plain silly. This had got to stop, especially as everyone was clamouring for free drink at our expense. So we called a council of war, that's Susannah, Tommy and me. The venue was the maternity wing of Hamptons.

Tommy was all for killing her off, Cindy that is. Susannah's a big-hearted girl, as well as everything else. She insisted Cindy lived, and I suppose I was with her on that.

I said, 'But we change the rules.'

'Rules?' Tommy looked shocked. The only Rules he recognizes is the restaurant of that name down Maiden Lane. 'We don't have any rules.'

'Which is precisely the problem.'

Susannah paused in siphoning up the Romanian antifreeze. 'Max is right. We've got to settle on who Cindy is before we write her into stories. She needs to be defined so that she's always the same sort of person. I mean, last week somebody had her in as a wino. A *wino*! Now that's just not on.'

She was taking this personally.

Tommy had a reasonable objection. 'But if she's always an antiques dealer, it'll end up boring and we'll never get her into stories.'

Susannah clucked her tongue. 'The job isn't the important thing. She can be anything – though not a wino. What does matter is the *type* of woman she is. What she looks like. That's what we've got to agree on.'

Tommy said, 'She's got big knockers.'

Susannah could live with that.

I suppose I was thinking about Mo Frew of supergrass fame. 'And she's a redhead.'

Tommy's eyes were over the sea and far, far away. 'Naw, she's Eurasian or something like that, really slinky and sexy with long black hair.'

'What's wrong with her being blonde?' asked Susannah, twirling her hair round her fingers.

Tommy, an expert in the area, was scornful. 'Because you never see blonde Eurasian girls, do you?'

I said, 'Yeh, and you don't get Eurasian girls calling themselves Cindy Reilly either.'

So blonde she was. The blue eyes were taken as read. From there we meandered on to Cindy's general character. Tommy and I both had her down as a good sort.

Susannah slapped a rider on that. 'But she's not a pushover.'

'None of them are,' Tommy mourned into his drink.

I called them back to reality. 'We're not hitting the button here. All we've done is made Cindy a blonde who likes her fun.'

'We've given her great boobs,' Tommy reminded.

Susannah said, 'We're agreed on the main things anyway. Any time we get her name in a story, we've got to say she's a blonde. Oh, and she's a Miss. Otherwise the story doesn't count and you can't claim a drink.'

Fair enough. But we were still missing something. I soaked up gin and inspiration came a-flooding. 'Her *voice*! That's what we need.'

'What does she want a voice for?' – Tommy.

I spoke as if I was dictating straight to Copy: ' "*Blonde stunner Cindy Reilly told last night of her marathon ordeal trapped in a store cupboard.*' Stop. New paragraph. '*The buxom thirty-year-old model escaped by stripping down to her undies and wriggling through a tiny window . . .*"'

Tommy said, 'What's wrong with that?'

It's hard to believe, but he's generally a sharp bloke. He only loses the plot when women are involved.

I sighed. 'Because it's still too easy. Any dipstick can get a busty blonde tagged into a story. What we need is a quote. A signature quote.'

Susannah chinked her glass down on the counter. 'Oooh, yes. I like it. And the exact same quote has to appear in every story we do on her.'

But what quote? We had to shift an awful lot of liquor before we hit it. In the interim we roadtested and crashed a good few dozen candidates. Here are a couple of examples, with the judges' findings in brackets. 'It was just like the Blitz.' (Too restrictive.) 'They ought to bring back hanging.' (Ditto.) 'It scared the pants off me.' (Ditto again.)

That particular line triggered off a bout of increasingly hairy innuendos from Tommy and me. They didn't help a lot, but they kept us amused. Susannah had gone quiet. All of a sudden she sat up with a crazed gleam in her eye. 'I've got it!'

We waited.

Susannah said, 'It was the biggest one I've ever seen.'

And we thought *we* were crude.

She was up and away now. 'Somehow or other it's got to go into every story, whether Cindy's talking about a bluebottle or a . . . a . . .'

'Bra?' Tommy supplied.

'Yeh. Well, whatever. What do you say?'

I said I liked it. Tommy didn't object. So we yipped for more drink and Massimo, the head honcho in Hamptons, stuck his nose over the bar. Massimo has a hooter that makes Barry Manilow look positively snub-nosed.

Susannah eyed it thoughtfully through her glass. 'Do you know,' she said, 'that's the biggest one I've ever seen.'

Peals of hilarity from her side of the bar. Massimo wrinkled his snoot. 'What are you lot on about?'

That set her going again.

He wagged the thing at her sadly. By this stage we were practically holding Susannah up. Tears were tripping down her cheeks. Massimo leaned forward. Not the smartest move in the circumstances. She collapsed in a gurgling heap. Every now and then she tried it on again. 'That's the big—' She never got any further than that.

At length she pulled herself half together and staggered off to the loo. We could hear her chortles all the way down the bar.

Massimo's nose followed her. 'What's the matter with her?'

Tommy said, 'You tell him, Max.'

I said, 'God knows. Maybe you forgot to water down the wine.'

Massimo snorted, swung his sail off westwards and tacked after it in search of intelligent life further down the bar.

Cindy Reilly vanished from newspaperland for a week or more. Then one morning Tommy rang me to say she'd resurfaced in a four-paragraph filler. There was no by-line on the story but it was clearly Susannah's work. That girl has too much time on her hands. This was the upshot:

City high flyer Cindy Reilly is used to bulls and bears as part of her daily work.

But the freelance financial consultant fled when she

opened her car boot and found herself face to face with a six-foot python.

The 30-year-old blonde said last night: 'I was absolutely petrified. It was the biggest one I've ever seen. Yak yak yak.'

The final paragraph explained that the snake was the fugitive pet of her neighbour's kid, Max. I've left out the python's name. But I expect you'd already guessed that. Monty.

I said to Tommy, 'Well, that's it. Susannah's got it all in there. We owe her a drink.'

Tommy wasn't too sure. 'She left out the boobs.'

He more than made up for that in his subsequent story of the hunt for American tourist Cindy Reilly who left one of her many suitcases in a taxi. The case contained all her new-bought undies, among which was a lacy bra. Yep. The biggest one the cabbie had ever seen.

Meanwhile various hacks tried to join the show but they invariably forgot to mention one or other of her key attributes. By now Susannah, Tommy and I had become the official arbiters. We called ourselves Cindy Reilly's Assorted Pals, though I don't want to explain why. It was our unhappy duty to tell thirsty candidates just why they didn't deserve free drink.

Naturally I had to sneak a story into our paper. Thus one morning readers found themselves ploughing through a yarn which began: *PSYCHIC Cindy should have seen it coming . . .*

That was my intro to the sad tale of a Dolly Parton-lookalike who had her crystal ball stolen at a motorway service station somewhere between Glasgow and

London. As crystal balls go, it was a whopper. Indeed, it was the biggest one she'd ever seen. I charged twenty-five quid on hospitality for that. And I copped a bottle of Hamptons' foulest.

In between times we also managed to write some true stories. Well, true-ish.

Among the latter was the funeral of Benny the Belly, down Mortlake crematorium. A bunch of hard-looking geezers in shiny double-breasteds were there to see him ascend to heaven in a puff of smoke. None of them wanted to talk to us but his missus, who was also outstandingly gifted in the belly zone, took over all weepy and yowling. It was hard to make out exactly what she was saying, but the general theme was that she wanted to separate Dave Stretch and Barry Frew from their private parts. That's what we wrote anyway.

This was said as she grazed through the acres of wreaths sent by the mourners. South London had done the boy proud, but a couple of the messages were a bit out of line. I'll quote from a livelier one: 'We'll get the bastards, Benny. God Bless. Jim, Jen & Family.'

A couple of days later the *Sunday Mirror* carried a minor follow-up. A new wreath had appeared on the corner of Coldharbour Lane where Benny had gone belly up. This time there was no card. But in the dead centre of the yellow flowers was an old snap of Maureen Frew. She looked different from she did in court. But I put that down to the bullet hole in the middle of her forehead.

*

We now fast-forward about three weeks down the road. I was in the office. I'd just got back from a drop-down-dead lunch with several evil cronies, so I was drinking black coffee and doing my best to be invisible. Angela Whipple saw clean through me.

'Max!' she yelled all the way across the newsroom.

I dredged up what I hoped was a happy bunny smile. At that distance she probably didn't see it. I steered a straightish course for News Desk. By the time I got there the smile was wearing thin round the edges.

'Yes?' I said. It was meant to sound sparky and keen. It came out more like a grunt.

She gave me a five-second stare. 'You've been on the razzle, haven't you?'

You've got to hand it to these News Editor types. Their powers of observation are downright uncanny.

I said, 'You've got a story for me?'

Another long appraisal. I filled in the time trying to work out what was on her mind. She hadn't summoned me all this way just to make cheap cracks about my lunchtime pursuits: nor was she about to have a routine pop at me about expenses. I knew that because I hadn't done any exes for a while. Therefore, I deduced, she wanted me to write up some half-baked story. There was nothing left of my smile.

Angie pushed back the big black leather chair and stood up. A little frown puckered between her eyebrows. She said, 'Let's go to my office. I've got a special for you.'

So off we meandered to the walk-in cupboard which serves as her office. That's not really fair. The cupboard has a window with an unparalleled view of the office car park. It also has a minibar where ocasionally I get to help myself. Not today.

Angie plumped herself down behind the desk. Without waiting to be asked, I took the other chair. She still had that frown lurking between the eyes. I'm guessing my frown was even bigger. It started when she said she had a special for me. Eleven times out of ten what that means is some dipstick like the Editor has come up with a lunatic idea. An innocent hack is then given the grim task of making the idea stand up. But no matter how hard the hack tries, the idea keeps falling on its backside. And guess who cops the blame?

I said, 'Whose idea is this?'

'The Editor's . . .'

Dear God.

' . . . and it's a peach.'

I'm not hot on peaches, not unless you drown the things in Drambuie. I just sat there cursing silently.

Angie said, 'Remember the Zeller Maine trial?'

Yes, Angie, I can actually remember things that happened almost three weeks ago. I nodded a yes.

Angie said, 'Did you ever see the boyfriend?'

'Whose boyfriend?'

She gave me a fishy look. 'The boyfriend of the supergrass. Who else?'

Oh, *that* boyfriend.

I said, 'Nope. The Old Bill had him and her all tucked away somewhere, so he wasn't talking.'

'He is now.'

I waggled an eyebrow.

Angie said, 'We're buying him up for eighty grand.

It's a cracking story. I want you to do the interview. The line is Living in the Shadow of the Gunman.'

Just in case I'd missed that, she explained, 'I mean Maureen Frew's going to be running all her life because her husband has put out a contract on her.'

Several questions were chasing around in my head: like, why does the boyfriend of someone like Maureen Frew need eighty grand? Like how come we were able to get to people on the witness protection scheme?

I said, 'Where is he?'

Another funny look from across the desk. 'Who? The boyfriend? How do we know? The police still have him and her hidden.'

This was getting beyond me. I said slowly and carefully, 'Then how am I going to interview him when we don't know where he's holed up?'

Angie sort of harrumphed. 'Honestly Max, I should have waited till you sobered up.'

That was plain unfair. I said, 'Okay, so we're doing this through a middleman.'

'Yeh. Maureen Frew's solicitor came to us with the idea and the Editor greenlighted it. The interview is actually with Maureen but we can't be seen to be paying money to a criminal. That's why you're supposed to be interviewing the boyfriend. His name is Stan Defoe.'

Let's see if I've got this right. I'm supposed to be interviewing Stan Defoe, but all the time it's Maureen Frew, but because she's under wraps somewhere, I'm really interviewing her brief? And we're forking out eighty grand for the privilege? Maybe I was missing something.

Angie said, 'It's a great one, isn't it?'

For the first time it occurred to me that Angie too might have been knocking it back at lunch. I gave her a steady look. She appeared sober, but you never can tell with Desk people.

I said, 'Where and when do I do the biz?'

'I'm just waiting to hear. We signed the contract today, so it's down to Maureen Frew now. There are a couple of minor things, like the police need you to sign an agreement that you will not divulge to *anyone* where she is.'

For a moment back there I thought I'd got it all together, but here it was, slipping away from me again. I took a deep breath, 'How can I divulge where she is when I don't know?'

Angie thumped her little white fist on the desk. 'For Christ's sake, Max – when you interview her you'll see her.'

I sat up. This was a first. 'It's actually a face-to-face interview?'

'What did you expect – telepathy?'

I smiled. Well, it was almost a joke. I said, 'I thought it might be a long-distance phone call.'

Angie went all snooty and disdainful. 'What – for eighty thousand? You don't think the Editor's that stupid?'

I smiled wider. Now that was a joke.

Angie said, 'We're getting the whole thing, words and pix.'

'Pictures too? So Mo hasn't had the plastic surgery yet?'

It was Angie's turn to lose the plot. 'What plastic surgery?'

I sighed. 'When they get a supergrass, the first thing they do is redesign his mug, or in this case, her mug. Then they build a whole new identity around it. If they've already fiddled about with Maureen's nose and given her boyfriend jug ears, there's no way they'd let us take a snap of them.'

She hadn't thought of that. 'Oh yes. Of course. Anyway, I expect the protection officers will want you to sign a whole list of provisos. And they'll insist on seeing what you write before we publish.'

Rats.

Angie got up. 'So that's the story. But you mustn't mention it to anyone else. We'd be in it up to here if this leaks out.'

I said, 'It sounds like Maureen's still in Britain.'

'You'll know before I do.'

I tried to look sage. 'I will?'

An impatient click of the tongue. 'We've given the protection people your numbers. They'll contact you. And you'd better have a word with her solicitor.'

'Oh.'

I was thinking to myself that as specials go, this one was not at all bad. I said, 'Just one thing you haven't told me. Who's the photographer?'

She actually smirked. 'Frankie Frost.'

For many reasons too awful to go into, Frankie Frost is regarded as a menace and a monster by his fellow man. Personally I think his fellow man might have a point there. But the odd thing is I'm on the side of the menace and the monster. Most of the time anyway.

So I smirked right back. 'Frankie? Fine.'

Angie shrugged. She probably thinks we deserve each other. She said, 'He doesn't know yet, and I'm leaving it up to you to tell him, but for God's sake warn him he's not to say a dicky bird about it, I mean not a *word* to anybody else. The Editor would blow a gasket if this one leaks out.'

I'd stopped listening. I was thinking that Editors' specials are wizard for expenses. You can rack up any old figure you want, and it gets through News Desk because they think it was the Editor's dumb idea. And they can never tell him how much money his rubbishy story cost. For the Editor must always, *always* be shielded from the truth.

Angie was saying, ' . . . and you can wipe that silly grin off your face. I've been told to pare all reporters' exes down to the bone.'

That meant I'd just have to make the bones bigger.

'So,' she breezed on, 'you can go and brief Frankie, and let me know as soon as the police contact you. Okay?'

Okay.

We marched back out into the newsroom and I peeled off towards Picture Desk in search of Frankie. But he was off frightening his fellow man again. I'd fill him in some other time.

Chapter Six

I got the chance soon enough. Next morning I was in my corner forging taxi bills for my mate Dinesh when Nige and his sheet of paper came scooting over. 'Max! We've got an armed siege in a council flat in Tower Hamlets. Pictures have already sent, so we need you to go down and do the words.'

'An armed siege?' I echoed.

'That's what I said. You'd better move it in case they start shooting.'

Nige is just like everybody else on News Desk: they've got the tee shirt all right, but they've never been there or done that. If he had, Nige would have known that *proper* armed sieges only occur at night, that is when the gunman has had plenty of time for a good snort down his local boozer. This one was probably sparked by some old dear who watched too much TV.

I didn't demur. I was getting writer's cramp from filling in all those taxi bills. So I took the address and drifted off to Flat 7C Billington House.

I rounded the corner of the street and there about fifty yards away stood a seven-foot-high meerkat. A meerkat armed to the teeth with cameras. Yup, Frankie Frost.

I rolled up alongside. 'Nothing doing?'

'Wotcher, Max. Naw. False alarm. Just some old biddy—'

I didn't want to know. I said, 'It doesn't matter. I wanted a word with you anyway.'

Frankie squinted down his bony nose. 'Me? If it's about that tenner, I've already paid you.'

'No you haven't. And it was twenty. But that's not why I need to talk to you.'

He was still suspicious but he eased a fraction. 'What then?'

'Let's find a pub and I'll tell you the whole bit.'

Frankie patted his bulging pockets. 'I'm boracic.'

As in boracic lint. As in skint.

I said, 'I'm buying.'

'Oh all right then.'

Frankie re-arranged his necklace of cameras and off we clattered through the streets in search of a boozer which looked like it might have two clean glasses. After a while our thirst got the better of us and so we just hit on the next one we bumped into.

We were both on pints of lager. I took a swig, lit a cigarette, and started talking. 'You'll like this. We're going on a special together.'

He grinned a truly awful grin. 'What sort of special?'

'An Editor's special.'

His whole face sagged.

'But,' I said, 'think of the exes.'

His chin came up again. 'Is it a Foreign?'

Foreign trips are much prized in our small community. Not only do they afford you mega expenses, they also keep you out of the office for a while. Sometimes you even get to see the sun.

I said, 'No. It's home-side.'

'Oh.' The chin went into freefall again.

I said, 'I reckon we'll have at least a week in a swank hotel with all the grub and drink we want.'

His weasel eyes flickered. 'Anywhere decent? I mean anywhere where there's lots of babes?'

'Probably not.'

The eyes flickered out.

Do you know, I can play this up-down game with Frankie's face all day long and he never twigs. But I was getting bored so I just took another gulp and told him the story. Unlike Angie, I put it in the right order. When I was all done our glasses were empty. I left Frankie brooding on the news while I ordered the top-ups, making sure he got the glass with the lipstick. That second pint swung the balance.

He was thinking out loud. 'You know, it mightn't be as bad as you make out.'

Who said anything about bad? I nodded anyway.

'In fact,' he said, 'you never know about the babes. There might even be some.'

True. For Frankie's definition of what constitutes a tasty woman is hugely liberal. Some of them even have their own teeth. I let him ramble on. And once he gets on to this wavelength, Frankie can certainly ramble. Right now he was telling me about some little rascal he'd scored while covering a job down Camberwell. I can only take so much. I butted in, 'What else have you been up to?'

'What? Women?'

There really is no hope for him. I sighed. 'No. I meant jobs.'

You could hear his brain changing gear without the benefit of a clutch. He got there in the end. 'Not a lot. Except last Tuesday . . .' His face split in half in a gruesome grin . . . 'D'you remember Cara's Cat?'

I did. This basically was the story: a little blonde fluffy-looking kid called Cara had a black and white cat which she called Mister Mew. Mister Mew was an ordinary moggie, but he was the most precious thing in the entire world to Cara. It should be explained around here that Cara suffered from some terrible disease which rendered her blind, therefore her world was somewhat proscribed.

Anyway, she and Mister Mew lived happily together down Wandsworth way until disaster struck. Mister Mew did a runner. Cara was heart-broken. And that might have been it, just another everyday tragedy.

But then the *Star* – big-hearted newspaper that it is – stuck up a five hundred quid reward for Mister Mew. Nothing happened for a couple of days and then a *Star* reader, for there is such a thing, rang them to say he'd found the missing mog. We got a tip-off from our mole on the *Star* News Desk to tell us there was going to be a big happy reunion of Cara and cat later that afternoon. Frankie with a freelance reporter in tow was immediately dispatched to snatch a pic of the memorable moment. But he knew there was no way the *Star* would let him near Mister Mew. Therefore he came up with an evil plan. This involved driving for half an hour around the pretty bits of Wandsworth until he spotted a cat licking its paws and minding its own business on its owner's doorstep. By chance it was black and white, but it was not exactly a dead ringer for Cara's kitty, being black where Mister Mew was white and vice versa. Still, as Frankie delicately put it, the kid was blind so she wasn't going to know that, was she?

I forgot to mention that earlier Frankie had conned the freelance into buying a pound of pork sausages. Armed with the sausages, Frankie coaxed the cat into his car. Once inside, he removed its little ding-dong bell, for Mister Mew didn't have a bell, and then he drove like a mad thing to Cara's place.

Her mum opened the door. Next she opened her mouth to say, 'That's not Mister Mew.'

But Frankie got in first, saying he was a snapper from the *Star* and this here particular cat was just for the photograph. The real one was on its way but the picture was slotted for an early page so he had to knock off a pic right now or else he'd miss the deadline. So maybe Mum could *pretend* this was the genuine article. Mum fell for all this and the upshot was the fake cat was handed over to Cara, who, under the impression this was her beloved Mister Mew, began stroking and petting him and tickling his chin. There was a slight snag here because the cat wasn't into all this touchy-feely stuff and wanted to leg it. But Frankie had a couple of sausages in reserve and after a while he managed to get a lovey-dovey snap. Then he and the freelance got well offside before the *Star* arrived. The next day a big three-column pic of Cara and the alleged Mister Mew beamed out of our page seven. If you examined it closely you could see what looked like a half chewed cigar sticking out the side of the cat's mouth. And that's it. End of story.

I had just one question: what happened to the phoney cat?

Frankie said, 'Happened? Nothing happened. I couldn't take it away again, could I?'

'Yeh. But for all you know, you might just have nicked some other kid's cat.'

I think that was the first time this might have occurred to Frankie. He thought about it for all of a second. 'So?'

I gave up.

I got back to the office fifteen mins before lunch. That was just to show Desk I wasn't spending all my hours in the pub. I hung around for a good ten mins and was about to slide off again when my phone pealed.

'Mister Chard?'

'Yes?'

'My name is Ernest Tullamy.'

I didn't know whether I was supposed to sympathize or what. I stayed silent.

He said, 'I am Missus Maureen Frew's legal adviser.'

Oh.

He cleared his throat. 'I believe you are the journalist who will be speaking to Mister Stanley Defoe, whom I also represent.'

I said I was the one.

Tullamy fluffed about some more before he got there. 'I would appreciate it if you would call and see me this afternoon. Shall we say three-thirty?'

I lied and said I was otherwise engaged then, but I could squeeze him in now. Much rustling of paper from his end before he finally caved in. The address was in St James's, which was nice for me because the Lamb and Flag is also in St James's and is a good place to drink strong drink. But business first. Tullamy's office was on the second floor of a newish building, the lobby of which had been furnished by either a minimalist or else a bloke without a lot of spare change.

I drummed on a cold grey door and a cold grey voice bawled, 'Come in.'

The office was a big affair with four titchy little cubicles, three of whose owners were off knocking back drink. That left Tullamy. He was not at all as expected. He had a soap pink face with corrugated lines all over his forehead. There wasn't much in the way of hair. He was decked out in tweeds with cherry red shoes. All very well, but definitely *not* in St James's. I began to have serious doubts about Ernest Tullamy's competence, maybe not as a lawyer, but as an exemplar of fashion.

We sat ourselves down, went through the usual rigmarole about the weather and then he got started. 'Naturally I wish to ensure that my clients are in no way compromised, or indeed placed in jeopardy, through your interview: that goes without saying.'

Don't say it then.

I said, 'Okay if I smoke?'

'What? No, that is I don't object.'

And just to prove what a liberal-minded chap he was, he went off and fetched a tin ashtray.

'Now, where were we?' he asked.

I said, 'You hadn't started.'

He gave me a stony look. 'I was explaining that it is imperative that your newspaper article does not prejudice my clients.'

I sat forward. 'These are the rules the way I see them. In exchange for us paying you eighty thousand quid I get to meet Maureen and Stan. They will tell me – or, for the purposes of the story, Stan will tell me – how it feels to have a price stuck on your head. These interviews – and for eighty grand we expect at least two or three – will be controlled by the police. Afterwards my story will be vetted by the police just so I don't drop Maureen and Stan in it. Those are the rules.'

I sat back again.

It was his turn to lean forward. 'And, Mister Chard, as their legal representative, *I* shall also require the right to approve your article before it is released for publication.' He patted a folder as thick as a Sunday supplement. 'You will find the relevant clauses in the contract.'

'That's a contract?'

He waved a pudgy hand. 'It is largely a copy of the terms of the agreement which have already been signed by your Executive Editor.'

I said, 'But you want me to sign it all over again?'

Tullamy nodded. 'Quite so. There are certain elements which pertain directly to you, for example, you will shortly be apprised of my clients' present location. The contract stipulates that you agree that you shall not publish, broadcast, relate or disseminate in any other manner this information.'

I said, 'That goes without saying.'

Tullamy was still spouting. 'And there is a similar contract which requires the signature of your photographer before an interview can be arranged.'

'Interviews,' I corrected.

He took it in his stride. 'I will relay your request to my clients, but your Executive Editor has signed the contract on the clear understanding there will be a single interview.'

Further proof that our Executive Editor should have his office Biro taken off him again.

I shrugged. 'We'll see how it works out. I'll take the contracts back to the office and have our lawyer run through them.'

Tullamy waxed expansive. 'I don't foresee any problems.'

I did. For eighty grand the Editor would expect a Monday-to-Friday series. Gifted as I am, there's no way I can spin out a single interview into a five-parter. Maybe I'd better start working on it now.

I lounged back in a chair which was not built for lounging. 'Anyway, now I've got the ground rules straight, what can you tell me about Maureen?'

Another worry line joined the mob up there on his forehead. 'I'm afraid I don't follow.'

It wasn't *that* hard. I said, 'The only time I've seen Maureen Frew was those couple of days in court. She seemed a very together lady. But that's all I know about her.'

He turned on a fat smile. 'Mister Chard, you know it would be quite unethical for me to disclose any information on a client.'

Unethical? For heaven's sake he was the brief for a gangster's wife, a woman who had laundered millions in nicked money.

I said, 'I take it you've been Mo's legal adviser for some while.'

He didn't disagree.

I pushed on. 'What about Stan – is he a new signing?'

The smile slipped off his chin. 'Really, I cannot discuss my clients in this way.'

We were having a communications breakdown here: I was being too roundabout. I edged the chair forward and favoured him with a matey grin.

'You see, Mister Tullamy, I have a problem. My Editor wants nine thousand words of copy. Unless Mo can rattle out three hundred words a minute, we're going to end up with an awful lot of empty holes in the paper.'

He did not exactly shed tears of sympathy.

I said, 'And if we end up with lots of holes, our lawyers might just say you haven't delivered on the contract. So goodbye eighty grand.'

That got him where it hurt. He pushed his lower lip up and down with a pink finger. I waited.

'Very well,' he said at last, 'I am prepared to give you some *general* information on my clients. But that is all.'

We started with Mo. I deliberately kept my notebook in my pocket. Mrs Frew, said he, was a witty, intelligent and charming woman. She was outgoing and friendly, always elegant and good-humoured. I was beginning to feel sorry I'd ever asked. Furthermore, he said, she had given the Old Bill invaluable information on a major crime.

I said, 'That must have taken some balls.'

Tullamy agreed, only in a more flowery way. 'Maureen – Missus Frew – was fully apprised of the personal risks that her actions might incur.'

'By whom?'

'Sorry?'

'Who "apprised" her?'

Shutters dropped over his eyes.

'The um police, of course. And she herself was aware of the possible consequences.'

I said, 'What about Barry Frew? The trial didn't give me much of a picture on him. What's he like?'

The shutters were still down. 'It is sufficient to recall that he consorted with David Stretch, a man known to be an habitual and violent criminal. Other than that I cannot say. I did not know the man.'

This was getting us nowhere. I came in from a different angle. 'You're not a criminal lawyer?'

'That is correct. I represented Missus Frew solely in civil matters.'

'What, like the paperwork when she bought a new house, knocking up her will, that sort of stuff?'

He said, 'Yes. I represented them in those matters, but you will understand that I cannot comment on specific aspects.'

'And what about Stan? Is this true love?'

Tullamy put it together in his head before he got round to answering. 'Missus Frew introduced Mister Defoe to me, and I agreed also to represent him.'

I said, 'He must be pretty hot on her to stick his life on the line.'

He didn't exactly go 'tsk-tsk', but that was the impression. 'Really, Mister Chard, it would be most inappropriate for me to discuss their personal relationship.'

I said, 'I expect you'll be handling Mo's divorce?'

'No.' He was firm about that anyway.

'No?'

'I am not a matrimonial lawyer.'

There was another five minutes of such jaw-dropping tedium before Tullamy wrapped up the two contracts and sent me on my way with a rubber handshake.

I eddied round to the Lamb and Flag, treated myself to a fragrant Gordons, and did a spot of pondering. I suppose what was uppermost in my mind was the great unanswerable question: why do lawyers always need to lie?

Chapter Seven

I whiled away the afternoon swotting up on Maureen Frew. The *Independent*'s profile on her was the best of the bunch and it wasn't exactly jampacked with snappy facts. But after reading it and any other guff on file, this is what I had.

Little Mo hailed originally from up north, either Durham or Cleveland, depending on which paper you believed. She and her mum, Mrs Marion Stoveley, came to London, Plumstead to be precise, when Maureen was fourteen. The dad didn't. Maybe they didn't have Newcastle Brown down here in those days.

Marion kept hunger at bay through a succession of bitty jobs, ending up as a 'hospital ancillary worker', whatever that might be. Mo was the only child and a solitary one by all accounts. No particular friends at school, no known extra-curricular boyfriends. She was bright enough and could have made university, but her mum sprung her from school in the final year. Mo got herself a job in a builder's yard, answering phones and tapping the typewriter. Her boss remembered her as 'a quiet and pleasant girl, but you could see she was ambitious. We always thought she would go far.' I don't think he expected she would go *that* far.

She stayed there a year before she and her mum went walkabout again, fetching up in Bournemouth. We know that because one of her old classmates once bumped into her there. Mo told her she was working as a hotel receptionist, which sounded likely enough.

After that Maureen Stoveley vanished. All the papers plugged the gap by saying she held a succession of low-key jobs. For all we know, that might even have been true.

Her next public outing was in the witness box at Southwark Crown Court, by which time she was Mrs Maureen Frew, copper's nark and estranged wife of runaway crook Barry Frew.

There was even less on him. He'd been raised by a granny in Clerkenwell following the deaths of his mum, dad and sisters in a motorway smash-up. Like Mo, he got around a bit, starting off as a trainee accountant in Mount Pleasant, and then branching out for himself as a financial consultant down Reigate. It looked like he'd found himself a nice little earner, for the Frews' marital home in Godstone was presently up for grabs for anyone with £800,000 to spare.

Around here I did a cross-check through our library files on Dave Stretch. There was yards of stuff on him, all of it bad. He'd served more porridge than Quaker Oats. Ram-raiding, knifing, extortion, and generally bashing people about. Anything violent, Stretch was game for it. His saving grace was he wasn't very clever at it, which is why he spent so much of his life banged up. Amid this catalogue of villainy, two minor details stuck out. The Zeller Maine job was the least violent episode of his whole career. Also, it was probably the only one he would have got away with, if it hadn't been for Mo the Mouth.

In the files I came across some familiar names, notably that of Benny 'The Belly' Sloman, last seen pegging out in Coldharbour Lane. But there was not a single reference to Barry Frew. Nor was there a file on Stan Defoe. That might just have been down to our library's customary ineptitude. We've got people in there who think John F. Kennedy is an airport.

I put aside the files and switched my brain on. Maureen stood to trouser £800,000 on her house, plus whatever else she had under the mattress. And when people go on the witness protection scheme, the Old Bill chucks sackloads of fivers at them. Why then was Mo flogging her story for another eighty thou? Maybe she just liked to talk.

I wasn't getting anywhere with this, but I suppose I always think better when I've got a glass in hand. I wafted over to News Desk and told them I had to see a contact. They knew I was lying but they were too busy cobbling together the splash – TOP JOCK IN BETS SHOCK. In case you're wondering, that was about a champion jockey, not the Chieftain of the Clan Mac-Tartan.

I took the back stairs down to the Stone dive bar and treated myself to a large one. It went down a bit swiftish, and just when I was thinking I deserved another, my mobile chirruped.

'Mister Chard?'

At least it wasn't the News Desk.

It was a bloke I'd never heard of before. He told me his name but I'm sworn to secrecy on that one.

Let's just say he was a senior Plod and his first name was Tom. Or that's what we'll call him anyway.

After we'd got the introductions out of the way, he said he'd like to see me on the subject of Mo Frew, as of now.

I said, 'Where? Down at the Yard?'

He had a much better idea. A pub in Petty France.

I said, 'I'm on my way.'

It was only when I was in a cab tooling up Victoria Street that I realized I had no idea what this Tom looked like. It wasn't a problem. There were about four or five drinkers in the pub, only one of whom was in a navy blazer. That was him all right. He came across, pushed a square hand at me and said, 'Mister Chard?'

So now we were acquainted. I lit a cigarette while he called for two pints of Fosters. He nodded his bonce in the direction of a cosy nook. 'We'll talk over there.'

He was buying. I didn't argue.

We sat opposite each other and for a few moments there was silence but for the sound of Adam's apples bobbing.

He said, 'You've seen Tullamy.'

I said, 'Yep. And I've got his contracts.'

Tom brushed that away. 'That's just between you and him. It's got sod all to do with us. We're in charge of the meet. You can forget him.'

I was warming to this Tom. I said, 'When is the meet?'

'You'll be told. Let's just say I wouldn't go on holiday right now if I was you.'

He pulled an envelope out of his pocket and peered

at the back of it. He must have been long-sighted. 'And your cameraman is called Frank Frost?'

'Yeh. Frankie.'

Tom said, 'He knows the score all right?'

'I've told him. I suppose you need us to sign some sort of confidentiality deal?'

He made a rumbling noise. It might have been a laugh. 'Bugger that. If anything goes wrong on this one we'll just shoot you. All you've got to remember is what we say goes. If we say, "You can't ask that question," then you don't ask it. And when you've typed your notes up, we take away your notebook.'

He took a gollop of lager. 'And when you come back you tell *no one* – not even your Editor – where the meet took place.'

I said, 'You'll be sitting in on the interviews?'

'There'll be protection officers present all the time. Oh, no tape recorder. Your photographer gives his film to us, we develop it and we say what photographs you can use. When I give the word that the meet is on, you must be ready to go. Immediately. There won't be any second chances. This thing is a big enough bollocks already.'

I pushed a cigarette his way. 'You don't go a bundle on this meet, do you?'

He ignored that. 'Your paper is also liable for any expenses.'

'What expenses?'

'Think about it Max. We transport you and your photographer there. We put you up and feed you. We're buggered if the taxpayer is going to pay for that.'

'Fair enough—'

He hushed me. 'To answer your question: no, we don't go a bundle on this. She's being greedy and your newspaper is just out for some tatty scoop. But she kicked up such a bloody fuss that we had to go along with it. And there are some idiots upstairs who think that if the story's handled right, it might encourage some other wives to start grassing.'

I said, 'It's a funny one. She couldn't need the money.'

Tom gave me a flat-eyed look. I think he was working out what he could tell me. I got busy with the Fosters and waited. After a while he said, 'It might not have been her idea.'

That's one I hadn't thought of. I pointed at his glass. 'Time for another?'

He looked at his watch. 'Why not?'

When I returned he said, 'All of this – what we're saying now – is not for publishing. Okay?'

I said, 'Okay. I've been going through our files and I can't find anything on Barry Frew, or on Stan Defoe.'

'You won't. Frew was one of those bean counters who keep their heads down and never get nicked. After Maureen came forward, we did a tax check on his business. It was squeaky clean.'

I said, 'So how does a bloke like that get involved with somebody like Dave Stretch?'

'Frew did his books, didn't he? Dave was running a car auction place out in Kent, the Isle of Sheppey I think it was, and Frew handled the accounts. They're legit too.'

I said, 'It doesn't hold together. I mean, if Frew was

such a down-the-line man, why didn't he pay Maureen her slice of the Zeller Maine job?'

Tom looked at me sadly. 'It was big money, Max. Big money makes you think different. The first thing he thought was he could dump his old lady for a newer model *and* keep her slice for himself. He picked the wrong wife to do it with.'

Okay, that hung together. I said, 'And what can you tell me about Defoe?'

'Stan the Man? What is there to say? He knows a good thing when he's onto it. Barry Frew might have thought Maureen wasn't worth shelling out a million for, but she's a real looker. And she's got money with it.'

I said, 'I just can't wait to meet the happy couple.'

He must have thought I was being serious, for he said, 'You'll see them soon enough.'

We glugged away in silence. Tom certainly liked his drink. A fragile little hope suddenly stuck its head up. I said, 'Will I need my passport?'

'No. No passports.'

So Mo was still somewhere in England, or Britain anyway.

I emptied my glass. 'One for the road?'

'It's my shout.'

I looked at him sternly. 'Surely the taxpayer should not have to pay for my pint.'

And just for the record, the taxpayer didn't.

Later, after Tom had crawled off, I got busy on the phone. I dug out Frankie first.

I warned him, 'Don't go getting pissed. We're on standby.'

'What for?' asked Mr Memory.

'The special I told you about.'

'Oh, the supergrass thing.'

Thank you, Frankie. Why don't you just get a megaphone and yell it from the rooftops?

I said, 'Keep it down. I've just been talking to some serious Old Bill and they're as twitchy as hell. So don't say anything on the phone.'

I amended that. 'Don't say *anything* to anybody.'

'All right. But this job had better not be tonight.'

'Frankie, it could be anytime now. Whoever she is, she'll just have to wait.'

'It's not a bird. It's Joe Dunwoody.'

I blinked. Joe, like Frankie, is one of our snappers. Unlike Frankie, indeed, unlike his whole species, Joe is a reasonably civilized bloke, except he hardly ever drinks.

I was intrigued. 'What are you doing with Joe?'

Frankie snorted at my ignorance. 'Joe got the award in the Ilford sports pix, didn't he? Tonight he's buying the lads a drink.'

Aaah. The sight of a photographer flooding the bar with drink is the sort of thing you can tell your grandchildren about, only they wouldn't believe you. No wonder Frankie wanted to be there.

I was unmoved. 'A couple of pints and that's your lot. I don't want you turning up half guttered.'

'What – with Joe buying?'

And I suppose he had a point there. I let it pass.

Next I called Angela Whipple and told her to scrub me off the News diary for a week or thereabouts.

'Great!' she raved. 'You've seen Maureen then?'

Hang on, Angie.

'Nope. But I've been warned to stick by the phone.'

'Where is she?'

Just how many times do you have to tell them?

I said, 'God knows. And when I find out, God help me if I tell anyone else.'

Angie was still not on message. 'I know, I know. It's just between the police and us.'

'No. It's between the police and *me*. Not even the Editor is allowed to know.'

'Oh, it's hush-hush, is it?'

'Yeh. You could say that.'

She said, 'Okay Max. Call me as soon as you know where she is.'

And we're supposed to be in the communication business.

I quit the bar and ventured out into the sunshine where the rest of the world was celebrating rush hour. Not a taxi to be found. In the end I had to walk all the way to Victoria and jump the cab rank there. With much parping of horns and running over of cyclists, it eventually got me to Battersea and Rosie.

'Hello,' said she, eyes all agog. 'What's happened – did you drink Hamptons dry?'

But she gave me a fluttery kiss anyway. I made it a proper one. When I finally managed to break free, I poured us each a hefty splosh of Gordons. We sat supping them side by side on the sofa. She was togged up in dinky little blue shorts and a scoopy-necked yellow tee shirt. Maybe that doesn't sound anything special, but it fair made my heart go boop-de-boop.

Sometimes I think Rosie dresses the way she does just to wind me up. She squeezed closer, flopped her curls over my shoulder, and said, 'So why are you back this early?'

'Because,' I intoned dramatically, 'I am going on a long and mysterious journey, and I may be gone some time.'

Her bluey-grey eyes came up. The blue was rapidly draining. 'Oh no. You're not going on another bloody foreign trip, are you?'

'Sadly no. But I've got a special to do and I reckon it'll take maybe a week.'

There was no blue left. 'Can you not get out of it? What old rubbish is it this time anyway?'

Whereupon I ignored all those prior warnings and proceeded to tell her the whole bit. Or at least the bit that I knew.

She was deeply underwhelmed. 'And that's going to take all week?'

'Depends. If they've got Maureen tucked up in Chigwell, I'll be out of there in a couple of days.'

'But?'

'If she's hiding herself in the Outer Hebrides, then . . .'

She sat herself up and pulled away. I lit a cigarette and waited for her to get on with it. She started off, 'Why you?' About ten minutes later she'd worked herself down to, 'Well, get back as quick as you can.'

I narrowed the gap between us and she didn't object. I said, 'And the reason I'm here early is so I can take you out and ply you with exotic foods and fine wines.'

'What – dressed like this?'

I suppose not. The way she looked right now, she'd be leched after by every waiter in town. I poured myself another while she went off to rummage through her finery. I filled the intervening hours by making dog noises at Blue the cat. Blue pretended I was dead. Rosie at last returned in an outrageously short buttery yellow dress. It wasn't just the shortness. I've seen snakes with more generously tailored suitings.

I said, 'Maybe we'd better stay in: I'll pick up a takeaway.'

Rosie said nuts to that, and off we went to blow my money. There's a new nosherie opened on the corner of Woolaton Road which I have so far managed to steer well clear of on account of the prices. But tonight, what the hell. Rosie likes her tucker. She opened with prawn crespelle, pushing on to grilled red mullet romescu, and I haven't the faintest idea what any of those things were. She liked them anyway. I skipped starters and made do with a thumping great slab of steak. All very tasty, but if the chef had a failing it was his tendency to go overboard with the salt. We needed a bottle of wine apiece to wash it away.

We were sitting there waiting for our coffee and grinning at each other across the candles. Rosie's eyes were at their smokiest and bluest, for food does things to that woman. I suppose I was feeling fairly frisky too. I stretched a languid hand across the linen and said, 'How's about we—'

'Brr-ddeeep, brr-ddeep,' went my mobile.

Bugger. I flapped it open.

'Max?'

The least welcome voice in the entire world.

'Hi, Tom.'

'You're on.'

I said, 'Now?'

'Get to Chelsea nick as fast as you can make it. Ask for a Mister Blackhurst. Okay?'

'Okay.' I didn't feel like thanking him. I switched off the mobile.

Rosie said quietly, 'Was that it?'

Yes.

In between yelling for the bill I called Frankie.

'Yuh?' said he. In the background there was the sound of snappers falling over.

I said, 'Thunderbirds are go.'

'You what?'

'Drink up. Meet me at Chelsea nick in half an hour. No later.'

'Bloody hell, Max. I've just got a fresh pint in.'

Somehow I didn't feel particularly sympathetic.

'Be there or I'm going without you.'

I cut him off mid-whinge. Rosie and I walked back to her flat without talking. She phoned a minicab while I went through my overnight bag, taking care to remove the tape recorder.

For once the cab was prompt. I stood in the hallway and let the bag slip from my shoulders. Rosie draped her curls around me and gave me a kiss. She pulled back and looked me solemnly in the eye. She said, 'Be careful – and come back soon.'

Then she kissed me again. I broke away. Honestly, the sacrifices I make for this job.

I waved goodbye as the minicab drove off into the

purple evening. Standing in the doorway she was as exotic, as radiant as a bird of paradise.

The driver said over his shoulder, 'Nice night for it, mate.'

Those five little words cut his tip in half.

Chapter Eight

The desk woodentop at Chelsea said, 'Mister who?'

'Blackhurst,' I repeated.

The duty sergeant came to the rescue. 'Are you Mister Maxchard?'

I'd already introduced myself. 'It's Chard.'

He said, 'Where's the other one?'

'Frank Frost will be here shortly.'

Grunt. These guys must go to charm school or something.

He went away and came back five minutes later, trailing behind a bloke in a lightweight suit, no tie. The new arrival didn't introduce himself, but I'm guessing this was the much talked about Blackhurst. He said, 'Where's—?'

And bang on cue, Frankie rolled in, cunningly dressed as a walking camera tree.

'I'm the photographer,' said he.

Blackhurst didn't seem as surprised by this as he should have been. He said, 'This way.'

He turned and marched off down a muggy yellowed corridor. Frankie breathed beer in my face. 'Where we going?'

I said, 'To Birmingham, by way of Beachy Head.'

Frankie, 'Wot?'

We played follow-the-leader with Blackhurst through the rabbit warren until we hit the back of the building. He swung open a fire door and the cool night seeped in. Outside, with its motor already ticking away, was an unmarked Ford. There was a driver up front. Blackhurst got in beside him. He didn't say anything but I got the idea we were supposed to fit ourselves in the back.

Frankie said, 'Can I put my gear in the boot?'

'We're running late.' From Blackhurst.

And off we shot with Frankie's cameras bashing the hell out of my knees. The Ford pitched and turned through a mesh of dark and nameless streets so it took me a while to figure out our general direction. West. I pulled out my Bensons. Without turning round Blackhurst said, 'No smoking.'

We were now out on Cromwell Road, still heading west. Up came the sign for the M4. Frankie jerked his nose at it and semaphored a Meaningful Glance.

I said to the back of Blackhurst's bean, 'I'm surprised you haven't blindfolded us.'

His bean pretended I hadn't said anything. I turned to Frankie instead. 'Good party?'

'Yeh. Loads of drink. Not many women, but you know little Jodie out of Showbiz? Well she was there.'

I preferred not to hear this, for I've always had a minor thing about Jodie. Frankie chuntered on anyway. It wasn't as gross as I'd feared. Jodie's charms remained unsullied. She had simply guzzled vodka until she was well out of her tree. Then she fell down.

It could happen to anyone. I've even been there myself.

We snaked on to the M4 and the driver stuck his foot down. The exit for Heathrow zipped past at ninety-five miles an hour, and with it Frankie's last hope of a Foreign. I heard his face fall.

Just after the airport the driver switched direction, taking the M40 towards Oxford. Oxford, yep, that sounded the sort of place they'd park a safe house. But Oxford came and went. About ten miles later we left the motorway and skimmed off down a dark and empty back road. I hadn't the faintest idea where we were and I'd lost interest anyway. I just wished we'd get there quick so I could have a cigarette.

A little red-edged signpost loomed up out of the night. Frankie prodded my ribs with his bony elbow and mouthed in my ear, 'Brize Norton.'

Thank you, Frankie. I can read too you know.

Five minutes later we were at the gates. Blackhurst got out and in a scant twenty seconds said more to the guard than he'd said to me in the past hour. We were cleared through to the terminal.

Blackhurst, suddenly waxing downright conversational, said, 'Collect your bags and follow me.'

The driver stayed put. We hared after our genial guide, all the way across the terminal to a boxy office where two civvies behind a table were puffing away on fags. And good for them. I lit up too.

Blackhurst said, 'Empty your bags on the table.'

We emptied. The civvies took one lot apiece and turned everything inside out, leaving us to repack.

'Now your pockets,' said Blackhurst.

As soon as I produced my mobile he whipped it off me and plopped it in a plastic sack. There was a matching plastic sack for Frankie's phone. Both bags were carefully tagged with our names. The civvies were through with me, but Frankie's toys exercised them hugely. My snapper had to demonstrate that each of his cameras was exactly what it looked like before the civvies surrendered. Then the cameras were heaped into an air freight box.

Frankie moaned, 'They can't go in the hold. They'll just get smashed up during the flight.'

'They go in the hold,' said Blackhurst. 'You pick up your phones when you get back.'

I said, 'Back from where?'

No answer.

I had another go. 'Give us a clue. Does it begin with a letter between Ay and Zed?'

Still no answer.

I said, 'Well, I can't just sit around here listening to you jaw on all night. There's a bar out there.'

Blackhurst looked at the wall clock. 'Be back here in fifteen minutes. No later.'

I heard that last bit as I shot out the door, hotly pursued by Frankie. In under a minute we were wading into a couple of pints. I'd have preferred my lager about ten degrees colder, but I'm not picky. Frankie surfaced with a blob of foam on the end of his beak. 'What about duty frees?'

'What duty frees? This isn't a Foreign.'

'Oh yeh. I forgot.'

We guzzled on.

I said, 'Your round.'

'There's no time.'

'Get your money out.'

Frankie griped a bit but he dragged out his wallet. Judging by the size of it he must have had the rest of the Zeller Maine haul tucked away in there.

We got back to Blackhurst three minutes later than promised. He didn't exactly emit a joyful whoop on our return. Then it turned seriously tedious. For close on an hour we were cooped up in that room without even a chair to sit on. Blackhurst and the civvies mopped up the time by watching Frankie. I don't think they'd ever seen one of him before. In our game we call photographers monkeys on account of the way they gibber and caper. This is grossly unfair to real monkeys, for you never catch them blowing their noses and then looking in their hankies. Frankie's clobber was also a source of wonder. His jacket had started off in life as some sort of army surplus job, with more pockets than you could find a use for. Its original khaki was now H-Block brown, liberally patterned with beer stains, food stains, blood stains and other stains which you didn't want to think about too much. Frankie was oblivious to all the attention. He just slouched against the wall, thinking his own dim monkey thoughts and counting his pockets.

At length Blackhurst stood up. Without even looking our way he said, 'Okay. Collect your bags.'

And off we trawled again, back through the terminal and across to the boarding gate. We were actually clunking up the steps of a Hercules before he let us in on the big secret. 'You're going to Akrotiri.'

Cyprus! I swung round and spread the glad tidings to Frankie. And was he happy?

'Sod it, Max. I could have got in some duty frees only you said it wasn't a Foreign.'

There's no pleasing some people. At least I felt chipper. The prospect of cheap drink and lashings of it loomed before me. But as I buckled myself in a sudden chill thought popped up.

I said to Blackhurst, 'We were told not to bother with passports.'

'You don't need them.'

'For Cyprus we do.'

'Not for Akrotiri. It's a sovereign base. It's British.'

'Aaah.' And the sun shone once again.

The flight was hardly the most memorable experience of my life. It was long, uncomfortable and mind-numbingly boring. But there was one hidden bonus: thanks to the racket of the engines and the ear-plugs I didn't have to listen to Frankie wittering on. The only thing to look at was the tonsils of a row of sleeping soldiers sitting bang opposite. After a while I followed their example, only I closed my mouth.

I woke up with Frankie's top teeth getting intimate with my tie. I pushed him back into his own seat and he awoke grumbling and growling. He still whiffed of beer.

'Have we got there yet?' he mouthed.

'What do you think?'

The Hercules was droning on, only now its nose was slanting downhill. The squaddies opposite had also surfaced and they sat there scratching their stubbly chins. On my right Blackhurst was already awake and fiddling with his watch, knocking it on a couple of hours. That meant we must be nearly there. On an RAF flight you have to guess these things for you don't get some silver-tongued pilot switching on the Tannoy and announcing: 'Good morning, folks. We will shortly be arriving at wherever we're going, where the temperature is ninety-nine degrees. Thank you for flying with us etc. etc.' Nor was there an in-flight magazine to help me keep the boredom at bay.

After an unconscionable time the Hercules bumped down. Bits of Cyprus jerked and skidded by the tiny portholes at 1,000 mph. From what I could see of it out there it was sunny and mostly made of concrete. The plane bumbled to a halt. Blackhurst waited until all the soldiers got off before he made a move. It was already hot.

At the bottom of the steps there was a chunky Range Rover covered in stripes and chequered markings and all the usual clobber to let you know this particular Range Rover was Old Bill. A pair of pink Plods lounged against its bonnet. Apart from the short sleeves, they were just the same as the Law back home, right down to the fancy peaked caps. But the cap badges proclaimed they were SBA police, as in Sovereign Base Area.

One propped himself upright and stepped forward. 'Mister Blackhurst?'

'Yes,' said the last of the great conversationalists. And turning to us he added, 'Get in.'

Frankie bleated, 'What about my cameras?'

'You'll get them.'

We climbed aboard. The Range Rover trundled along past a bunch of bods tinkering with a helicopter. Other equally industrious souls were charging around the place in petrol tankers and jeeps. It made you thirsty just to watch them.

I said, 'When do we get to eat?'

The copper in the front passenger seat said, 'We're heading for the base. Once you've cleared security you can have a bite, unless you want to shower first.'

Yes. Frankie was getting a bit ripe.

We left the flatness of the airport and the road twisted away through crooked trees in the direction of a young mountain. Gradually the landscape cheered up, with here and there a sun-splashed taverna, half hidden behind flowers and vines and general greenery. Even at this early hour you could spot the locals irrigating their throats. I could get to like it here.

I said to the chatty cop, 'How long till we get to the base area?'

'You're in it.'

I peered out at the scrubby trees. '*This* is an army base?'

He laughed. 'Everything you see. There's even a Cypriot village in the area. And a couple of great beaches.'

I said, 'Nice posting, this.'

'Aye. I've been in worse.' He had a Liverpudlian accent so I had no doubt he was speaking from bitter experience.

We were now skirting along the shoulder of the mountain and behind us the sea sparkled blue all the way to Africa. But as yet no sign of the army base. And then we broke through a covey of trees and there it was, way, way down in a hidden valley.

I said, 'Wow!'

'Yes,' agreed the Scouser. 'Nice place, isn't it? There's a cricket pitch down there, or you can ride horses, play rugby, football, tennis, or even—' and here he put on a brass-hat accent, '—have a chukka of polo, old chap.'

He wasn't kidding. Slap in the middle of Happy Valley was a full-scale polo ground. It lay all green and lovely, fringed about with nodding chestnut trees or something similar.

My new-found mate asked, 'Why are you boys here anyway?'

Blackhurst plumped in. 'They're with me.'

End of guided tour.

We passed muster at the security gates and then we corkscrewed down the hill, past uniform ranks of white bungalows. You might as well have been in Potters Bar. Even the street names were English. Hereford Road. Dorset Avenue. I fell to thinking: somewhere behind these laced up little windows Mo the Grass was waking to another day in hiding. It was a good place to stash her. The Range Rover pulled up in front of a two-tier barracks and we clambered out. The white buildings bounced the heat back at us. I draped my jacket over my shoulder.

Blackhurst said, 'Wait. I'll be back in a couple of minutes.'

Frankie remembered why he was here. 'What about my gear?'

Blackhurst didn't feel like answering. He stomped off leaving me to placate my monkey. Yes, I told him, you'll get your cameras soon, yes, they sell sun cream, and yes, you can buy me a drink when they're open. That shut him up.

Our genial host returned. 'Breakfast,' he said.

We ate in the corner of a large and airy mess hall. I ploughed my way through sausage, beans, chips, the works. Blackhurst finished first. He pushed away his plate. He'd scoffed the lot, except for a lone porky sausage parked on the rim.

I'm not at my sunniest this early in the morn. Also, I could have done with an extra two hours' sleep. Whatever the reason, I was growing more than a mite grumpy. I lit a Bensons and puffed smoke across the plastic table at our charmless escort.

I said, 'If it's any consolation, I don't like you much either. And Frankie feels likewise. What do you say, Frankie?'

Frankie said, 'You finished with that sausage?' His fork was already hovering two inches above it.

Blackhurst ignored him. 'Look, my job was to get you here. You're here. Okay?'

No, not okay. I said, 'Somebody upstairs in the Yard, somebody way upstairs, thinks this is a good idea. They guaranteed us full co-operation. But so far you've failed to deliver. Now unless you stop effing about, I'm going to knock this whole thing on the head. And somebody in the Yard will get very cheesed off indeed. They're going to start asking what went wrong. And we're going to tell them it was all down to some sourpuss detective constable. Are you following me on this?'

Blackhurst said, 'Detective sergeant.'

I shook my head. 'When they're through, you'll be a Dee Cee again, if you're lucky.'

Frankie clumped in, 'Yeh, and what's happened to my cameras? That's what I'd like to know. Can I have your sausage?'

I said, 'So when do we get to see the bloke who knows what co-operation means?'

We were building up to a head-on spat when a skinny type with a long narrow jaw pulled up at the table.

'You Max Chard?' he asked.

'Yes. Who're you?'

'Clovis.'

That helped a lot. He pulled himself up a chair, got out his Rizlas and began rolling himself a cigarette. Without looking up he said, 'We'll get you settled in first, then we go and see her. She knows you're coming all right.'

I said, 'Are you the minder?'

Clovis nodded at his cigarette. If anything he seemed even less chirpy than Blackhurst.

I said, 'I was just explaining to your Dee Cee here that the Yard has promised us all the help we need.'

He still didn't look up. 'So what do you need?'

'Frankie's cameras for a start. And a background fill-in on Maureen.'

Clovis said, 'It's no use asking him. He knows nothing. If you're finished, let's go.'

We left Blackhurst sitting there. He didn't kiss us

goodbye. Outside there was a dark green Rover. Clovis did the driving. I did the talking, or most of it. I reckoned a minor lie might come in handy. 'When I saw the Assistant Commissioner he was really up for this story. So how come we're getting treated like the outcasts of the island?'

Clovis said, 'Maureen was a right villain and no mistake. A lot of people think she shouldn't get paid a penny for boasting about what she did.'

'What about you?'

He shot me a sidelong glance. 'I'm just the minder. It's got nothing to do with me.'

I said, 'And what about Stan Defoe?'

'Ask me that again after you've met him.'

So Clovis didn't like him.

We jerked up outside a bungalow. It didn't exactly have *Mon Repos* emblazoned on the wall, but it gave that impression. Two doors along at an identical bungalow a fat woman in ill-advised shorts was bending over her herbaceous border. Clovis said, 'It's got all you need – fridge, cooker, washing machine.'

More importantly, it had two bedrooms. Clovis hung around in the living room while I made merry with the shower. Even Frankie hosed himself down. He still looked grungy. His cameras had turned up in the meanwhile and we were keen to get going.

Clovis said, 'No hurry. I thought it better that you got together over lunch and then you can size each other up. We'll be at a restaurant, so no cameras and I don't want you to start asking her nosy questions.'

Me? I said, 'I suppose Maureen has got some sort of false identity. Like a new name and so on.'

Clovis said, 'There'll be six, maybe seven of us. Maureen and the boyfriend, you two, me and Kay. Kay's a minder too.'

'Who's the seventh?'

'There's Doctor Coadwell. He's the psychologist. He might be there too. When you write your story you don't even mention him. Okay?'

'Never even heard of him. Now, where do we get drink around here?'

Clovis rolled himself another spindly cigarette while he thought it over. 'The beer's better in the NAAFI, but you get a better view at the taverna.'

I argued Frankie down, and so twenty minutes later we were bumping across the sand in the direction of a big sprawling place covered in drink signs. We picked a table out on the seaward side and waited for a waiter. Clovis had gone quiet and then I suddenly remembered my manners. I slipped him a straight hundred quid. 'Look after the bills for us – we don't have any Cypriot money. And let me know when that runs out.'

Clovis got talking again. 'In public you call Maureen Doctor Lawn. Or just Meg. And Stan is Doctor Simon Green. It might be a good idea if you called yourselves some other names too, like you could be Mike, and—' Clovis pointed at Frankie.

I said, 'Frankie.'

'All right, he's Fred or something.'

I said, 'Fred's fine. Remember that Frankie: from now on you're called Fred.'

His mouth said yes, but his eyes said duh? Sometimes he has difficulty remembering the Frankie bit.

Clovis said, 'Mike and Fred. Right, that's settled. Maureen's cover story is that she and Stan are stress counsellors with the Ministry of Defence and they're over here to compare notes with Doctor Coadwell. But don't ask them anything about their work. Talk about the food, the weather, any old crap, but nothing serious. Just one last thing: you won't recognize her.'

He got that right. A couple of hours and several miles later we turned up at a place called the Kyrenia Taverna, still within the base area. Upstairs there was a big busy verandah looking out on to about a mile of beach where there were maybe half a dozen sun worshippers in the whole expanse. The actual sea was about three hundred yards out. The taverna was largely peopled with Brits from the base. Officer caste. They all bellowed at each other so you could hear them half the way to Egypt. They were deeply interested in their own bellowings and they didn't notice Clovis or me as we threaded our way through, but a couple of the womenfolk rolled startled eyes at Frankie as he racketed off the tables. Without his customary carapace of cameras he looked even more stained than usual. The table we wanted was in the shade, right at the far end. Four people were already parked there. In the centre were two women. One was Mo, but I had to guess it was her.

They'd given her a curly black wig and a pair of Jackie O shades. The way I remembered her from the court, she had a normal complexion, but now the wig and the shiny black specs made her look as if she'd been washed in one of those biological powders. Also, she was wearing a black vest thing which didn't help.

She watched us come towards her. She had her mouth set straight across. I think I was wearing my polite smile.

A big bloke camouflaged as a deck chair and with his back to us was the only one talking. You could see him beginning to sense that the others had lost interest. He twisted his neck round and saw Clovis.

'Ah, Derek,' he said. 'We were wondering when you'd get here.'

Clovis just nodded and pulled up a chair. On the far side of the table a blonde with a cheeky grin let me know we were welcome to join the frolics. I ended up sitting next to the big bloke who did all the introductions. He was Ralph Coadwell, the blonde was Kay, Mo was Meg, Stan Defoe was Simon.

I said, 'I'm Mike, and he's Fred.'

Frankie said, 'Yeh, Fred.' But I think that was just for his own information.

The man known as Simon who was really Stan Defoe got hold of a waiter, and God only knows what *he* was called. Bottles aplenty appeared. This was more like it. I settled back with a Bensons and a beer. I'd already worked out the strategy. I was not even going to spare a glance for Mo and partner.

I looked straight across at the blonde. 'So, what's the swimming like?'

There was nothing particularly Sherlock Holmesian about this. She was rigged out in a turquoise bikini which just about held all of her together.

Kay pursed up her little lips as if she had to think about that one. 'It's great, once you're in the water.'

I said, 'Yeh. I find that's generally true about swimming.'

There was a hee-haw from my left. That was Ralph Coadwell chortling. He took off his horn-rims and waved them beachwards. 'What Kay means is that it's too hot to actually get to the sea. You burn your feet on the sand. It must be about thirty degrees down there.'

I took a swallow. 'And what's that in English money?'

Stan Defoe said, 'Eighty-six Fahrenheit.'

So much for the weather. I was still looking at Kay and she was looking at me, but that might just have been because she didn't want to look at Frankie.

I said, 'I suppose a lot of people have property hereabouts.'

Coadwell seemed to think that one was tossed at him. 'I have a small place at Pissouri, on the way to Paphos. D'you know Pissouri? No? Well, it's very popular among people on the base, though I fear it's become a trifle too touristy, and property prices there are going through the roof. Still, it's a better element than you would find, say, in Ayia Napa, or, if you were to go west, at Paphos. Though there still are some undiscovered spots on the west coast.'

If I'd wanted all that, I'd have asked the Cyprus Tourist Board.

Kay said to me, 'Why – are you thinking of staying?'

Anybody earwigging our table might have noticed something odd. Only Kay, Ralph Coadwell and I were doing any talking. Mo and mate were sitting there acting dumb. Clovis had his head down, fiddling with cigarette paper and Frankie was leering at Kay with saliva dripping off his tongue.

I said, 'That depends on some people I've got to see. If they make me feel welcome, who knows, I might just stick around for a while.'

Kay was deliberately pushing it. 'And do you feel welcome?'

'Yesss!' drooled Fred/Frankie.

The waiter whizzed out another pile of Carlsbergs and gins and we drank on for maybe an hour without anything interesting being said, but that was largely because Ralph had the floor. Further along the verandah the bellowers had cleared off but you still imagined you could hear them in the far blue yonder. The verandah backed onto a long and high window. Now the sun had switched direction the glass mirrored the group at the table. From time to time I tossed an idle glance at the window. It told me that Maureen Frew had so far soaked up one and one-quarter gins. Her boyfriend had about four times as much. The window gave me a profile view of him. He was wearing a lemony short-sleeved shirt in that sort of waffle weave. He kept his hands under the table except when he needed one of them to hoist his glass. Both he and Mo were sitting square in their chairs, not tense, but not easy either. They didn't talk to each other. You just caught the occasional glance. It gave you nothing to go on. The afternoon dribbled past.

And then Mo spoke. 'We're going back.'

She stood up and looked directly at me. 'We'll see you tonight – our place – around nine.'

Kay jumped up too and Ralph Coadwell sprung

himself out of the chair. Stan Defoe lingered a moment over the last dregs of his gin. He measured out a thin grin at the rest of us. 'See you later.'

The four trooped off. Defoe had a strange way of walking, chest puffed up and his arms sticking out from his sides, as if he was about to lift a car by the bumper. Maureen was wearing white baggy shorts which were too long to give you a good idea of her legs. Kay's little cheeks wiggled and bounced under her turquoise bikini bottom. She knew what she was doing all right. I don't remember anything about the men's legs.

When they were all gone I said to Clovis, 'That Mo is going to cop laryngitis if she doesn't stop yakking all the time.'

'She'll be okay later.'

Frankie remembered he could talk. 'Hey, what about Kay? Is she game or what?'

Clovis turned black eyes on him but didn't say anything. I was getting interested, for I am a keen student of sexual dynamics. So far it was clear that Ralph the walking deck chair was slavering after Kay. It was even more obvious that Kay was more than interested in a spot of mischief, though not with Ralph, and you could hardly blame her for that. Who with then? I had no illusions. All that eyelash fluttering at the table was not for my benefit. It was designed to make somebody else jealous. That probably meant Clovis. But he wasn't playing. Why not? The whole show was seething with sexual undercurrents. Except for Mo and Stan, the only known lovebirds in the ensemble. Maybe Clovis and Mo . . . I took a squint at his blue jaw and pinched-in cheeks. No, surely not. But women are funny sometimes.

Clovis said, 'Do you get paid a lot of money in your game?'

Frankie said, 'Nine o'clock is too late for me. I'd have to use flash so the pix would be rubbish.'

I soothed him. 'Don't worry. You'll get the chance tomorrow.'

Clovis was still following the money. 'What happens when you're reporting an assignment like this? Do they give you advances, or do you make a claim when you get back?'

I said, 'Have you any mates on the Fraud Squad?'

A bleak smile. I read that as a no.

I said, 'We just think of a figure and then we double it.'

Frankie mourned, 'And then the office cuts it in half.'

I said, 'But we know they're going to do that anyway so the first figure is double what it should be.'

Clovis followed all this with the occasional serious nod of the head. 'Then it pays well?'

'Well enough. And just in case you're wondering why Frankie here never buys a drink, that's because he had all of his bunce locked up in Zeller Maine.'

Clovis actually laughed.

Chapter Nine

In the intervening hours we did many things. Clovis wouldn't let me off the base to buy any summerweight gear but he drove us to a shop where I stocked up on tee shirts and stuff. Frankie treated himself to a safari jacket which scored high on the pocket count. We ate. We drank some more. We had another shower. We changed. Enough fine detail.

Clovis drove us through the trim suburban streets surrounding Happy Valley. You caught the occasional glimpse of kids falling off bikes. Otherwise the place was deserted. We swung a left corner into a backwater that called itself Bournemouth Avenue. I said, 'Well, well, well. Now there's a coincidence. Mo used to work in Bournemouth.'

Clovis, staring straight ahead, said, 'You think that's funny? They had an IRA supergrass out here and they billeted him in Londonderry Lane.'

He chuckled to himself. I guessed those were the sort of jokes Clovis liked.

The safe house was just like all the others in the street, except a hefty bush covered in big yellow flowers lounged against the wall. Kay opened the door and wafted perfume out into the evening. She was happy to see us. We felt likewise. She had on a patterned sarong-type thing with a matching top. The top looked like the sharp end of a bikini. 'Come *in!*' she pealed.

Seeing we were half way down the hall that was a bit redundant. Mo's hidey-hole was a square two-storey house. The decor was about as bland as a cheapo TV soap opera set. The hall was one of those creamy colours, the carpet was grey or maybe green. There was a framed painting of some rural English scene. Otherwise nothing. We followed Clovis into the living room. Stan Defoe was there, still in his shirt and shorts, still with a glass in his hand. His hair was a straw thatch but his eyebrows were black. Either they'd given him a wig or they'd sprayed his eyebrows. No sign of Ralph Coadwell. And then there was Mo. Minus the black curls, minus the shades. She was turned out in a dead simple dress in what I think you call sage. She had a pair of big loopy earrings to match. She looked absolutely knockout.

'Drinks, lads?' asked Stan.

We hung our tongues out and he filled the glasses. I got the impression he liked dishing out drink he didn't have to pay for. By now we were seated on vaguely patterned sofas. Mo was in a chair on her own. She had her eyes battened on me. It wasn't the chummiest gaze I've ever had.

She said, 'My name is Maureen. It is *not* Mo. *Nobody* calls me Mo.'

So we were off to a promising start. I got out my Bensons. Stan helped himself and Kay joined in. Mo didn't.

I said, 'If your name was Jo or, say, Kim, we wouldn't have a problem. But Maureen has seven letters. That's long. Also, in newspaper print the M is half as big again as an ordinary letter. So that means Maureen is seven and a half letters long.'

She said, 'It's still Maureen.'

'And a name that long doesn't fit in headlines, not in a tabloid anyway. That's why we call Paul McCartney Macca, and Gascoigne is Gazza.'

She thought about that for a second. 'But you call Clinton Clinton and that's just as long as Maureen.'

I sighed. I wasn't expecting to have to give a lesson on newspaper subbing. 'The "l" and the "i" and the "t" each count as only half a letter. That means Clinton is a five-and-a-half letter word. I'm just explaining how it goes.'

Her mouth was a straight line. The mouth was at least half a letter too wide for her face. But it still looked good. She said, 'You're only talking about headlines.'

True.

'So there's no reason why you can't call me Maureen in the rest of the story. Is there?'

Also true. I gave in. She eased herself back in the chair and took a dainty sip. Then she sat forward again, back on the attack.

'And you must never refer to me as the wife of Barry Frew. I am the *estranged* wife.'

I said, 'You've got a legal separation?'

She had very fine, very grey eyes. Right now they were shooting ice at me. 'That's not important. We no longer live together. We are estranged.'

I rolled over on that one too. These were small

fishes. I wanted to get to the main course. I said, 'Okay, tell me about your *estranged* husband.'

'You want to know about the Zeller Maine robbery?'

That could wait. What I wanted first was all the grit about their sex life, for I know just what our readers like. This is why I will never become Editor, but I can live with that.

I said, 'Correct me when I get it wrong, but I suppose you were madly in love with him, at one time anyway.'

She turned on her first smile. 'At one time. He was very handsome and charming. And tender. Of course I was in love with him. He was such a funny man, I mean he could always make me laugh.'

Judging by what I'd seen of Mo so far, this Barry Frew must have been a right comedian.

I said, 'You said he was tender. Are you talking about lovemaking?'

I threw this in deliberately just to see how Stan Defoe reacted. He didn't.

Mo swung one leg over the other. She said, 'Yes.'

Terrific. How was I going to spin a couple of thousand words out of that?

I took a long pull on my gin and then spelt it all out. 'Tabloids like ours are interested in just three things: sex, sex and sex. In that order. Sometimes there isn't enough of it around, which is why we have to fill up the paper with stacks of rubbish. What I'm saying here is . . .'

'I know what you're saying. You want to know if Barry was good in bed.' Her smile was wider. 'The answer is yes.'

'How?'

'How? As I've already mentioned, he was tender and thoughtful.'

I said, 'Aren't we all?'

She laughed. It was a deeper, richer laugh than you might have expected from her. I had another dekko at Stan Defoe. He didn't seem fazed by all this between-the-sheets stuff. Though Clovis didn't look too happy.

Mo said, 'Do you give your wife two dozen yellow roses every Friday? Do you buy her sexy lingerie, do you shower her with gifts? Do you pour her pink champagne in crystal goblets?'

Frankly I don't. Rosie's happy enough with a stiff gin.

I said, 'So every Friday . . .'

She swung a white sandal to and fro. 'Yes, every Friday . . . every Friday, Barry would come home with the flowers. Then we would have dinner – you probably want it to be candle-lit. Okay, we lit the candles and we had, now what did we have? I suppose it was usually something cordon bleu. I didn't even have to cook because it was delivered from a restaurant. And afterwards—'

And afterwards things got more than a bit steamy. On occasions four-times-a-night steamy. I'm leaving out the gory details because many of you might even have wives of your own and know the score already.

Throughout this hot and humid saga Stan Defoe sat more or less unmoved. Sometimes he smiled sadly. Mostly he just drank. Yet the way Mo painted it, superstud, superhuman, supercrook Barry Frew was a tough act to follow.

We panted to a full stop somewhere gone midnight. By now Mo was relaxed and chipping in stuff without me having to ask. She even got quite girlish at one stage, giggling when she said, 'I'm sure you thought I looked a fright when you saw me this afternoon.'

Well, yes, but I was hardly going to say that.

She said, 'They – I mean the police – came up with that dreadful hairpiece, and the clothes. But this dress is my own. They were going to put us somewhere else but they changed their minds at the last moment and I didn't have anything suitable for Cyprus. I'm now having to buy a whole new wardrobe by mail order.'

Clovis cut in. 'You don't write anything about that.'

Rats. And there was me going to make that the big story.

Mo stood up to show that the audience was over. Frankie said, 'I'll do the snaps tomorrow?'

She frowned. 'I've no idea what to wear.'

Frankie had that already worked out. 'You could always borrow Kay's bikini.'

'We'll see.' That meant no way.

I said, 'And I need to talk about the Zeller Maine business.'

Mo had her hands on her hips and there was a sharp mischief in the grey eyes. 'I thought you said your paper was only interested in sex, sex and sex.'

I said, 'Yes. But there wasn't enough of it to go around.'

She was the only one who thought that funny.

*

Clovis dropped us off at our holiday chalet. As we clambered out of the Rover, he did a wondrously kind thing: he passed me a litre bottle of Grants. Glenlivet might have been even more wondrously kind, but this is an imperfect world.

I cradled the bottle lovingly. 'How much do we owe you?'

A crooked grin. 'Twice what you'll charge on expenses.'

He drove off.

And so Frankie and I sprawled out in the living room, lapping up scotch from those tubby little glasses you can bounce down fifty storeys and they still don't break. I breathed a contented sigh. Through every minute of the last twenty-four hours I'd had one or other minder perched on my shoulder. It was good to be free of them.

Frankie was thinking much the same. He pulled his snoot out of the whisky. 'You know, Max, this is the first time we've been alone together.'

I said, 'What exactly are you suggesting here?'

'Leave it out. I mean, I'm getting pissed off with Clovis and that lot listening to everything I've got to say. We can't even talk about how we're going to do the job.'

I draped a leg over the arm of the chair and swigged scotch and puffed cigarettes. Sometimes just for the hell of it I did it the other way round.

I said, 'So how do you see it then?'

There are times I forget that Frankie is a pro snapper. There are even more times when I forget that snappers can think. They set you straight on this by thinking out loud, which is what Frankie was doing right now. 'Clovis won't let me take her in a bikini, because that shows she's somewhere hot and they're not going to give out any clues. That means they'll want me to do the pix indoors, but that's just boring.'

I said, 'Unless you get to snap her in the shower.'

There was a five-second silence while he pictured that. 'Naw. She wouldn't go for it.'

He returned to his brooding. I was having trouble too. I was thinking thus: luscious redhead, pink champagne, four-times-a-night, crimson satin sheets, five million in stolen smackers, fugitive hubby, death threats, various murdered villains. Try sticking all that together in one tight paragraph. No, I couldn't do it either.

Maybe she'd come up with a quote that would turn the whole thing round. Or if she didn't, I'd just have to do it for her.

The day dawned bright and blue but that's the way things generally happened out there. We were collected just gone seven by Kay and transported to the mess hall. I was not looking my best, being dressed in a royal blue tee shirt and lighter blue shorts. They were okay for the scene. It was the white arms and whiter legs sticking out the corners that looked like they belonged somewhere else.

Over my second coffee I said to Kay, 'So what's the inside track on Stan?'

She looked stern. 'We're in public' – there was no

one within screaming distance of us – 'call him Simon. You'll need sun cream. You can borrow some of mine.'

Frankie, following his own sordid line of thought, asked, 'Did you lend wot's-er-name your bikini?'

Kay got even sterner. 'She's called Meg. No.'

I said, 'Tell me about Simple Simon, then.'

'Well, I wouldn't call him simple. He's quite a bright chap. But he's no problem, though she can be a bit of a bother sometimes.'

'How?'

'You're not writing this, okay? You probably think Meg's, well, she tried to make a joke of it last night when she was talking about the hairpiece, but when she first saw it she blew her top. Simon just rolls along and doesn't really fuss about anything. By the way, he's joining us this morning; Meg wants to leave the next session to the afternoon.'

I said, 'They're not exactly Romeo and Juliet.'

'Not in public.'

'Uh-uh. Not even in private. Like last night. She chirps her head off about what a right old time of it she had romping around with Barry Frew. And Stan just sits there looking gormless.'

Kay smiled an enigmatic smile. 'Last night was public. I don't know what they do in private, but it sounds like they're not quite as unromantic as you're making out.'

I said, 'Do you stick a glass against their bedroom wall, or is this just one of these things that A Woman Knows?'

A chirp of laughter. 'A woman knows.'

Yeh. I thought as much.

We trawled off to a sports club on the base. There was a freshly washed swimming pool hidden away at the back with a decorative border of those yellow-flowered things just like the one outside Mo's place. The Army must have been off practising how to walk for we were the only punters around. Kay said, 'You two make yourselves at home here while I go and get Simon. Now don't move.'

Frankie and I were already laid out on a couple of sun loungers. A skittish breeze chased over us. Just behind me a waiter with a big silver tray hovered to take our order.

Frankie was baffled. 'Why should we move?'

It was a full hour before she returned with Simon. He was arrayed in a purplish shirt and red and green checked shorts. There's no accounting for taste. I hadn't given him a proper look over before so now I took my time examining Simon, also known as Stan Defoe. He wasn't tall, say five eight, five nine, but he was solid. He probably had a set of weights parked under his bed. I couldn't see his eyes because they were hidden behind a pair of those dumb mirror shades. He had a taut grin across the visible half of his face.

'Hello again. You men look as if you're enjoying yourselves.'

I said, 'We are masters at concealing our true feelings.'

A chuckle of sorts. He pulled up a lounger and stationed himself on my right. Kay did likewise, so that she was on his right. I would have preferred it the other way round. Especially when she whipped off her dress and revealed a sketchy pink bikini.

The waiter hove up with a couple of beers for Frankie and me. Stan Defoe shook his head. 'No. Nothing. Too early for me.'

Maybe he was still on London time.

I said, 'It's a good place to hide.'

'Yep. We've no complaints. But we're not here for good.'

I said, 'How did you two meet?'

'What – me and, uh, Meg?' He laughed a laugh which was for his own amusement only. 'Well, she didn't give you the *whole* story last night.'

'What am I missing?'

'You've got to remember she's still frightened of Frew. I mean, you can't blame her. He was a right sod sometimes.'

I said, 'So she left that bit out. And what else?'

'Us. She left us out too. God, it's hot.' Defoe sat up and whipped off his shirt. Underneath it he was wearing a black fur vest. Closer inspection revealed it to be the densest, blackest forest of chest hair ever seen on a human being. He looked more like a Barbary ape. Maybe they'd given him a chest rug too.

Kay meanwhile had fallen into a sunbaked coma, with only the gentle rise and fall of her bikini letting you know she was still alive. It was a good time to ask questions.

I said, 'So why don't you tell me about "Us".'

He told the yarn with many a self-satisfied chortle. It started well over a year back. That was when Barry Frew recruited him to landscape his back garden with trees and roses and things like that. Naturally in the course of this work he got to meet Mo. Picture the scene: there's stolid Stan out in the dandelions brandishing a pickaxe when Mo leans out the window. 'Yo-ho. Can I fetch you a cup of tea?' That's the way I imagined it anyway.

Possibly Mo had a weakness for human gorillas. At any rate, a month or so later they were having naughties. Serious naughties. They were helped in this by the fact that Frew was away a lot on business, which meant his garden went to hell. Before long the affair had moved on from plain old-fashioned lust to something worse. L-o-v-e. Stan started putting the squeeze on Mo to dump her old man and leg it with him. She was wibbling and wobbling over what to do when one night Barry Frew came home when he wasn't supposed to and found Mo and Godzilla cavorting on his crimson sheets. Sharp rush of adrenalin all round. Frew thumped the nearest thing which came to hand. Unfortunately that was his missus. Stan, the way he told it, leapt from the bed and gave his boss a right pasting. For, as Stan explained, 'He wasn't up to much, but I can look after myself.'

Frew went bouncity-bounce-bounce down the stairs, repainting the walls a fetching blood colour as he passed. Somehow he was still capable of speech. 'You slut,' he squealed up the stairs. 'And you, Defoe, get the hell out of my house.'

As an afterthought he added, 'And you're fired.'

I put this together. 'So, that's the *real* reason he cut her out of her share on the Zeller Maine deal.'

Defoe shrugged. It looked like a yes.

I said, 'I haven't figured out the timetable here. This must have been some time after the robbery, for she had been helping him launder the money.'

Another shrug. I took a deep swig of lager. 'But you didn't even know she was involved?'

He turned his mirror eyes on me. 'That's right.'

Yeah, and my favourite drink is Babycham.

I said, 'And of course you had nothing to do with the laundering.'

Just a nod. I supposed it saved him having to tell more lies.

I lay back and gazed at the wide and empty sky. I said, 'You're lucky you weren't involved . . .'

'Too right, mate. Look what's happened to those three guys who got topped.'

'And Mo – Meg – got nothing.'

His mouth turned down. 'Not a cent. Not a bleeding farthing.'

We might have continued in this vein, but all of a sudden Kay sat up. Ever-so-sweetly she asked, 'Would one of you kind gentlemen rub some sun cream on my back?'

No. Neither of us kind gentlemen would. We left that to Frankie.

At lunchtime we had a switch of minder. Kay tripped off and Clovis turned up. Much as I missed her, I was glad to see him.

I said, 'I want to talk to – to interview Ralph Coadwell.'

'No.'

I said, 'Hear me out on this. I want him to tell me how he prepares a supergrass for a new life. I want to know the techniques, the whole caboodle. I will *not* quote him on this. I'll just say Meg is getting counselling. I'll even say it's a woman counsellor.'

'No.'

'No?'

'No.'

I said, 'That sounds like "no" to me. I need to speak to Assistant Commissioner Hilden.'

Barring the odd press conf. I've never talked to AC Hilden, but I wanted Clovis to feel the man was never off my phone. You see, Hilden is the great bright hope of Scotland Yard. All right, I know that doesn't mean much in the real world, but it sets cops back on their heels.

Clovis rolled a matchstick-thin cigarette. 'What do you want to say to him?'

'The brief that I got was this story is aimed at making some other wives and loved ones dish the dirt on their partners. If I can write how there's a whole support programme for supergrasses, then that's a Good Thing.'

Clovis was unconvinced.

I said, 'Look, for heaven's sake, if I write anything that Hilden doesn't like, he'll just rip it out. He has the final say-so.'

Clovis looked at me steadily. 'I'll phone somebody.'

'Who? Hilden?'

'No.'

Thank God for that.

I settled back in the lounger just as Ralph Coadwell

steamed into shot. He was wearing a shirt that looked like a cross between Southampton's home strip and Arsenal's away kit. I made a mental note to get myself a pair of sun specs.

'Well, well, well,' said he. 'And where's the fair Kay?'

Nobody bothered to answer. The shirt of many colours lowered himself onto a neighbouring lounger and flagged for beer.

Clovis said to me, 'By the way, we've been in touch with your Editor to let him know where you are.'

I spilled good lager. 'You told him we're in *Cyprus?*'

A warped grin. 'As if we'd say that. He thinks you're somewhere in the north of Scotland.'

I said, 'Let's hope they're having scorching weather in the Mull of Kintyre.'

Clovis didn't care if it was snowing golf balls thereabouts.

'Because,' I continued, 'when we return all bronzed and beautiful the Editor's going to think it a bit odd.'

He thought that over. 'Then tell him we flew you on somewhere else. But not Cyprus.'

I said, 'It's bloody hot here in Gibraltar.'

'Yeh. Gibraltar. I like Gibraltar.'

So we lounged on, draining the bottles and listening to Ralph Coadwell splosh around like a drowning steamroller.

We didn't get to see Maureen Frew until gone three. This time Frankie had all his toys with him. Not to be outdone I had a notebook and pen. We almost looked like tabloid journos again.

Stan Defoe was standing by the big flowery bush. He gave us 25 per cent of a smile.

I said, 'Just love your garden, Stan.'

'What? This yellow thing? Bloody horrible, isn't it?'

He turned and stomped off down the hall with his arms sticking out. It looked like he was trying to waft air up his armpits. Over his shoulder he asked, 'Are you taking the pictures now?'

'Some of them,' Frankie said ominously.

Defoe braked sharply. 'Well I don't want any taken of me.'

Frankie's jaw dropped. I suppose mine did too. I said, 'That's part of the deal. We're paying you for words *and* pix.'

Defoe dug his heels in. 'You can do Maureen, but not me.'

Clovis was standing by with an evil little grin on his face. He was enjoying this.

I said, 'What's the problem? Frankie takes pretty snaps.'

Okay, it was a lie, but we had to get the pix.

Stan shook his straw hair. 'I don't want anybody back home recognizing me.'

The way Frankie takes snaps, there was little chance of that. But I didn't say so.

I said, 'Let's see if I've got this straight: if anyone's going to put the kibosh on you it will be Barry Frew. Remember him? Because he most certainly remembers you – and he knows *exactly* what you look like.'

Stan said, 'He's the only one. I never met the people in his gang.'

I wasn't making the connections. 'So?'

Stan said, 'He hasn't got a picture of me. And the police made sure I got rid of all my photographs. But if you have a picture of me in your paper, his people will know who to look for.'

By now I was getting more than a bit cheesed off. I said, 'You're wearing a wig, right? You look different already.'

'Not different enough.'

'Okay then, borrow Doctor Coadwell's specs.'

Frankie added, 'And we could draw some lines on your face with Maureen's mascara. That'd alter the whole shape.'

Nice thinking, Frankie.

Defoe didn't agree. I did. But it was the sudden appearance of Kay that turned the whole show around. She said, 'Why don't you just try it, Stan? If we make you up and you still feel it doesn't work then we'll try something different.'

'Like what?'

'Well, there must be an amateur dramatics company on the base and we could get things from them. A moustache, for instance, or a beard. How about it?'

Frankie gave Kay a thank-you leer. And Stan the pillock went off for a make-over. For reasons best known to himself, Coadwell followed them out. All this while Maureen had been sitting in the same chair as last night not saying a word.

I parked myself opposite and took her in. She was wearing a blue long-sleeved shirt with butterflies or somesuch fluttering all over it. Most of the rest of her was covered up in white trousers. She said, 'I suppose I'd better put this on.'

And the bell of rusty red hair disappeared beneath the shapeless black hairpiece. It was as if somebody had turned off the light. Her face was narrower now, and older. She might have been a humdrum housewife. Still, that was Frankie's problem, not mine.

He sorted it. 'Your old man must have pictures of you. You don't have to wear the syrup. Does she?'

The last bit was addressed to Clovis. He wagged his head in a way that might have meant yes, no, or just maybe.

Mo took it as a yes and off came the rug. That was better. She rested her chin on her knuckles and looked up at Frankie. I think she was trying to pose.

He stared at her with his mouth turned down. 'Are those the best clothes you've got?' he asked in that suave diplomatic way of his.

'Yes. Unfortunately I had to leave my fishnet tights and French maid's outfit back in England.'

Good grief. The woman had actually cracked a joke. I let her know I appreciated it. One of us had to, for I think Frankie thought she was serious.

Clovis broke his silence. 'All of the photographs must be taken in here.'

'But I'll have to use flash and they'll turn out all grainy,' Frankie bleated. And off we went on another argument. In the end Clovis agreed she could be snapped in the minute back garden. She didn't seem to care where it happened.

While Frankie geared himself up I kept the conversation going. 'Last night you told me about yourself. Tell me about Stan.'

She wasn't happy. 'Why?'

'Because I'm writing about both of you. Tell me how you met, that sort of thing.'

She was slow, doling out pieces of the story like so many crumbs. It added up to much the same as he'd told me, only she put in lines like how she was 'swept off her feet' by the hairy one. She left out the episode of how Stan knocked her hubby topsy-turvy down the stairs. I thought it only fair to remind her. She was not particularly grateful. She patted her knees demurely and with her head down she said, 'Yes. That's the way it happened. But I don't want to talk about it.'

'All right, what do you want to talk about?'

Maureen gave me the cold grey stare. 'Wait until Stan gets back.'

So I contented myself with smoking and watching Frankie go through his routine. I've got to hand it to him, he tried his best but she still kept her blouse on. She did switch the trousers for a skirt, so he got some nice leggy shots. He took her in profile, he took her head-on. He shot her smiling, and he shot her like she'd just had her lips sewn up. He got her every way except one: she never once looked sexy.

After about five rolls of film, Maureen said, 'That's it. No more.'

She had a lot to learn. Frankie just kept on popping. Then Stan Defoe turned up in specs and painted-on sideburns and a little 'tache. He didn't half look moronic. But at least he looked different. The photo shoot commenced anew, this time with Mo and Stan holding hands, kissing, cuddling, and that's just about as far as they were prepared to go on camera.

Clovis was deeply absorbed in Frankie's caperings. I'd lost interest. I'd seen all this before. Many, many times. I rolled off in search of Ralph Coadwell. I ran him to earth in the kitchen where he was drowning a tea bag. 'Cup for you?' he offered.

And this man is a psychologist? I indicated that something livelier than PG Tips was called for, and he, heroic soul, suggested I tuck into the beers in the fridge. I duly tucked. We sat there sipping for a couple of minutes until I judged the time was right.

'So, how do you get involved in a business like this?'

'Psychology?'

Well, that would do for starters. He warbled on for some distance about his CV. It was stodgy stuff, but he felt safe with it. Also, he was enjoying this sudden attention. I showed only polite interest.

Coadwell moved on from the general to the specific. 'But the major tool in this field of my work is undoubtedly the application of social and psychological identity profiling. It enables one to—'

I checked him. 'Social and what?'

A blokish laugh. 'I forget you are a layman. To put it crudely, what it means is we can create a new psychological profile in a person, yet a profile which does not conflict with their original persona.'

He wanted to breeze on, but I needed this chopped up into bite-sized pieces. I said, 'I suppose it's like giving someone a new hair style that still suits them.'

Coadwell didn't think it was even vaguely like that.

I did. He chewed his tea for a moment. 'Let's see. Say you had been taken hostage in Beirut and you had been held captive for some considerable period of time, on your release it would be found that there has been a significant personality change.'

I couldn't see where he was going with this but I uncapped another beer and smiled winsomely.

Coadwell said, 'The critical aspect from the psychologist's stance is that your personality had been altered to enable you to survive your incarceration. Now, what we have identified is that the hostage is subconsciously able to recognize the *need* to change, purely to continue to exist in this hostile environment.'

He saw my eyes begin to glaze over. 'If we move on from there to, let us say, a situation where one must make a *conscious* choice to change one's psychological profile in order to survive: the essential element is to ensure that the new identity does not conflict with one's underlying characteristics.'

I nodded wisely. 'So what you're saying is that Maureen is having a personality change.'

He stroked an invisible beard. 'That is a huge oversimplification.'

Maybe it was. But it was true.

I said, 'How do you go about changing someone's personality?'

The way he smiled it must be a doddle.

He said, 'The initial step is to alienate the subject from his or her surroundings.'

I took a dekko around the poky kitchen. Well, they'd done that all right.

Coadwell saw my glance. 'Not merely the physical

environment. That can be changed by simply hopping on a bus. The alienation has several strands. As far as is possible, relationships with those who were previously friends or colleagues must be relinquished. To put it simply, it is like walking out of a room full of such friends and closing the door on them for ever.'

This was more like it.

He said, 'So now the person is on his own, in much the same way as a hostage in Beirut. A personality change has already begun to develop, but there is a grave danger that this change might be detrimental to the psychological well-being. If you like, it might manifest itself as a siege mentality.'

He didn't read many tabloids, that man.

I said, 'So what do you do?'

He upped his chin and stared at the ceiling thoughtfully. He had little blond hairs sticking out of his nose. After a while he said, 'It is my role to establish the various traits which make up an individual's overall personality, for want of a better word. Some of these characteristics may have been deliberately or artificially repressed or perhaps even amplified by the subject's previous circumstances.'

I weighed in, 'So you tweak some up and you tone some down.'

He didn't like it put that way but he couldn't think of a better way.

I said, 'Does that mean you can turn a shrinking violet into a right little raver?'

An indulgent guffaw. 'Hardly. Unless the shrinking violet is actually a repressed "raver", as you call it.'

I'd liked that line about closing the door on the past. 'How do you set about this alienating job?'

'Alienation? You cease to make available to the subject anything which refers to his or her previous existence.'

'That means no TV, no newspapers.'

Coadwell beetled a brow or two. 'Among other things. Letters must perforce be scrutinized. We seek to discourage phone calls.'

I said, 'But now you have me here, getting Maureen to rabbit on about her past life. That must put the mockers on alienating her from it.'

His cheeks split wide open in a smug grin. 'But that is *precisely* why you are here. I advocated it.'

No. Eighty grand was why I was here.

Coadwell said, 'One could liken your position to that of a priest: Maureen is making her confession to you, after which she receives absolution.'

And eighty big ones.

I said, 'So once she's spilled her heart out to me, that's it? She forgets everything?'

More or less. He said, 'It is a public renunciation. She has publicly renounced her past.'

Yeh. I got that the first time. I said, 'And when you've done your biz . . .?'

'The subject is free to start a new life with a new name and a change of persona.'

'An altered image?'

Coadwell wasn't having any of that. 'A change of persona.'

The door dunked open behind me and Kay stuck her head round. She had more spikes than a hedgehog.

'Hello,' she said, all bright eyes, 'and what are you two talking about?'

I said, 'Bad women.'

She tossed her head, showed us her teeth, inhaled visibly, shrugged her shoulders and vanished again. She probably thought we were jabbering about her.

I turned back to Ralph. His teeth were frozen in a blistering smile. All for Kay's benefit and she'd already gone. So there was no sense talking to him. My bottle was empty. I got up to unburden the fridge.

Timing is everything. That's what they say. Timing when you're drinking is even more important. If I had not developed a raging thirst at that particular moment, or, if the fridge had suddenly run out of cold ones, I would have missed it.

It doesn't sound much now, but here's what happened. I opened the fridge, whipped out a can and, as I snapped the jigger up, I glanced out the window. My highly trained eyes told me that Frankie was no longer there. Nor was Stan Defoe. Just Mo, and not very far behind her, Clovis. She had on a happy sunshiny look. This might just have had something to do with the fact that Clovis had his right palm cupped around half her bottom.

The lager can was still ten inches south of my mouth. It stayed there, almost forgotten. Out back in the scratchy little garden Maureen turned towards her minder and said something. His hand dropped. But they were both still smiling.

Chapter Ten

That night I whopped it back like a Trojan. Red wine, beer, local gin, and something which called itself brandy but wasn't. If the waiter had bothered with underarm deodorant I would have whiffed on that too.

This was a subtle ploy.

Frankie whacked down just about as much, though I don't think he had any particular ploy in mind.

We were all, the whole mob of us, out together in an open-air restaurant where fronds dangled in front of your face and crickets fought to make themselves heard over the racket of a band playing several variations of *Zorba the Greek*.

This was my treat. I'd insisted on it. I even did the seating arrangements. I was north, Mo was due south. Clovis was on her right, Ralph Coadwell on her left. Up at my end I had Frankie to one side and Kay to the right. That was just to stop him pestering her. Between Kay and Coadwell was Defoe. So now you have the scene.

The conversation was not exactly littered with witty aphorisms and all that. Mostly it was about drink and the affects thereof. I contributed a tale or two. One affect which I carefully neglected to mention is that under the influence you begin to see things which aren't there.

By now my guests were beginning to see a semi-guttered Max Chard. See what I mean? Funnily enough, Frankie twigged it. He went reasonably quietish.

Psycho Ralph stampeded into every gap with stories that began: 'I remember once . . .' but never lived up to their early promise. Meanwhile I was watching the rest. Mo was close to sparkling and just every now and then she tilted her head towards Clovis. Sometimes he glanced her way too. But there was never a direct exchange. Straw-thatch Stan was operating on his own channel and not broadcasting a lot, except to Kay. And whatever she had to say to him she said it so soft I couldn't catch.

The band quit their plonking and the other diners took the hint. Apart from us and an underage waiter, the place was empty. Maureen cut across whatever Ralph was saying and tilted her wineglass at me, 'That's it, Max. You've got everything you're going to get. No more questions. Okay?'

The drink made her eyes rounder, harder.

I said, 'Not everything.'

Clovis broke in, 'We don't talk here.'

Maureen swung her curly wig round at him. 'I've had enough. I—'

Clovis jumped on her, 'We don't talk here.'

Ralph Coadwell snatched the ball. 'What say we go back and have a nightcap?'

At least the waiter was all for it. He stuck a bill down in front of me. The bottom line read close on a hundred and eighty quid. Not bad for seven thirsty scoffers.

Stan Defoe read my face. 'That's *Cypriot* pounds.'

So?

Ralph said, 'That's nearly two hundred of our pounds.'

Stan pretended he hadn't spoken. 'Which comes to about two hundred and twenty-four sterling. Call it two fifty, when you add on the tip.'

I still wasn't complaining. Anyway, it was no longer my problem, for Clovis picked up the bill and flashed me a meaningful look. It read: 'You now owe me two hundred-odd quid.'

He pocketed the bill. Fair enough. But I did have one minor quibble booting around. How was I going to rake up expenses if I didn't have a wodge of hooky receipts?

This conundrum teased me all the way to the car. Clovis, Frankie and I were in the green Rover, the others in something else. We shot off with a squeal of rubber and yawed through a 25 mph corner at about twice that and a bit besides. He was a snappy driver, was our Clovis. If he was trying to impress or even scare me, he was wasting his time. Just remember, I've driven with Frankie Frost and, so far, have lived to tell the tale.

We zig-zagged down a hillside in silence. When he spurted out of the bottom zag, Clovis said, 'You want Maureen to tell you about the Zeller Maine business – is that it?'

'And the rest.'

Half a mile more silence, then, 'What rest?'

In the back seat Frankie woke up. 'Yeh, and I want some decent snaps too. That stuff I got today is just crap.'

Crap was a euphemism.

I said to Clovis, 'Right now I need your help. Mo's too wound up. You tell her to take it easy and we'll have this all sorted tonight. Pix and words.'

He had his face set straight ahead but I could see the edge of a crooked grin. 'And why should she listen to me?'

I said it deadpan. 'Because it is generally my experience that women are prepared to listen to men who squeeze their bums.'

Now there was serious silence. He gummed his right foot to the floor. Villages, trees and things that might have been trees zipped past the window. I turned my head round and there was Frankie with his mouth wide open. He was sticking together what I'd just said.

About three minutes later I heard him go, 'Bloody hell!'

Still nothing from our driver, but he'd eased off the revs. I spotted a familiar-looking taverna. We were nearly home.

Clovis said, 'Is that what you want to talk to her about?' His voice had no tone, hardly even a question mark.

'No. That's between you and her. Nor am I interested in the possibility that Kay and Stan are also up to mischief. I just want you to sweet-talk Mo so I can get the story stuck together.'

'And the decent pix,' from Frankie.

'And the pix.'

Clovis said, 'Just as long as I know what you want to ask her.'

We were back at Dun Thievin'. I was in the living room cradling a proper Gordons. Stan, Kay and Dr Strangelove were sprawled hither and thither. They were not used to this drinking league so they were all a tad cheery, and I was acting likewise, right down to laughing at Ralph Coadwell's alleged jokes. Clovis and Frankie were in the bedroom with Mo and by the sound of things they were enjoying themselves in there too. Or at least she was. Every so often I caught a merry peal of laughter. Once I heard her say, 'Oooh no. I *could*n't.'

Oooh yes, for eighty thousand she damn well could. Next came the whizz-whirr of a Canon motordrive, followed by Frankie's: 'Lovely. Now, put your leg here, no the other one, yeh, higher, and look up. That's it. Big eyes, *big* eyes. That's it. Belter. All right, and . . .'

I've never figured out how he does it. Women must be different. I mean, if some Amazonian on stilts came up to me with her Sureshot and invited me to strip down to my boxers, I'd tell her I wasn't that sort of bloke. Well, not unless she went first.

Sometime in the early hours Frankie had had enough. The happy threesome reappeared, though Clovis wasn't looking too sunny. Mo was wearing a silky greeny-goldy kimono thing and I'm prepared to bet there wasn't very much underneath it. She was all coy and cute, and more than a little tickled with herself. That's why I got Clovis to set up the snaps before I did my stuff.

I jumped up and weighed out a monster gin for Mo. I added an inch of tonic, pouring that very carefully on top so she wouldn't notice the mix.

Clovis was already briefed. He said to Kay, 'Max here has just got a few details to iron out with Maureen and Stan. Why don't you give Ralph a lift?'

Ralph said, 'Right-oh!'

I don't think Kay was quite so hot, and Stan was a shade deflated.

Kay said, 'Okay then, I'll come back as soon as I've dropped Ralph off.'

I was sitting in the swivel chair. All I had to do was swing this way and that. Clovis caught it. He said, 'No need, Kay. Take an early night. See you in the morning. G'night Ralph.'

And off they went. Kisses, hugs, steamed-up glasses, all that. So now there were just four people left: Clovis, me, Mo and Stan. Frankie doesn't count.

Mo was on the sofa beside Stan. There was a yard of cushion between them. She had a hefty belt of gin and she pulled her knees up and all you could see was her pink toes sticking out from under the kimono thing. The toes curled prettily over a pinker cushion and her head canted forward my way. Her hair fell over in a fringe so I couldn't see what her eyes were up to.

She said, 'Do you know, tonight's the first time I've really enjoyed myself here?'

I'll bet.

You might not believe this, but Frankie is sharp as

a fox. He was fiddling around with the buttons on the hi-fi. 'Let's have some music. What does everybody like?'

Mo perked her chin up. 'Sinatra.'

'Frank Sinatra?'

Yeh, that Sinatra.

It creamed out of the speakers. *Start spreading the noos . . .*

Karaoke Mo joined in, only in a decent accent, ' . . . I'm leavin' todayyy . . .'

She didn't get any further with it because it suddenly struck her as the funniest thing she'd ever said. I could believe that.

Ol' Shut Eyes chuntered on in the background while some of us let our hilarity run riot. After a while Maureen sussed that I was chuckling less than some of us.

She said, 'Come on, Max. Loosen up.'

I dished her my brightest beam. 'Fill me in on the fine print, Maureen, and I'll sing tenor.'

I have to hand this to her. She knew what I wanted. 'Turn the music down, Frankie. Max wants to be *see*-rious.'

And dead right too. I got my notebook out just to show how *see*-rious this was. It was even worse than that. I'd only three cigarettes left. I said, 'I want to launder five million quid. How do I do it?'

She drew in the kimono so the goldy bits stood out. Or maybe she was just breathing. She said, 'It's all in my court evidence. You know this already.'

Bits. I knew bits. I still didn't know how she washed five mill.

Maureen hiked one leg over the other so now I could take in a fair length of thigh. I stayed just the same as I was. She studied me for a long moment then she said, 'Go and sit in the chair, Stan; I want Max over here beside me.'

He got up making a sort of 'humph' noise. Maureen patted the cushion. 'Come on.'

I sat down very close to her because that's what she wanted.

She laid warm white fingers flat on my thigh and gave me the full treatment with her eyes. She was trying to make them soft but they were still a shade tigerish. I bet she was a right handful.

She hauled in a sigh which went all the way down. 'All right. Write this down. You put it in a bank.'

I said, 'Just out of the blue you stick five million in your cheque account and the bank manager doesn't suss there's something funny going on?'

A big self-satisfied smirk. 'Not if you use the right bank.'

All right, Mo. Tease me, flirt with me. I'm still asking questions.

I said, 'And which is the right bank?'

By now she was mainstreaming on neat gin so she thought that was a silly question. A giggle, a finger wagging at me.

'Your *own* bank.'

I batted an eyelid. 'You bought a *bank*?'

'Too bloody right. We bought three of them. It's not as hard as you think, Mister Know-It-All reporter. It only costs you about ten thousand pounds a time.'

I lit my pre-penultimate Bensons. 'So, it's as simple as that?'

Over in the chair Stan chuckled to himself.

Mo said, 'No, it's not that easy. First of all you buy a string of different companies in all sorts of places.'

'Such as?'

'Such as Liechtenstein, the Caymans, Hong Kong, Panama . . . everywhere you can think of. Some of them hold shares in each other, and they own the banks. But the names of the directors are false so the authorities can never establish who owns what.'

I was writing all this down. I was also trying to work out how on earth I could make this simple enough for our readers to understand. I was having problems there because I didn't understand too much of it myself.

I said, 'Is that where the Zeller Maine loot is now – tucked up in your banks?'

'God, Max. You haven't got the faintest idea.'

Stan came to the rescue. 'What Maureen told me was that the money had to vanish and turn into something else.'

She slapped him down. 'As soon as we got the money we wired it to the banks. Then we instructed them to convert it into different things, like negotiable bonds and shares. These were wired on to the dummy companies and they turned them into something else again.'

I said, 'So now it's in dozens of iffy company accounts all round the world.'

'No. Now it's clean. Now it's in legitimate banks and nobody can touch it.'

'Where?'

'Ah.' More finger-wagging. 'Wouldn't I love to know. Barry's plan was to switch it into the People's First Fiduciary Trust of Hong Kong – because the Chinese don't care where the money comes from. He also had slices going to Bulgaria and Pakistan, as they're just as easy. But I know that once he ran off with that little tart of his, he'd have moved it somewhere else.'

Stan said, 'He had it in so many accounts that he forgot some. That's how the police were able to get some of it back. There was sixty-eight thousand in Luxembourg and another thirty in Guernsey. But the rest is . . .' He shrugged.

Maureen leaned her head back on the cushions so I could admire her bumps. 'And do you want to know something really funny – it took us precisely one hour and thirty-six minutes to launder every penny.'

High finance is too abstract for me. I said, 'What about the rest of the stuff in the safe deposit boxes, the jewellery and so on?'

She still had her eyes on the ceiling. As if she was reading from a tele-prompt she said, 'The rest went to the shell companies and they turned it into cash. I don't know too much about that end because I was only handling the money.'

Stan said, 'I expect they did deals with other off-shore banks, using the stuff to raise loans and things like that.'

I had my pen still loitering over page one of my notebook. So far I'd used up maybe ten lines. I shot a glance across at Clovis. He was rolling a cigarette. It looked like he had a lot of loose tobacco to spare. Frankie was just pouring drink into himself.

I was the only one looking for sense around here. I said, 'And did you get to keep any of the trinkets, Maureen?'

'Uh-oh. That bastard took the lot, but his little trollop is probably wearing a ring as big as an egg.'

I think she was talking about the size of the actual sparkler. I said, 'Tell me about her.'

There wasn't a lot on file, largely because Maureen had seen her just the once. Her name was either Sonia or Tanya. She had bottle blonde hair and all the usual trimmings. She was in the company of Dave Stretch, and Maureen, innocent little wife that she was, assumed that Tanya/Sonia was just one of his minor distractions. She assumed that all the way until about a month after the robbery when one day she got an anonymous phone call.

'Your old man's having it off with my Sonia,' said the caller. Or it might have been Tanya. He didn't say anything else.

That night Barry copped an earful from his beloved wife, who, it must be remembered was already disporting herself with Hairball Stan. Frew denied everything and calmed Maureen down with tales of what he and she would do with their cut of the Zeller Maine stack.

Two weeks later came the fateful night when he found Stan and Mo making whoopee.

I said, 'And he walked out.'

Maureen looked at me as if I was the sozzled one around here. 'Barry was too cold-blooded for that. After Stan left that night we sat down and talked it over. You see, the big problem was I was helping him shift the money. I knew too much.'

I had a reasonable question. 'Why didn't you walk out?'

Stan chortled. Maureen's hand renewed its acquaintance with my thigh. She said, 'Max, oh Max, just think about it: we weren't just husband and wife – we were *partners*. His share of the robbery was three million, and I was due a big cut of that.'

So over the kitchen table Barry and Mo worked out a deal. The partnership would continue until all the cash had been through the washer. She'd get her chunk – a million – and then goodbye. In the meantime she would kick Stan into touch and behave herself. It sounded a fair exchange. Next morning she was back on the phone wiring money all over the shop. Barry Frew forgot his bruises and insisted she lodge her million with a bank in the Dutch Antilles.

A couple of days later he shipped her off to Lugano to lay a false paper trail on the Antilles money. Mo was gone four days. When she returned, Barry had skipped the coop, taking with him all his clothes, papers, the works. Her slice was no longer in the Antilles and the bank there had clean forgotten where it had gone to. Frew had also gone over their house with acetone – the place stank something rotten – wiping every surface so there wasn't even a fingerprint left.

But, said Mo, what really brassed her off was he'd nicked their wedding album. Women are weird, aren't they? You would have thought that was the sort of thing she'd junk in the bin. I said as much.

She turned stroppy. 'You just don't understand how

it feels; it feels like a piece of yourself has been stolen. I mean, he took *everything*, our holiday snapshots, pictures of me on my own, every last scrap. It's like I don't even have a past.'

A heartfelt groan spilled out of Frankie. He'd been counting on a clutch of her old snaps to beef up his own pix.

'But,' said Maureen with acid glee, 'at least the police know his DNA. They got that off his hairs on the bedroom carpet.'

Terrific. So if Barry Frew ever breezed into New Scotland Yard demanding a short back and sides, they'd have him.

I said, 'If you had to make an inspired guess, where would you say Frew was right now?'

She lobbed back a ration of gin and her eyes went all thoughtful. I hung around waiting. After a while she said, 'It would be somewhere hot, 'cos he's really into that sort of thing. And that little blonde bitch looked as if she spent her life sunning herself in Marbella. But I wouldn't say Spain. Somewhere more glamorous. Rio? The Virgin Islands? Christ, that's a joke, him and her in the Virgins.'

I was already out of cigarettes and nearly out of questions. I said, 'So there they are, lounging by a pool in Costa Rica. She's pouring Cuba Libre into herself. What's he drinking?'

'Frew didn't drink,' Stan burbled.

Mo was still off in her own imaginings. 'I don't think it would be the Med. Too many English people around. He might bump into someone . . .'

A little light flickered in the grey eyes. 'God, it would be awful if he was here. That's frightening.'

I said, 'Yeh. Especially when you think of what happened to Benny Sloman and the others.'

Clovis – remember him? – jumped straight out of his seat. 'Okay. That's enough. You've got all you need.'

Mo said, 'Why? What—?'

Clovis moved across so he was between her and me. He swung his back to me, 'Maureen, you're tired. It's late. If he's got anything else to ask, he can do it through me.'

Actually I did have something to ask: why was Clovis suddenly so uppity?

He swung round my way and gave me the black look. 'No more questions, okay?'

I know a no when it means no. I said, 'Okay, you're the minder.'

There was a sardonic edge to 'minder', but it went right past him.

'I'll drive you back.'

In his quiet corner Frankie turfed a quintuple scotch down his throat just like that. Stan got to his feet, rubbed his hands on his trousers and held out one of them for me to shake. So this was goodbye. I didn't mind. I was already thinking of the pack of Bensons awaiting me.

Mo was a touch more emotional. 'You're good fun, Max. I'll miss you.' Gin suited her.

She held my hand all the way out to the door. Stan stayed put. Clovis crowded our steps.

At the door she put her hands on my cheeks, pulled me towards her and kissed me smack-dab on the lips.

Then her arms went round my neck and she buried half my face in her hair. That's what Clovis saw.

But he didn't hear her whisper in my ear, 'What happened to Benny?'

Nor did he hear me whisper back, 'Nothing happened.'

She gently pushed my face away, still with her fingers curled round my cheeks. Her mouth was smiling straight up at me, a little wide, a little wanton. But her eyes were chill grey. We held that for a second, maybe more. Then she kissed me again.

It wasn't lust or love or any of those daft things. It was simply a tribute from one bare-faced liar to another. But it was fun all the same.

I walked away.

Back in the Rover, Clovis had become Man of Stone. That left Frankie for small talk. He was full of it. 'She was an absolute darling. You ought to see the snaps I've got. Knock your eyes out.'

It sounds cruel, but sometimes you have to bring monkeys down to earth.

I said, 'Did she whip her kit off, Frankie?'

'No, not all of it, but ah—'

'—How much?'

'She was wearing this lacy thing, it was nearly see-through, and she was posing—'

'Nearly?'

Frankie said, 'Yeh, well that's all right, innit? We can paint the nipples on later.'

Clovis spoke for the first time. 'That was just bloody stupid.'

Frankie said, 'Come on, you was in there too. You were even helping.'

Clovis said, 'Not you. Max was stupid.'

Everyone's entitled to his own opinion, no matter how ill-informed that opinion might be. I settled back and waited for the rest.

Clovis said, 'You should never have mentioned Benny Sloman. Maureen has no idea about him being killed and it would screw her up if she did know. That's something we have to shield them from.'

'Why?'

For once he was driving slowly. He went even slower and he turned his face round so he could look at me. 'I'm her protection. She's got to have absolute trust in me so she feels she can't be touched. If she hears that Barry Frew has been going around killing people, it makes her nervous. She starts thinking she could be next.'

I said, 'And she stops trusting you?'

No answer.

We rolled up outside our resting place. Frankie gathered all his clobber together and did his acclaimed impersonation of an Anglepoise lamp escaping from a matchbox. I just got out.

Clovis was on robo-speak. 'I've checked with the Yard. You can write a piece on Ralph Coadwell providing you don't name him.'

I said, 'It's already written.'

He wasn't listening. 'Tomorrow you'll be on the first flight out. That'll get you back to Brize Norton around seven. You make your own way back from there.'

I said, 'Thanks for the lift.'

He pushed that away. 'You owe me for the meal. And the whisky.'

I counted out £300 and spread it on the passenger seat. 'That's for the grub and the grog and anything else I might owe you.'

A sideways flick of the head. 'That's too much.'

'I know.'

He took it anyway. I watched him drive off. Frankie said, 'What's going on, Max?'

Where do you start?

Chapter Eleven

In the morning I spring-cleaned my brain. I vacuumed out all the words I'd heard over the last how many days. I thought about real things, like Rosie, and football, and my various mates around Fleet Street. I had to do that before I could think about the story.

Frankie was on cracking form. He even bought drink. We were round at the officers' club basking and gargling. Frankie was staging his one-act one-man play, involving various off-stage girlfriends who had done this, and, you wouldn't believe it, that.

The fact I wasn't speaking all that much helped. And so he rattled on with me supplying the chortles. I meant them too, for Frankie is the best seven-foot-high comedian in the land. Like, there was this one doxy . . . no, maybe we'd better leave that.

Somewhere around noon he twigged that I wasn't coming back with equally untoppable tales. He looked at me with furrowed concern. 'Are you out of drink?'

No I wasn't. I was in the grasp of a deep and hideous envy. This is an awful thing to admit, but sometimes hacks wish they were monkeys. Naturally we would never tell them that. This envy can even happen on a daily basis.

Here's how it goes: the hack and the monkey go out together to do a story. The one with the office ballpoint writes down all the words in his notebook. The other one goes pop-pop-pop with his moron-proof camera.

And that's where his day's work is done.

But it's only just beginning for the poor hack. He has to rifle through a dozen scrawled pages, dredging up interesting words and sticking them in the right order. More often than not the person he's been interviewing has about as much imagination as a streaker in a nudist colony. Therefore the hack has to invent what he really should have said.

And then he has to ring Copy and somehow or other keep the copytaker awake until he's got the story across. All this while the monkey is down the pub wallowing in it.

Right now I was feeling dead envious. Ahead of Frankie lay the awesome task of flying home and popping his stuff in the darkroom where one of the lost souls would develop it, print it, wipe out the shadows, paint in the eyes, and generally make it into something closely resembling a photograph. Ahead of me lay 8,000 or more words, all painstakingly strung together by me and me alone. So far I hadn't even got one word in my head.

It would come, it would come. I got up and went looking for an English newspaper for it had been too many days since I'd last seen one and I was beginning to twitch. There was a stack of various day-old papers in the bar. The waiter invited me to help myself, so I bagged the lot.

I had not missed much, but then you find that's always the way. Here's a rough cross-section: Lib-Lab Pact in Peril over Euro. Glasgow Intercity Derailed – not many sober. Britons Escape French Flash Floods. Plot to Kidnap Supermodel Foiled. Not a sausage on Zeller Maine.

I turned to the sports pages for more challenging stuff. Chelsea were shaping up well for the new season and Man. Utd had lost out in the race to sign some Italian hot-shot. I was beginning to feel better. And then I chanced upon a yarn about Arsenal racking up the price of a season ticket. Sometimes I think that Arsenal should pay people to watch them. Other times I reckon if you're an Arsenal fan you deserve all you get. I was halfway through the story when I hit upon this outrage:

Loyal supporters last night branded the swingeing price hike as 'sheer greed'.

One mother said: 'My two sons have supported Arsenal through thick and thin, but now they can't even afford to go to watch them.'

Mrs Cindy Reilly added . . .

Mrs Cindy Reilly! *My* Cindy Reilly. I had breathed life into her, I had patted her fondly and sent her on the road to stardom. I'd seen her make her first appearance as a freelance antique valuer. I'd foolishly indulged her various careers as mugging victim, road accident eyewitness, schoolgirl, mystic, and all the rest. But the mother of an *Arsenal* fan? No, *two* Arsenal fans. Now that was just plain out of order. And which-ever malevolent sports hack penned this vicious libel had left out all the true stuff, like her age, her hair, her bust measurements and the signature quote. But *Arsenal!* Sometimes I'm ashamed of my profession. I chucked the paper away with an angry growl.

Frankie said, 'What? – my round *again?*'

He got them in, but it didn't do any good.

Kay came to collect us. No sign of Clovis.

'He's looking after Maureen and Stan,' she explained without me having to ask.

I suppose I was still feeling righteously bitter over the Cindy Reilly slur.

I said, 'I thought you did all the looking after Stan.'

Her eyes sparked. 'That's not funny.'

'Yeh, and Clovis didn't think it all that hilarious when I saw him squeezing Mo's bum.'

Frankie was up on his elbows, his head swinging from Kay to me and back. She was side on in one of the sun loungers with her sunglasses parked on top of her blonde spikes.

'I don't know what you're talking about.'

I said, 'Take it easy, Kay. I've already promised Clovis I wouldn't write a line about it.'

'You'd better not.' She was all flinty now. 'Because it's not true.'

I shook my head. 'But it *is* true. I'll tell you what's *not* true. What's not true is a certain woman police protection officer telling me that behind closed doors old Mo and Stan are a right pair of lovebirds.'

She was silent.

I rambled on as if I was thinking out loud. 'I suppose I could just about swallow that line. Or I could, if I hadn't seen Clovis playing pat-a-cake on her bottom, or if I hadn't seen the way she looked at him. That's when I knew you'd told me a whopper. But I didn't know why. Were you just covering up for your boss, or was something else going on here? So I started watching you and Stan. You probably know this already, but Stan takes over all funny every time you walk in the room. And when you walk out, we have to mop up his tears. Just out of morbid curiosity, were you and he playing footsie under the table in the taverna last night?'

She sat stone still, looking at me hard.

I let the silence lie there. She wasn't going to say a word.

I said, 'Thank you, Kay.'

The eyes sharpened. 'What for?'

'For not lying.'

After that things got more than slightly strained. She and I were both about as talkative as Marcel Marceau with lockjaw. Only Frankie, the great big daft Labrador puppy that he is, kept on yapping and grinning his head off. But she'd gone right off him too.

The last time I saw her was when Frankie and I went through the flight departure gate. She was taut and chill. If she was heartbroken at our leaving she did a good job of hiding it. I said, 'Cheer up. Your secret is safe with me.'

She had the shades over her eyes now so I couldn't see what she was thinking.

I said, 'I can see what Stan sees in you, but not vice versa. Unless you've got a thing for men with dead bears glued to their chests.'

Not a ripple.

I blew her a goodbye kiss anyway.

On board the Hercules we were strapping ourselves in when Frankie turned to me. 'This is where we've really got to do some thinking.'

We?

'Yeh, we haven't worked out how we're going to knock up our expenses yet.'

Hell's teeth, he was right. I forgot all about Mo and Clovis and Kay and Stan, for I had more important things on my mind.

England, or at least Brize Norton, was sweet and soft and sunny as we lurched in just gone seven. Our first priority was to hit the bar for a couple of swifties before we sorted out a way of getting back to London. But the Old Bill had other plans.

'Mister Chard?' a skinny civvy queried.

I owned up.

'I'm Dee Cee Pembright. We've got a car waiting.'

He also had a whole string of demands. 'You are to give me your notebooks and all your cameras and film. They will be returned to you within the next day or so.'

Balls to that.

I said, 'You can't have the notes because I need them to write the story.'

DC Pembright did not live up to the second half of his name. His brow crinkled. 'But—'

I trampled over him. 'My agreement with the Yard is you get the notes *after* I write the story.'

He was still all set to argue the toss. 'But,' I added, 'you *can* take possession of Frankie's film and gear now.'

'Thanks a bunch, Max.' From Frankie.

Pembright was only half convinced and I had to mention the names of a few senior woodentops before he caved in on the notebook issue.

The car was a green Rover. Don't they do them in any other colour? Another CID bod was picking his teeth behind the wheel. On the back seat were two matching plastic bags containing our mobiles. I snatched mine out.

'Okay if I make a phone call?'

Pembright said, 'Who are you calling?'

I wanted to say 'Your missus', but he didn't look like he had a sparkling sense of humour.

'My girlfriend.'

I was halfway through dictating a torrid message into Rosie's ansafone when she cut in. 'Max! Hi! I've *missed* you.'

That sounded promising.

She stopped long enough to breathe and then she got busy with the questions. 'Where are you? Where have you been? Did it work out all right? Tell me all about it.'

The truth could hold till later. I said, 'I've just flown down from Aberdeen. I'm at Heathrow right now so I'll be there in about an hour.'

She couldn't wait. The feeling was mutual. I told her to uncork the Gordons, splash me a tall one and I'd be there before the ice had melted.

I hung up. Our driver was watching me in the rear-view. He was thinking thus: 'Why's that geezer looking so chuffed with himself?'

I didn't feel like explaining.

And there *was* a bubbling Gordons awaiting. I let it bubble, for Rosie and I were otherwise engaged. She's big on the welcome homes, is Rosie.

After a while we got ourselves curled up on the sofa, much to the disgust of the vile Blue who had been kipping there. Rosie said, 'So, tell me where you got to.'

I told her.

She's never been to Cyprus. 'What's it like?'

I could not lie. 'It's jammed full of topless bars and massage parlours. Yeh, pretty nice place.'

'Tell me what it's *really* like.'

From there we moved on to Stan, Mo etc. It was not quite the full picture. I neglected to mention that Mo was more than a bit tasty and a terrific kisser. Also I left out the fact that Kay looked like something out of Baywatch. There are things it is wiser not to tell Rosie. Most of the time I was talking to the top of her curls, for she was now stretched out across the sofa, her toes tickling the far end. It was pleasant like that and she was having a fine old time too. It was promising to get even finer when all of a sudden her doorbell went ding-dee-donng.

She flicked a startled blue gaze up at me. 'Who on earth is that?'

Frieda and Lori, that's who. They hurtled in, both yattering away at 70 watts per channel.

Normally I'm right in there with the merry quip, the saucy aside, when Frieda and Lori come a-knocking. Tonight the smile was a trifle strained.

Rosie said, 'Hi' without using an exclamation mark. They didn't notice.

Lori widened her big black eyes at me. 'Max! We thought you were off somewhere on a story.'

'I *was*.'

'And now you're back,' said Frieda, the renowned thinker. 'Where were you anyway?'

'Scotland, just for a few days.'

Back to Lori. 'Scotland! You've gone all brown.'

Considering that Lori hails from Bridgetown, Guyana and has the most gorgeous, blackest skin imaginable, I was surprised she even noticed.

Frieda was reproaching Rosie. 'We thought you were all a-*lone*. We're just heading down to Sparks and thought you'd like to come, you know, for a bit of a laugh.'

I know Frieda's idea of a bit of a laugh. It wears trousers.

Rosie said, 'Aah, that's sweet of you, but no, we're staying in. But what about a drink now you're here?'

Can you believe that? I mean, just imagine I am with Rosie in my own drum and things are getting lively. Suddenly there's a knock on the door. I open up and find my best mate whom I haven't seen for ten years. I tell him to call me some other time for I have my hands full right now. He winks and says, 'No prob.' And off he goes whistling.

But if instead I invite him in for a sharpener he'd think I was some sort of perv.

Women just don't think like ordinary people.

And so Rosie poured gin down their gullets while they chittered on and the world spun slowly round. I thought they were there for keeps until Frieda disengaged her mouth for a second and glanced at her watch.

'Lori! We'd better be going.'

She'd had this horrifying vision of her bit-of-a-laugh legging it with some other fun-seeker.

There was a long and emotional farewell. Ending with, 'Call me tomorrow.' 'No, I'll call you.' 'That's what I said.' 'Oh, I thought you were going to call me.' 'Okay, then. I'll ring you in the morning.' 'Better leave it until later because . . .' 'On second thoughts, you call me . . .'

I turned away, my teeth biting the hell out of each other.

And then the door closed and the chirruping was no more.

Behind me I heard a long whooshing sigh. I turned round and there was Rosie leaning with her back to the door. She put her hands up under her curls and splayed them all down her wrists like blue-black waterfalls.

She said, 'I thought they'd never go.'

'Go? For God's sake, you invited them in.'

She let her hair flump down and came towards me. You could just catch the white of teeth on her bottom lip.

She said, 'So now you should appreciate me more.'

I was appreciating all right two hours ago.

*

In the morning Rosie went off somewhere with a sheaf of designs. Blue got offside too. I gave Frankie a shout to remind him that we'd spent the last several days in Gibraltar, not Cyprus. I had to say it a couple of times before he got it straight.

He'd had a sleepless night. 'What are we going to do about these exes?'

I'd already worked that out. We have a stringer called Ed O'Neill down in that part of the world. I said I'd call Ed and have him send us a load of dodgy restaurant receipts, the bigger the better.

'Ace,' said Frankie, and off he went, his every care banished.

Next I called News Desk. Angie jumped down the phone at me. 'Where are you calling from?'

'Battersea.'

'So you're back, then?'

No, Angie, I'm interviewing Mo Frew round the back of Battersea Power Station.

'Where did you go?'

I said, 'I've been warned not to say anything on the phone.'

News Editors just love it when you act conspiratorial. It makes them think they're in on the secret.

She lowered her voice six inches. 'So when will you be here?'

I fobbed her off, saying I wanted a good browse through my notes.

'You mean you haven't written anything yet?'

Argggh. There are times when I really land myself in it. I said, 'I'll need a couple of days to knock the story into shape. I just got back ten minutes ago. I haven't even slept yet.'

Angie didn't care. 'This is slotted down for a Monday-to-Friday run next week. We need the copy now.'

This time I thought before I spoke. 'You can't have it. The Old Bill have got to see it first.'

'They'll just have to wait. I need you to put together the Day One piece and I need it by this afternoon.'

I said, 'Angie, there is a large and extremely inquisitive police officer in my flat. Would you care to explain that to him?'

No, I didn't think she would. She went away, griping and grizzling. I got out my notes, lit the first Bensons of the morn and ordered my brain cells to call up reinforcements. A pretty useless bunch they were too.

But coming up lunchtime I had at least mapped out the structure. I knew we'd run a Page One piece, probably a double-column, on the first day, with a centre-spread inside. The front-pager would be little more than a long picture caption. I could make that up without any bother. On the spread I'd need half a dozen paragraphs of standfirst as an opener. The standfirst is the bit that tells you why you should waste your time reading the other 1,500 words in the main copy.

So what was the main copy? I brewed myself a mug of tea and stood at the window watching the world stagger by. It was a hot day out there and the girls were making the most of it. I lingered awhile lost in admiration before turning with a sigh towards my laptop.

In the meantime my brain had been thinking its own sordid thoughts. 'Sex!' it yelled. 'That's what this story's all about.'

And so it was. I pictured the big snap we'd run on the centre spread. That would be Mo sprawled out on the bed showing you more than is good for you. I started plikking the keys.

RAUNCHY redhead Maureen Frew last night revealed why she kissed goodbye to a cool MILLION smackers.

'I wanted a real *man,' she disclosed.*

Maureen ditched her gangster husband, Barry Frew – and her share of the Zeller Maine cash – for hunky handyman Stan Defoe.

But incensed by their fatal attraction Frew has put out a £100,000 contract on their lives.

Last night in their heavily guarded love nest, sultry Maureen said: 'We know he has sworn to kill us.

'The shadow of his hired gunmen is there every day of our lives.'

She smiled wickedly and added: 'But the nights make it all worthwhile.'

Like it? No, I don't suppose I thought it a Pulitzer prize winner either, but then our readers can't get enough of this sort of stuff. I steamed onwards:

'Barry thought he was a four-times-a-night superstud, but he was a wimp in bed. He doesn't know how to please a woman.'

And cuddling new lover Stan, Maureen said: 'I was due £1 million from the robbery. But I walked out on that without regrets.

'Stan makes me feel like TEN million.'

And so it rolled on. Just in case a stray intellectual

picked up our paper at the barber's, I included a chunk about theirs being a Lady Chatterley bonk-a-minute affair. Okay, so we know that Mo and Stan are not in the same stable, but I couldn't tell the truth, could I? Not with Scotland Yard pencilling through all the good lines. I also told a whole string of other lies, among them a crack about the pair of them disporting themselves in Florida. That lie was chiefly for the benefit of Plod.

By mid-afternoon I had trotted out Day One and was sifting through the second bite. This time hairy Stan was doing the quoting, for our readers like to get both sides of the story. It opened with how he and Mo were playing doctors when Barry Frew walked in on them. Lashings of bloodshed followed. And that bit was actually true.

I hit a pause. I'd rattled out a fair old whack and I deserved a break. But first I had to don my martyr's suit and head down to the office. I copied the story-so-far on to a floppy disk and skimmed off to Docklands.

'Max!' squealed Angie. 'I thought you were sleeping.'

Yeh. That was the main idea, Angie.

I said, 'No, you told me you needed to see it today. I can get my head down later.'

They fall for it every time.

Angie said, 'Ooh. I didn't mean it *literally* today. Let's go and have a drink and you can fill me in.'

Any excuse and she's down the pub. I nodded like an automaton that's been up all night. 'Okay. If you've got time.'

She made time, just for me. We were down in the

darker reaches of the Stone dive bar and she was buying. I wanted a pint, but I also fancied a high Gordons with a bubble of tonic frolicking in it. She was feeling guilty. She got me both.

'Right,' she said, wriggling her bottom on a stool. 'What was she like? What's the boyfriend like?'

Apart from the Cyprus thing, I told it the way it was, right down to Mo getting her cheeks squeezed and lusty Stan's lust for Kay. I also told her that none of the above would appear in my copy.

She wasn't fazed. News Editors get a buzz from running stories which they know to be patently untrue. It makes them feel smarter than the average reader, and God knows, they need all the help they can get.

Angie said, 'Sounds great. When can I have a look at it?'

I slapped the disk on the bar. 'That's Part One, and part of Part Two.'

Whereupon Angie downed the rest of her glass and said, 'Let's go, then. Finish your drink later.'

I finished it sooner. We trolled back up to the office and straight to the computer room. Barring the Editor's office, it is perhaps the least charismatic place in the whole building. Unlike the Editor's office, it serves a useful purpose. All of us hacks, all of the subs, even a few of the Monkey Desk keepers, have access to the same computer system. That means you can snoop on everyone else. All you need is their password and sooner or later you get it. I mean, I already know that Angie's sign-on is *Danielx*. I haven't the faintest who Daniel is, or was, but that isn't the bit that matters.

What mattered at that moment was letting Angie

have a taster of my floppy disk without the whole office going, 'Hey! Come and have a butcher's at what Max Chard's been writing.'

In the computer room Systems Manager Cyrille was tending the shop. Cyrille is a bloke who looks like an American football heavy and he's not much given to talking. But he knows what computers think.

I explained the situation. 'We need a print-off of this disk but it must not get onto the system.'

Cyrille grunted and pushed buttons. As my first part was chattering off the printer, Angie was reading it on screen. She said, 'I like it, Max. I *like* it.'

I think she especially liked the stuff about Stan. I just stood there smiling faintly and wishing you could smoke in the computer hole.

Cyrille tugged out the paper and read the first scorching page. Not even a 'Cor!' Maybe it was as hot as that every night of the week down his place.

Angie finished. 'And what have you got for the rest of the series?'

I said, 'I'll tell you later. Cyrille, can you kill this?'

He sat himself down, played an arpeggio, and that was it; it never existed. The only evidence was in Angie's sticky little dabs. Cyrille lumbered away to wipe the rest of the Watergate tapes.

Next she wanted to see the snaps. I told her Mr Plod was presently examining them through a steamed-up magnifying glass.

'Well, tell the police I need them tomorrow afternoon by the latest.'

Oh, sure.

'But first, Max, I want you to go home and get a good night's sleep. You look more dead than alive.'

It's amazing what people see if you tell them to see it.

I smiled wanly. 'Thanks. I've just got a couple of things to do first.'

I ended up doing them in Hamptons, where Susannah was already in residence and gargling Sancerre. Judging by the happy hello I got, she must have been kicking around in there some while.

I went straight at it. 'Who wrote that crap about Cindy Reilly being an Arsenal fan?'

Lewis Cranston. A friend of hers.

'*Friend?*'

Well, just another freelance hack she knew. After he got it in the paper he even had the brass neck to show up in Hamptons and demand free drink.

Susannah said, 'But we, especially Tommy, gave him a real dressing-down, then Lewis started mouthing off at Tommy and Tommy thumped him and . . .'

And in the end Cranston got kicked out in the gutter. I still wasn't satisfied. I would have preferred it if they'd killed Cranston before they chucked him out. Still, life is filled with such little disappointments.

Susannah said, 'It's about time you got another Cindy story in. Did you see Tommy's one on Monday?'

Er, no, I'd missed that.

Susannah gave me a fill-in. 'That was absolutely brilliant. It was about a woman who took her niece to Whipsnade and they were watching the rhinos when one of the male ones started trying to have it off with a female. The story was all about how the little girl was shocked.'

I didn't have to ask how Tommy had introduced the 'biggest one I've ever seen' quote.

'So,' said Susannah, 'it's your turn for a Cindy story. You'll have to come up with something special to match that. Anyway, what you been doing recently?'

'Just this and that.'

'What sort of this and that?'

I said, 'Too boring to mention. Time for another?'

'Why not?'

I got back to my own place early. Well, early for me. I trampled roughshod over the heaps of junk mail and freebie newspapers cluttering up the hall without even seeing them, for I was gnawing at a problem. These were the basic bones of it: the first couple of chunks I'd knocked out on the Mo show were bang on the button for our lip-smacking readers, but not quite what Scotland Yard had in mind. Yet they had to give full copy approval before we could run it. Now, how could I get round that one?

I opened a Bud, slung myself on the sofa and picked at the poser. I got up, opened a second Bud and picked it around a bit more. A straw suddenly stuck out. I grasped it firmly with the mitt that wasn't holding the Bud. Ah! That's it. I'd got it.

The chief problem, you see, was that I'd fired off the series with all the steamy stuff. But just say . . . just say I knocked out a relatively po-faced bit on Mo's custom-made personality change, and I marked that bit Part One. Then I followed that up with a yawnsome yard on how she laundered the spoils. There's Part Two. For Day Three I could lead off on their safe house somewhere on the Gulf Coast of Florida. I'd have to pad all three pieces out with acres of flimflam. And then, almost as an afterthought, I'd tack on the bits I'd already written.

Now, just imagine you are the senior flathead landed with the job of approving the Memoirs of Mo. You plough through the opener. You think: 'Solid bloke, that Max Chard, but he doesn't half go on some.' You move on to Part Two. No, nothing there to fret about. By the time you reach Day Three you've got a nagging headache and you've had your fill of Mo Frew. So you just skim through the rest – which is also heavily padded – and give it a gold star.

Back it comes to us. Scotland Yard have pronounced all five episodes fit to run. *But* they have not specified that we have to print them in that order. Furthermore, they've cleared all the copy, which means we can't add anything to it. *But* we can take stuff out. So I take a machete and hack them all down for maximum oomph.

I hauled out the laptop and started flannelling.

Chapter Twelve

Two days later I had the whole thing wrapped up, well the bonking and biffing side of things anyway. But I was having trouble with the piece on how Mo and Barry laundered the money. I needed expert advice. I have this mate, we'll call him Gerry, for he's the shyest of men. By profession Gerry is a tightrope walker. The tightrope he walks is the one strung between tax avoidance and tax evasion. Every so often he falls off the line, hence his shyness. I gave him a call and we arranged to meet in the Melton Mowbray up in High Holborn.

Gerry breezed in rubbing his hands and reeking of freshly squeezed money. We rabbited on for a bit about Chelsea's new line-up and then I got down to what I was here for.

I said, 'Imagine I've got five million and I want to wash it, how do I go about it?'

'Just give it to me.'

I said, 'But just say I don't know you. Who do I turn to instead?'

The way Gerry told it, I could go to half the people in the country – fund managers, bond salesmen, solicitors, offshore bankers, investment advisers, the works, and they'd all wash my money whiter than white.

Somewhere in there he'd said solicitors. I was bemused. My personal knowledge of barristers and lawyers is confined to those loons who lurch nightly into Hamptons and drink their clients out of house and home. Personally I wouldn't trust them with a fiver.

I said, 'Why solicitors?'

'Because they're protected by law.'

Eh?

Gerry was patient with me. 'The privilege between a solicitor and his client is absolute. That means the solicitor is banned *by law* from disclosing anything his client might have told him.'

I had to ask. 'Who made up them rules?'

'Lawyers.'

I said, 'So I go along to my brief and I say, "Here's five mill from the Zeller Maine job. Do me a favour and clean it up." I could do that?'

'No. A lawyer is also barred from handling money he knows to be the proceeds of a crime.'

I thought about that while I ordered a vodka (his) and a gin (not his).

I said, 'Then if the lawyer suspects it's dirty money, he won't touch it?'

Gerry can be a right supercilious git sometimes. This was one such time. 'You're not listening. The solicitor will not handle it if he *knows* it's hot.'

Aaah.

I said, 'But if he only suspects . . .?'

'Then nobody can touch him.'

'So I wink at him and say, "Here's a bundle my great-aunt Jemima dropped me. Put it through the wringer." And he winks back "Okay"?'

'That's about it.'

I was still having problems joining solicitors and financial acumen in the same sentence.

Gerry said, 'They're the perfect middlemen. They can set up front companies for you, and the beauty of it is they are legally bound to keep it all secret. But that's just one way of doing it, there are millions more.'

'Like?'

'Think of a business which deals in hard cash.'

I thought. 'A bar?'

Gerry waved that one away. 'Too small. Think *big*.'

I couldn't be bothered. I let him do the thinking for me.

'Take an auction house – not one of the name ones – the type you find out in the sticks. Many of them deal only in money. No cheques, no plastic. Now just say you have twenty grand you want to vanish.'

I said, 'I've got twenty grand that I want to vanish.'

Gerry hunched his shoulders and got conspiratorial. 'The very first thing you do is turn the money into something else. So you go to Auctioneer A and you buy ten reasonable paintings. You then put them up for sale with Auctioneer B.'

I tugged at a flaw. 'Just say nobody buys them?'

'They get bought all right. Because you arrange for Rosie to buy them back with more dirty money. And Rosie pays twenty-five thou.'

I could feel a headache coming on. 'But I've just lost about twenty-five grand on the deal.'

'How?'

How? If he couldn't see that, how come he was such a financial wizard.

He said, 'Think about it. Auctioneer B gives you twenty-five, minus VAT and seller's premium, and it's all clean.'

'But that's my own money. And I'm down twenty.'

Gerry shook his head in sorrow. 'No it's not. It's *clean* money, and you still have the paintings which you put under the hammer with Auctioneer C. You can keep on doing that ad infinitum. Sell them four times and you've washed one hundred thou plus.'

I said, 'Sounds a lot of work. What about these offshore shell companies?'

That was his opener for a twenty-minute idiot's guide to finagling. I ran past him the stuff that Mo had told me and he filled in the gaps. Gerry reckoned the system was clean, safe and fast. The drawback was it involved too many people and they all took a whack as it passed through.

'There is,' he concluded, 'an even better way where you get to keep it all.'

'And that is?'

He turned on a sharkish smile. 'Pretend the money never existed.'

That one was just too Alice in Wonderland. I said, 'Let's talk football instead.'

*

With Gerry's expert tuition I stitched together a whole screed on the Frews' home laundry business. The yarn was complete. I returned to Cyrille, got him to copy my floppy, and, with the floppy copy in my pocket, then proceeded in a westerly direction towards Scotland Yard. Tom, the big geezer, who had originally briefed me about the story, printed it out, and had a quick shufti through the first few pages before deciding we both needed a drink. Just as long as I was still sparing the taxpayers the burden.

That was no problem. We wound up in a bar opposite Victoria station and started turfing pints into us. Tom had the print-out with him. He said, 'You made her out to be a bloody hero.'

'Heroine. Wasn't that what you wanted?'

'Not what *I* wanted.'

We're in the same business here, Tom.

I smiled a sad smile. 'It's never what *we* want. It's what somebody up behind a desk thinks *they* want.'

He tugged out the print-out and much to my alarm he started reading the saucy stuff in the final pages. He let loose a whistle, then a 'Bloody Nora!' I just sat there trying to hypnotize him to sleep.

After a good five minutes he slapped the print-out on the table. 'You've gone and turned it into a soft-porn love story, like that was all there was to it.'

'Do you want the truth instead?'

Truth is not a word to use in polite police company.

He swallowed on it, but it was hard.

I said, 'All right, then. Let's try it this way: "*Supergrass Maureen Frew turned her husband over because he caught her having nookie with the gardener."* Is that what you want? For that's the truth.'

Tom was still twitchy about the T-word.

'No, but come on, Max, she was in it up to her bloody arse. And she never even came across either, did she?'

I lowered my glass, keeping my eyes on him. 'She *lied?*'

Lies. Now I was talking his language. He leaned back, grinned fatly at me like he was a magician with a kangaroo up his sleeve, leaned forward, and then produced precisely nothing.

I wasn't disappointed. You get to expect this from coppers. But I smiled in my own quiet way. 'I'm glad you told me that, for I believed every lying word she had to say.'

A hearty har-har from him. 'I expect she told you she didn't get anything for herself. And you believed her and all?'

I said, 'How much?'

But Tom had run out of drink. I got them in sharpish. Even so, by the time I got back he'd remembered he was a senior officer in Her Majesty's constabulary, therefore he should not be talking to folks like me, except in the sanctity of the lodge.

I said, 'How much has she got?'

He was too busy quaffing to answer. I lit a Bensons and puffed. And puffed.

He lifted his big square head up. 'What do you want me to tell you – that the conservative estimate on Zeller Maine was upwards of eight million, maybe ten? That all Maureen could give us was peanuts? That she's got herself a new cushy number with the handyman? I mean, it makes you wonder, don't it?'

It was about time we had some facts. I said, 'Who put the "conservative" figure on it?'

Tom said, 'Give us a cigarette. I'm meant to be giving them up, but—'

I slid the pack across. I gave him a light.

I said, 'Whose estimate?'

The freebie Bensons relaxed him. 'Don't ask me. Ask Customs.'

There are times you have to be downright rude. 'And what do Customs know that you don't?'

Oooh, that hurt. He pulsed out smoke like a macho man. 'Customs – and this isn't for you writing up – they've been after a bloke who's been flogging gold, only he's been avoiding the VAT.'

Not the most glamorous of crimes, I grant you, but I was still listening.

I said, 'And?'

Tom stuck his arms behind his head and leaned back with the cigarette held hard in the corner of his mouth. 'Let's just imagine that this bloke they're after had a bundle in Zeller Maine.'

I imagined. Next I imagined how big this bundle was.

Tom enlightened me. 'Call it three million.'

I am not by nature a pickety man, but I said, 'A fifty-pound note is the highest currency in the realm. A million quid in fifty-pound notes is as high as this ceiling. How do you get three million in a little teensy safe deposit box?'

'Who said it was in sterling? Who said it was in hard cash?'

I reeled it back to him, all he'd told me. There was ten million in Zeller Maine. Maureen had cut herself a slice.

I said, 'Is Barry Frew still gunning for her?'

Yep. Him and Dave Stretch and all their cohorts. Tom had nothing to add on who the hitman/woman might be. I returned to the matter of my story.

'Otherwise, what I've written is okay?'

He squidged out the cigarette. 'Yeh. I suppose that's the way they want it upstairs. But you reporters take the biscuit. Maureen never said half these things, did she?'

I eyed him steadily. 'Course not. It's what you policemen call verballing a witness.'

He didn't even blush.

I pulled the same back-to-front stunt with Mo's lawyer, Tullamy, dropping off a printed copy in person. That was a right waste of time. His secretary, a frosty type with butterfly specs, said, 'Mister Tullamy is in conference with a client and cannot be disturbed.'

I offered to wait around. She shook her head. 'He is not in the building. The conference is taking place elsewhere.'

I said, 'But he told you not to disturb him anyway.'

'Yes.'

I could see Tullamy's cubby hole, its door was half open.

She was pushing me.

I said, 'Let's hope your boss doesn't catch a cold.'

She opened the door. 'Sorry?'

I said, 'It's pissing it down outside. But he's left his jacket hung up in the corner.'

'Good afternoon, Mister Chard.'

It wasn't an entirely fruitless journey. I nipped round to Savile Row and treated myself to a shirt in the Gieves sale.

It took Tullamy three whole days to get back to me. 'I have read your articles and whilst they are substantially acceptable, I have been obliged to make several amendments.'

Oh yeah?

He said, 'I am dispatching the amended manuscript to you by courier. You shall have it this afternoon.'

I wasn't having any of that. 'Scotland Yard have approved every single word. No amendments. Our lawyers have given it the okay. More to the point, I told your client, Maureen, what I was writing and she was happy.'

He burbled around for a second. 'What about Mister Defoe? Has he approved this? I also represent his interests, you know.'

The only way to talk to lawyers is to chuck law at them. I said, 'Let's get this straight: Mo is your client. She likes the story. *If* – just if – Stan didn't like it, and you started messing about with Mo's story, isn't that a conflict of interests?'

He tried to weasel out. 'I know that Mister Defoe is concerned that he is not portrayed in a derogatory manner.'

'He's not.'

'I have only your opinion on that, Mister Chard.'

'And the opinion of the Chief Commissioner of the Metropolitan Police. Now, if you want to keep arguing, why don't you fight it out with our own lawyer? He's the one with a cheque for eighty thousand in his safe.'

Hmm. Tullamy went quiet. When he came back on line he wasn't quite so bumptious. 'I have rendered various alterations for the sake of greater accuracy. I would hope you would give them due consideration.'

Half an hour later a biker weighed in with the revised story. I gave Tullamy's changes their due consideration. I binned them.

So the story ran more or less as described, except I reversed the order and took out all that guff. What with Frankie's doctored pictures it looked a right corker, and it duly played to packed houses. After Day One hit the news-stands, the Editor sent me a typed herogam. I reprint it in its entirety: 'Well done.'

I made the most of such lavish praise. I got a trunk-load of blanko receipts from Gibraltar supplied by the great Ed O'Neill and bumped in £800-plus in exes. Frankie followed suit. There were dark mutterings from Angela Whipple, and Belker, our foul Executive Editor, was all for setting about them with a meat cleaver. Just in time he remembered that the Mo Frew yarn was all the Editor's bright idea. The exes went through.

Which was just as well, because I'd been chalking up a massive slate in Hamptons, caused in part through Susannah getting two more Cindy Reilly stories placed. My mate Olly in the *Mirror*, newly enlisted among the ranks of Cindy Reilly's Assorted Pals, had also scored. In his he had Cindy as a stripagram girl on holiday in Paris where she'd been chased by a crazed axeman. She said, 'He came at me with his chopper.'

And I don't have to tell you what she said next.

Anyway, Olly, Susannah and sundry others were

all quaffing away one night in Hamptons when she started having a go at me. 'You've only done one story on her, Max. You've left it all up to us to get Cindy mentioned, but you're doing nothing.'

I reminded her that I was buying buckets of drink.

She was not mollified. 'That's *easy*. We're taking all the chances.'

The Assorted Pals nodded and mumbled general agreement. I waffled about being away on the Mo Frew job where I couldn't have stuck her in the story without Scotland Yard saying, 'Who's this Cindy bird?'

All to no avail. In the end, Susannah, who can forget herself when she's half cut, pronounced, 'Unless you can get a good one in on Cindy within a month, I vote we blackball you from the club.'

I knew she'd apologize for that in the morning, if she remembered. But that wasn't the issue. I had to deliver. I left Hamptons that night a considerably more sober man than the circumstances warranted.

The summer simmered away. Sometime around the cusp of August Rosie dragged me off for ten days in New York where she and her deranged sister who lives in those parts went shopping, while I drank Manhattans with the American bureau hacks in Eamonn Brannigan's. Weather great. And a good time was had by all. End of postcard.

So now I was back in the real world, churning out fiddly stories of no import. But I still hadn't come up with the definitive Cindy Reilly spoof. I wasn't concerned, for most of the Assorted Pals were off punishing their livers in foreign parts. The story could wait till they returned.

One morning when I was in my corner and tweaking up a minor league drugs bust at a posh school, my phone gave voice.

'Hello, Max.'

Whoever she was, I didn't recognize her.

'And hello to you too.'

'You don't recognize me, do you?'

I've just said that. The accent had a sort of west of England wobble. Not Zummerzet, but big on the vowel sounds.

I said, 'Listen, Cameron bloomin' Diaz, if you don't stop pestering me like this I'm going to set the Old Bill on you.'

She laughed. And the laugh gave her away.

I took a beat and then I said, 'My, how you've changed. I never thought I'd hear *your* dulcet tones again.'

'Well, it just goes to show, doesn't it?'

Show what? I said, 'So how are things faring?'

'Better than average, I'd say. And you?'

I said, 'Oh, you know, nothing's changed. I'm still mixing it with the murky criminal underclass.'

'Is that how you see me?'

I lit a Bensons and said, 'I take it you're not ringing to tap me for a fiver.'

'Nooo. I'm perfectly well provided for, thank you. I just wanted to let you know we loved your story.'

'What – all four of you?'

'Four?'

Come on, you know what I'm talking about. I said, 'Four. We mustn't forget the man who rolls his own cigarettes and fondles ladies' bottoms. Nor should we leave out the blonde who flirts with other people's partners.'

She said, 'You don't miss much, do you?'

'I like to think not.'

There was a little pause. I didn't feel like breaking it. I heard a clock chiming way off in the background.

She said, 'We don't see as much of them as we used to.'

'That must be a real downer for you.'

She found her laugh again. 'You know what it's like with holiday romances. They only last as long as the holiday.'

'Some people have longer holidays than others.'

She made a tut-tutting sound. 'Anyway, I thought you'd like to know how much we liked your articles.'

'I liked your articles too.'

'Naughty. Still, it's a shame that we can't all get together some time.'

I said, 'Maybe you should suggest it.'

She actually did sound regretful. 'Uh-uh. They wouldn't agree. You know that. But it's been nice talking to you again. Look after yourself, Max.'

She blew a farewell kiss and the line went dead. I looked up at the clock. 10.10 a.m. Her clock must be slow. But that wasn't what intrigued me. I'd counted ten chimes. Either she was ringing from New Zealand late at night, or else Maureen Frew was somewhere in these islands.

The weeks rolled into September. In the meantime the only thing of note was the Editor's wife had her handbag snatched while prancing down Oxford Street. Judging by the fuss the Editor kicked up, you'd have thought they'd nicked the wrong bag. At any rate I was hauled back to the office from Hamptons to churn out 600 instant words on evil sneak thieves preying on the rich and fatuous. I finished it with twenty minutes' drinking time still left on the meter. I charged out the door, scanning the horizon for a friendly taxi.

Instead, a car of unknown parentage peeled up alongside. The driver stuck his head out. 'Mister Chard?'

He was not anyone I knew. Nor did I recognize the other two geezers with him. The driver was the only one smiling. He said, 'Get in.'

And one of the doors flapped open.

I said, 'I think you've mistaken me for somebody else.'

The back-seat passenger slid out. 'You heard what he said. Just get in the bloody car.'

If he sounds a bit like Michael Caine to you, that's because he sounded that way to me too. He didn't look like him though. He was wide and knobbly and I don't reckon he earned his living in the limelight.

By now I was more than a shade edgy. I said, 'My name is Belker. I don't know anybody called Chard.'

The passenger type said, 'All right, Mister *Belker*. Get in the bloody car.'

I would like to report that he had a bazooka aimed at my head and a stiletto in the other hand. But he didn't. His hands were empty. Or they were until he grabbed me by the shirt and pushed me backwards into the car. I banged my head off the far door.

At about the same time the passenger clambered in, shutting the other door and the car skimmed off. The driver called back, 'Make sure he's belted in nice and safe, Harry; we don't want Mister Chard coming to no harm, do we?'

I sat up and took a glance out the window. There was no one out there I could scream 'HELP!' at. That's one of the buggers of working in Docklands. Any old bunch of kidnappers can snatch you off the street whenever they feel like it.

I tried to sound outraged, but I think that was mostly to hide how I really felt. 'What do you think you're doing?'

'You'll find out.'

Call me innocent, but I honestly had no idea what was going on. Whatever it was, I wanted out of it. I tried again. 'You're making a dreadful mistake. I'm going to report you—'

The driver, a failed comedian, said, 'You've done enough reporting, old son. We just want to talk to you a little. And then when you've done some talking too, we'll drive you right back to where we picked you up.'

Reporting. The only serious reporting I'd done in two months was the Mo Frew story. And I certainly didn't feel like talking about that. So I went quiet instead and began absorbing all I could about the car and its crew. It was a Vauxhall, maybe dark blue or black. The bruiser called Harry, sitting to my right, has already been described, though I left out the bit about his body odour. The driver had dark curly hair and saggy jowls. The front-seat passenger took a size 17 collar. All three looked like they'd been knocked up by Dr Frankenstein on one of his off-nights. The car was licking along through anonymous back streets but I guessed the rough direction was Wapping. Nobody else was talking so I said, 'Where are you taking me anyway?' My voice sounded a bit off.

The driver let the question hang for a moment. Then, 'Do we tell him, or do we just keep him in suspense?'

They chose the latter. Meanwhile I was motoring on neat adrenalin because certain images had sprung to mind, chief among which was a picture of the Old Bill carting off the bleeding carcasses of Belly Sloman & Co in Coldharbour Lane. My imagination, which never knows when to leave off, conjured up another vivid tableau. This time Max Chard took centre stage, lying in a lake of blood with his several limbs spread out all wonky. I swallowed hard and started chewing over my options. Top of the list was to get the hell out of the car. That was a non-starter right now because we were still bowling along and I didn't fancy smacking into the pot-holes at forty miles an hour. But . . . I told myself, sooner or later we'll run into a traffic light or a stop sign, at which juncture I can whizz open the door and belt off into the gloaming. Another but surfaced. Just say the three bandidos had pearl-handled revolvers or the like stuffed down their waistbands?

About eighty yards ahead I could see a junction looming up with a big fat welcoming GIVE WAY sign. To flee or not to flee, that was the question. The driver solved the problem for me. 'Ooops. I've forgotten the child-proof locks.'

Plick. The door button slotted down. I looked for

other options. I suppose I could always bounce the driver's head off the windscreen, while simultaneously kicking both passengers where they'd feel it. Nope, not even Bruce Lee could manage that one. There weren't any other options.

The driver had also been reviewing the scenario. 'Don't get any clever ideas, Max. It might turn out to be not too clever, if you follow my meaning.'

I followed. The car swung right on to what I think was Westferry Road. I saw a couple of *Telegraph* delivery vans scoot by. Otherwise nothing, but at least there were lights here. Not for long. We did a sharp left up a street you wouldn't want to walk down in daylight. No houses, just square black blocks of buildings that might have been anything. The car was a mite jumpy too, for we were trundling along slowly, as if the driver was looking for something. He found it. Another left turn, this time into an industrial estate. I'm guessing that's what it was.

I'd been doing some thinking just to cheer myself up. Cutting it down, here's what I'd come up with: the three blokes all seemed fairly relaxed, therefore their main plan was not to mow me down in a hail of bullets. So far there'd been no real menace. That meant there was no serious mischief on their agenda. All right, it was not the most logical thinking I've ever done, but it made me feel better. The car stopped and the lights clicked off. The driver turned to me. All I could see of him was a black head silhouetted against a marginally less black backdrop. He said, 'So let's you and me have a little natter, Mister Chard. Get out.'

I found hidden reserves of stupidity. 'I can't. You locked the sodding door.'

Harry slapped me hard on the face. 'Don't get lippy, son.'

The door button popped up and I got out. The front passenger was out before me. He grabbed my arm and pushed me round to the front of the car. The driver unclunked his belt and joined the party.

My stinging cheek said, 'Keep quiet.' My mouth said, 'Okay if I smoke?'

'Okay if he smokes?' echoed the front passenger, his first contribution of the evening.

'Sure,' said the driver. 'I think we could all do with a spark-up. Maybe you'd like to share them around, Mister Chard.'

I shared. I even lit the damn things for them. The glow of the lighter told me little about my new-found friends, except that the front passenger had a drooped-down left eyelid.

The driver said, 'Now, where did you meet that slag Maureen Frew and her scummy boyfriend?'

I was expecting as much. Without a flicker I said, 'On a ship.'

'You met them on a boat? What boat?'

My stupidity answered that one. 'Well, it wasn't the bloody Woolwich Ferry.'

Wrong answer. Harry hit me another bat round the dimples.

The driver cupped the cigarette in his paw and took a puff. 'Let's start again. What boat?'

I said, 'The HMS *Aardvark*.'

'The what?'

'It's one of the Navy's A-class frigates.'

I was banking on them not having a copy of Jane's Fighting Ships tucked in their hip pockets. Luckily they didn't.

'And where was this *Aardvark*?'

I got glib. 'The Yard told me to fly to Gibraltar. I was in the Colony hotel when they came and picked me up for the meet. All the interviews were done in the wardroom on the *Aardvark*. I think it had just sailed in to Gib, but I don't know from where.'

The driver sounded sad. 'Now why do I think he's making all this up?'

Harry said, 'Because he didn't write nothing about a boat.'

In the darkness I wasted a superior smile on him. 'If I'd mentioned the ship, the police would have gone spare. They told me to write she was in Florida.'

The driver said, 'And Stan Defoe was on this boat too?'

'Yes.'

I could see his head wagging up and down. I don't know what that meant. After a long silence he turned to Harry. 'Smack him around a little.'

Wallop! This time there was none of that playful slapping stuff. Harry took out a concealed blacksmith's anvil and belted me full in the stomach. Just as I was straightening up from that he landed a cracker on my ear. God, that bloody hurt. They *both* bloody hurt. Also, my cigarette had gone flying off into outer space.

The driver said, 'You're a nice boy, Max, and we don't want to give you any grief. Just tell us the truth and we'll leave you alone. Now, where did you see them?'

I got as far as, 'I met them on—'

He cut in, 'If I was you, I wouldn't say a boat.'

I could sense Harry shaping up for more frolics.

I said carefully, 'If you were me, where would *you* say I met her?'

He came very close so I could feel his breath on my face. 'I'd tell the truth, Max. I'd say Cyprus.'

Jesus!

I said, 'Why Cyprus?'

'Because that's where they was, wasn't it?'

The front passenger opened up, 'That's where they was seen.'

So it wasn't a lucky guess. I swallowed. I was feeling my way here. I said, 'If you've been told that's where they are, why're you trying to beat it out of me then?'

He was ever so patient with me. 'Because Cyprus is a bloody big place and we can't go knocking on all the doors, saying, "Excuse me, is that little prick Stan Defoe and his toe-rag girlfriend hiding here?" That's just not on. But you could save us a lot of bother by telling us exactly where they are.'

I stayed quiet. He said, 'Or let's put it another way: you could save yourself from a proper pasting if you just said the word.'

I said, 'Pissouri.'

The one called Harry must have thought I'd said something else because he came muscling in. The driver gently pushed him back.

'Where did you say again?'

'Pissouri. It's an upmarket holiday place halfway between Limassol and Paphos.'

'What're they in – a house, a hotel, what?'

I winged it. 'It's a holiday villa. There's no name or anything. But it's three doors down on the left from a place called the Aphrodite Taverna. About two hundred yards off the beach road.'

'How do you spell Pissouri?'

I spelt it. Then I spelt Aphrodite.

He said, 'And what's their armour like?'

'Their what?'

The front passenger decoded. 'What sort of protection does Defoe and Maureen have?'

I said, 'I saw four of them, but there might have been others.'

'And I suppose they were tooled up?'

'Yeh, they had guns with them all the time.'

Next I had to describe the house, right down to the big yellow shrub by the front door. No, sorry, I didn't know which was Stan and Mo's bedroom. We carried on like this for five minutes without Harry feeling the need to rattle my teeth again. It was time I started asking questions.

I said, 'She's got away with some of the Zeller Maine money, hasn't she?'

'You said that, Max. I'm not saying nothing, except they're dead when we find them. Now, you've done good telling me what I wanted. But just a little piece of friendly advice, don't you go running to the Jack and Jill about this. Understand?'

I understood that Jack and Jill equalled the Old Bill.

I said, 'About what?'

A heh-heh-heh from our driver. 'Very good, very funny. Right, now we're going to leave you here 'cos I've got another appointment and I don't have time to run you home.'

My imagination came back on line. It said, 'What he means is they're going to leave your bleeding corpse here.'

The driver turned away, took a single step and pirouetted right round. 'You got a mobile phone?'

I didn't have to answer. Harry pawed me and found it. The driver said, 'We'll take this, just in case you get any silly ideas about calling anyone.'

As if I would.

Harry said, 'We'll take these too.'

'Yeh,' said the driver, 'those things are bad for your health.'

And the buggers trousered my Bensons. Various words came to mind but I didn't say a thing. I just stood there and thought bitter thoughts.

The three folded themselves back in the car. The headlights flashed on, thereby blinding me. I stayed absolutely still while the car backed off, trapping me in its beam. Even now I half expected Harry to jump out and let rip. Then it did a three-pointer and vanished round the corner. I heard it rev off and listened until it merged with the general traffic roar.

I took a deep, deep breath and let it all out in a whoosh. It was only then I realized my pulse was ticking like a Geiger counter at Chernobyl. I could use a mega drink right now. I could do with a Bensons too. I'd even like to see the Law.

I pointed one foot in the general direction of the blackness and started walking.

Scotland Yard were their usual helpful selves. Top cop Tom was home, saying his prayers. No, they could not call him. No, none of his deputies was available to listen to me. And they couldn't call them either. It was, they reminded me, after midnight.

I was in a minicab firm down Poplar High Street. I gritted my teeth and said, 'This is an emergency.'

The switchboard operator disagreed. 'Yours is not a nine-nine-nine call. Should you require urgent police assistance, contact the emergency services.'

I gave up. I had no intention of ringing the nearest Plod. They'd just stick me in an interview room in the local nick and ask me to run through the whole thing from point A to whichever point we're at right now.

I hung around waiting for a cab. At length a bloke detached himself long enough from his mug of tea to do the honours.

'What happened to your face?' he said.

I could have asked him the same thing.

For some reason I felt like company. It was nearly one in the morning when he dropped me off in Battersea. There was still a light on in her bedroom. I leaned on the bell. I had to lean on it twice before a voice came from the other side. 'Who is it?'

I wasn't up to playing jolly japes. 'It's me.'

'You? Are you pissed? Do you know what time this is?'

I answered yes, no and yes. She was already

winding up the portcullis and undoing the various gizmos which I insist on her having. Some hours later the door creaked open.

'Oh my God, what's happened to you?'

First things first. I treated myself to a corker of a gin and a cigarette. Rosie meanwhile was sponging my face with a flannel. She meant well, but that woman is no great loss to the nursing profession. I trotted out the story with many a pause, largely because the flannel kept getting in the way of my mouth. Also, she insisted on asking daft questions, such as: 'Why didn't you run?'

When I was all done, she said, 'Right, I'll go and get changed.'

I've neglected to mention that she was wearing a skimpy dusty blue nightie thing which I bought her in Kuala Lumpur. I got the impression there was little if anything under it. It looked fine by me.

'Changed?'

She was all brisk and bossy. 'Yes, we'll get a taxi and go down to the police station.'

I had a much, much better idea. And after a solid ten minutes of arguing, she caved in. 'All right, but tomorrow . . .'

Tomorrow would just have to wait in line.

Tom got to his office at precisely nine twenty-six. I know that because he said, 'Hold it, I'm just in the door.'

I let him get settled and then I reeled off a snap

précis of my abduction. That woke him up. He said, 'Where are you? I'm sending a car.'

And not very long after that I was in Tom's office on the fifth floor. There were two other Plods there. They weren't introduced, but one of them looked suspiciously like Harry of the night before. They sat around drinking tea while I ran through the whole thing. Then they were silent because they couldn't think and talk at the same time.

Tom said, 'They couldn't have seen her in Cyprus. Maureen always wore that wig and stuff when she was not in the safe house. Even her own mother wouldn't have known her.'

I said, 'Maybe they didn't see her.'

They put on matching frowns.

I said, 'Maybe they saw Stan. Harry and his mates said *they* had been seen.'

That set them thinking again. No, that wasn't on either. Stan too was always covered up.

Tom said what they were all thinking. 'Are you sure *you* didn't let slip that it was Cyprus?'

I let them know I was mortally insulted. 'I got this black eye for telling them Mo was in Gibraltar.'

'Yes,' said one of Tom's chums, 'but they did threaten you.'

'Only with a bit of a bashing. No guns. No knives.'

Tom shook his head. 'It doesn't make any sense. You start lying to them and they know you're lying. So then they ask you about Cyprus and you make up this story about Piss-whatever-it's-called. Why should they believe you?'

That one had me foxed too. I said, 'My only guess

was they were letting Maureen know they were still after her. They reckoned I'd go running to you and you'd warn her.'

'Well, we're not. She doesn't need to know. But Cyprus. How did they know it was Cyprus?'

One of the resident brains pondered, 'It's possible that a soldier on the base – maybe somebody who's linked to Dave Stretch or Barry Frew – saw her in the safe house, I mean when she wasn't disguised.'

I said, 'In which case would you like to tell me why those three last night wanted to know *where* in Cyprus she was?'

He lost interest in the conversation.

Tom shrugged. 'We'll have a sniff at it, but I'm not hopeful. Anyway, it doesn't matter now. We moved Maureen and Stan well offside after you saw them. That was just in case somebody did try to screw anything out of you.'

'Or you let something slip,' added his chum.

I smiled at him sweetly. 'Or some copper did the slipping.'

Tom stood up. 'Don't worry about it, Max. They'll probably leave you alone now. Maureen's safe and that's the main thing. So no harm done.'

Try telling that to my black eye.

I'd counted on spending the morning thumbing through mugshots of villains called Harry and other villains with a droopy left eyelid. But they didn't seem interested. I headed for the office instead.

Angie was in morning conference but Nige let me know he found my biffed-up face richly amusing. He said, 'Been in a bar brawl again, have you?'

'Yeh. Everybody in the pub said you were a plonker, and I just had to stick up for you.'

I walked away before he could thank me.

The next priority was to get myself a new mobile. Anybody else in the country can just walk into the nearest Dixons and buy one. I had to fill in a three-page form from our managing editor, detailing exactly why and how and when and where my mobile and I had parted company. I also claimed I'd been relieved of a Dunhill lighter and a Dupont pen. Well, I reckoned I deserved something for the state of my face.

Chapter Thirteen

The puffy purple faded to blue, then it took on a greenish tinge, after which it went sort of yellowy. One morning about a week later I woke up and the skin around my eye was back in the pink. But inside I was still smarting. I was chiefly narked because the Old Bill had not nicked my three attackers and strung them up by the toes or whatever else came to mind. But then I wasn't surprised.

I had heroically failed to write anything for the paper on the abduction, for I didn't want the same three loons hanging around outside every time I slipped off for a sharpener. Also, Rosie had threatened to black my other eye if I landed myself in trouble again.

So I just got on with the job. The big feature of the moment was Doctor Death (not his real name), whose speciality was helping old dears top themselves. His Old Bailey Defence team painted him as an angel of mercy, bringing peace and deliverance to those who felt Life was a shade overrated. The Defence tended to skirt round the fact that his ex-patients were also delivered of buckets of cash in return for a handful of barbiturates and a plastic bag. The Prosecution picked away at that.

'Doctor Shurittow, is it not a fact that you received from Miss Marie-Louise Piedmond the sum of etc etc?'

Ur. He couldn't remember. That's all right. They could. And so it continued for ten days until the jury got tired of each other's company and found him guilty.

That night I was back in Hamptons and somehow or other the saga of Cindy Reilly bubbled up. Possibly the Assorted Pals were under the influence of the Doctor Death trial. Whatever the reason, the general mood was: 'Let's kill her.'

I suppose the joke had just about run its course, but I was still hedging. You can blame Susannah for that. She said, 'And when we've killed her, we'll decide which was the most outrageous story we had in and then we treat the winner to a slap-up lunch.'

As an afterthought she added, 'You don't have a hope, Max.'

I couldn't argue. All I'd achieved was my long-ago story about psychic Cindy and her lost crystal ball. What chance did that stand against Olly's strippagram girl or Tommy's randy rhino yarn?

I was a touch despondent – not because I was a non-runner for the freebie lunch award. That would probably be one of Hamptons bowel-loosening specials. What really brassed me off was the prospect of losing. For it would be seen that my peers had been more imaginative than I. I didn't like the taste of that at all.

So, that night when I pitched up at Rosie's, I was not at my sparkiest.

'Hi-ho,' said she, 'and why are you so down in the dumps?'

Sometimes Rosie thinks I live a life of unalloyed glee.

I helped myself to the bottle. 'Just a lunatic idea. Nothing you can help with.'

I forget that Rosie is firmly convinced she has the exact solution to every problem known to Max Chard. She stopped scraping pink paint out from under her fingernails. 'What is it?'

'Oh, it's a woman.'

I had her undivided attention. 'What sort of woman? What does she look like?'

There are moments when I take my life in my hands. 'She's got big blue eyes and a mighty pair of bazoomas and her hobby is men.'

A taut silence. Rosie stopped the business with the nail file. 'What's her name?'

'Cindy. Cindy Reilly.'

'And what does this "Cindy" have to do with you?'

We were both on the sofa and I moved a fraction distant. I didn't like the way that nail file was pointing.

I said, 'When you were a little girl, did you ever have an imaginary friend?'

'How do you know this Cindy?'

'And did you talk to your pretend pal and get her to join in your games?'

Rosie was in question-only mode. 'Is she one of your ex-girlfriends?'

No such luck. I said, 'And was this little friend so *real* that you used to lay out a bowl of Sugarpops for her at breakfast?'

'Just stop burbling and tell me who Cindy Reilly is.'

I'd pushed it far enough. 'All right, she's my imaginary pal.'

Rosie jumped up. She was breathing smoke. 'You've got a *fantasy* woman?'

You could put it like that, but only if you wanted a nail file in the ribs. I said, 'She's a joke we made up.'

'Who made up?'

I waved a hand. 'Oh, Tommy, Susannah, Olly and a few others.'

'Who's Susannah?'

'Tommy's girlfriend.'

Which is news to both of them.

Rosie sat herself down again but she still had that nail file glinting at me. So I explained the whole story, doctoring it here and there so that Susannah didn't feature too strongly. When I was finished, Rosie gave me a cool, pitying stare. 'You've actually been writing stories about a woman who doesn't exist? You men are just a bunch of overgrown kids.'

It's not just us men. It was Susannah's idea in the first place. But I thought it best not to mention that. I said, 'Now the problem is I've got to get in a story on Cindy before she's killed off.'

A harrumph, which I read as: 'If you think I'm going to help you, you can forget it.' Most of the time Rosie is sweet and soft and squeezable and all sorts of things beginning with S. But not where other women are concerned. Not even imaginary ones. They make her mean and moochy and all the rest.

I said, 'Anyway, what shall we do tonight?'

'I've got a lot of work to finish.'

This was a wicked lie. Rosie *never* works at night. She was just exacting her revenge. Sometimes she can be dead childish.

I did the decent thing and jumped through hoops to get her back to body temperature. But she was still only semi-thawed. I said, 'How's about we go back to that rip-off restaurant we were in the night I got sent to Cyprus?'

Her little nose was high in the air but I saw the nostrils twitch. I was on the right track here. I said, 'And we'll wrap ourselves round a few bottles of wine and chomp on sea bass and profiteroles.'

Profiteroles. I often get bothered about them. All it would take is a bloke with a suitcase stuffed full of profiteroles to come a-knocking on her door and she'd be off with him like a shot.

Rosie said, 'All right, but I'd better change.'

I sighed a two-tone sigh, part relief and part exasperation. Do you know, if the Last Trump was sounded, Rosie would say, 'Hang about while I go and change.'

I poured myself another Gordons and prepared for a lengthy slice of hanging about. But I hadn't counted on the cabaret. I was stretched out on the sofa rattling the ice cubes around when Rosie wafted in from the bedroom. She was wearing knickers and a floppy-necked blue sweater. Nothing else.

'What does this look like?'

It looks like the sort of thing your favourite fantasy woman might wear. I said, 'If we're going out maybe you'd better stick on some jeans.'

'What about the sweater?'

'I'd prefer you without it.'

She clicked her teeth. 'But is it all right?'

I told the truth. 'It's great. Suits you down to the drawers.'

Whereupon she whipped the thing off, thereby revealing what my imagination had already seen.

'Won't be a sec. I just need a quick shower.'

I sat up and watched her bob off. The ice cubes were clinking around without any help from me. Rosie always brushes her teeth before she showers. She thoughtfully left open the bathroom door so I could admire her bridge work, via the hallway mirror. This is hard to credit, but a back corner of my brain was meanwhile beavering away on the vexed question of Cindy Reilly.

The answer came to me in a flash. And I mean flash. It happened when Rosie swung around and was caught in profile by my mirror which she lets me keep in the bathroom. It's one of those shaving jobs that magnifies your chin five times its normal size: only now it was magnifying a fair curve of Rosie. The reflection bounced off the hall mirror. By some weird trick of perspective it threw off a bizarre image. Not to go into too fine detail, one side of her was huge, and the other normal. Rosie vanished into the shower, but the image was locked in my mind's eye, except now I'd placed Cindy Reilly's head where Rosie's ought to be. Now . . . I thought to myself . . . where could I go with that story?

A long, long time later we got to the poncy restaurant. It's one of those places that likes to pretend it gives value for money, so there were candles everywhere, fat creamy napkins and leather-bound menus.

On a distant side table was a chunky tub of yellow flowers.

'Aha!' I said. 'Mo had a whole bush like that outside her place.'

Rosie craned her neck round. 'Yeh, but I bet her bougainvillaea was real. That's just a plastic plant.'

I'm an innocent, I truly am. We gnawed our way down the menu and presently Rosie was making mincemeat of the promised profiteroles and was back to her usual breezy blue-eyed self. She dabbed cream from her lips. 'Have you thought any more about this Cindy thing?'

'What?'

'You know, the joke story.'

'Oh, that. No. Why?'

She said, 'I think it's missing the point. I mean, all you're doing is putting a name into a story you've made up.'

I told her that was the general idea.

Rosie waved her curls around. 'Yes, but nobody knows what she looks like.'

Yes they do, they know she's got this and that and everything else besides.

Rosie, who doesn't read newspapers, said, 'I know if I read a story about Cindy Reilly I'd want to see what she looked like.'

'See?'

Another forkful of profiterole, then: 'Yes, like a picture.'

I nearly dropped my glass. 'You mean a *photograph?'*

That's precisely what she meant. Something in my

head went: 'Wow!' A snap. A *real* pic of an imaginary woman. The idea defied all known logic. It was a perfect honey.

I was in the presence of true genius. I said in awed tones, 'A photograph. You are an absolute beauty. You are the wonder of the Western world.'

She just smiled. I suppose she already knew that.

I leaned across the table and planted a kiss on her little red lips, thereby almost setting myself ablaze on the candles.

The next question was how could I get a real pic of a woman who wasn't. It was the morning after and I was tipping back machine tea and fresh out of clever thoughts. I don't run well on unleaded. And this wasn't the sort of conundrum I could share with a fellow hack, for you could bet your boots he'd nick my cracking idea. All right then, Rosie's cracking idea.

The best I could come up with was to dig out a suitable snap from the library, take it back to Wonderwoman and get her to doctor it with her paintbrush. But here I ran into another snag. I'd already framed the story I planned to write on Cindy and the picture had to match that. I was pretty sure Rosie's talents didn't stretch that far. What I needed was one of those computer morphing things.

My desk phone began tinkling and I stuck Cindy back in her box.

'Mister Chard, please.'

A bloke, but not one I knew. 'Who's speaking?'

'It's personal.' London accent. Well that narrowed it down some.

I said, 'I'm sorry, I need to know who's calling before I can put you through to him.'

The bloke said, 'Just tell him it's about Maureen Frew.'

'This is Max Chard.'

A chopped-down chuckle from him. Then: 'You got it wrong about her. Unless there's a lot you left out.'

I don't take kindly to critics, especially at ten in the morning. 'And which particular lot might that be?'

He said, 'How much do you pay for a good story?'

Oh, one of them. I disabused him pretty sharpish. 'Maureen Frew is history. There's no interest in her anymore.'

'What? Not even if she's getting away with murder?'

'Whose murder?'

He said, 'I thought you journalists read your papers.'

'We just write them; we leave the hard bit to the readers.'

He turned grouchy. 'Look, are you interested or not? I'm offering you a great scoop for free.'

'No you're not. You're trying to flog it.'

He said, 'The money's not the main thing. I just want to set you right on a couple of angles.'

'Such as?'

'Like the money she's still got. That and the killing.'

I lit a cigarette and thought about it. I'd painted Maureen as a bad girl turned good, or at least goodish. I couldn't very well go back and paint her black again. Not without a certain degree of embarrassment on my part. But what if the Unknown Caller was telling it straight? Just imagine the embarrassment of Plod – and the Editor – if I turned Mo over. The idea tickled.

I said, 'What have you got then?'

He didn't want to talk about it on the phone. But how about me meeting him at a pub I'd never heard of up in Cricklewood? I pitched that suggestion out the window. The last thing I wanted was to turn up at some backstreet hellhole and find this stranger waiting for me along with Harry and the driver and the one with the eyelid. I suggested instead the dive bar of the Stone. He hummed about over that but in the end he said okay. Eight tonight. I said, 'And what do you call yourself?'

'Charlie. Just Charlie.'

I don't know how, but I got the distinct impression his Mum called him something else. I was about to ask how I'd recognize him, but he said, 'I'll know you. I've seen your picture in the paper.'

He went away. I had nothing much on my plate so I turned on the library screen and started poking through all the Zeller Maine cuttings, or the early ones anyway. What I was after was the size of the score. Nearly all the papers put it at ten million. That's what I'd got from a mate on the Robbery Squad, and maybe the others had the same contact. In the long months between the job and the court case the figure yo-yoed, hitting as high as twenty million and dropping back to ten, depending on the quantity of drink consumed. But never below that. Not until Mo popped up in the witness box and said it was only five-and-a-bit. Hmmm. Another conundrum to add to the Zeller Maine mystery. I frowned. What I needed was something to cheer me up. Or a drink might do instead.

Five minutes later I was brightening up over a cool gin and looking for bad company. My fellow hacks were still chained to their keyboards and the only company in sight was Ferdy from Promotions. Despite his humble calling, he knows some cracking jokes. Not today. He had his moustache half buried in a pint of London Pride and it looked like it would take a barrel of the stuff to get him back to his usual perkiness.

I shared out the Bensons and asked him how things were faring in the twilight zone of the Promo Dept.

He said, 'Take it from me, you don't want to know.'

That bad, huh?

'Worse.'

Personally I like other people's problems. They make me forget my own. So I rustled up another pint of Pride and pressed him for the grisly details. He started off slowly. 'Well, you know we've got this big push on in Ireland?'

I didn't. He duly enlightened me. It seems that the circulation riff-raff had been running their slide rules over our latest sales figures. They showed we were steadily losing readers in England, Scotland and Wales. Nothing new there. But for some bizarre reason we were holding our own in Ireland, north and south. Now, if I were the circulation boss I'd be dreaming up smart ideas to win back readers in England, Scotland and maybe even Wales. But that just goes to show how little I know about selling newspapers.

What they decided instead was to beef up the Irish edition. Whenever Circulation come up with a crackpot notion like this, they get every other department hooked in too. So Editorial was running extra Irish news pages in the edition. Sports had a change page, Features had shipped off a couple of scribes to Dublin, and so on.

But the real brunt of the push fell on Promo. I got thus far with the story before Ferdy fell silent.

'And?' I prodded.

And it all came out. The hard core of the promotion drive was to be our never-ending Bingo-Banko competition which delivers anything from a fiver to a million quid if the number on your scratch card matches the number printed in the paper. We don't get many big winners, largely because we make damn sure the right number doesn't appear on *any* of the cards.

But one afternoon in a head-banging session prior to the Irish push, Ferdy came up with his masterstroke. 'What if we have an Irish Bingo-Banko winner, a big winner?'

The other wastrels took turns pushing it this way and that to see if the wheels stayed on. They did. And so the competitions manager arranged to send all the big winning scratch cards to Ireland. Among their number was one which stood to make its owner a millionaire.

I thought I'd sussed out why Ferdy was so gloomy. 'But no one claimed the prize?'

His moustache drooped over his chin. 'That's just the trouble. Somebody did.'

'But?'

'But he's not Irish. He's from bloody Huddersfield.'

I said, 'Then how did he . . .?'

'Get the winning ticket? The berk was in Ireland on a fishing holiday.'

Call me unfeeling, but I laughed out loud. Ferdy didn't seem to notice. 'And now I'm right in it for wasting a million of the promo budget. I got a real rollocking this morning, as if I'd meant him to win it.'

I said, 'Still, look on the sunny side. It probably boosted the sales in Huddersfield.'

'Down two per cent.'

'What about Ireland?'

'Down four per cent.'

I got reeled back out of the pub because Desk wanted me to dress up some half-baked story about a couple of joyriders out Acton way stealing a hearse which they promptly pranged into a bollard. Only one dead. And he was already dead anyway, seeing as how he was all laid out in his coffin in the back.

I polished that one off and tidied up no less than five cruddy court stories which would never appear in the paper. I knew that. Even Desk knew that. But it served their prime purpose of stopping me zapping hell out of my liver. They can be ever so thoughtful sometimes.

Round about six they ran out of duff stories for me. I sauntered over to Angela Whipple and told her I had to see a contact.

She pivoted round in her big black chair and squeezed her eyes at me. 'I don't suppose you'd be meeting this contact in a pub?'

Envy is a terrible thing. I smiled with both decks of teeth. 'As it happens, I am.'

'Who's the contact?'

She didn't really want to know. She just wanted to watch me lie. I disappointed her. 'There's a whisper going round that Mo Frew is still sitting on a bundle of the Zeller Maine loot. Also, that she's mixed up in the murder of those three blokes in Brixton.'

Angie's frown said she was suffering from information overload. 'What three blokes?'

I cut it down as tight as I could. 'Three villains from the Zeller Maine lot were murdered in June. The Old Bill haven't a clue who set them up. Plus the word is Mo still has her share tucked away. Then today I get a call from a man who calls himself Charlie. He says she set up the killings.'

All the while I was rattling through this little speech her mouth was opening wider and wider. So were her eyes. Her mouth got back in shape first. 'Jesus, Max, do you know what you're saying?'

I knew all right. The question was, did she?

She said, 'My office. We'll talk there.'

As soon as we were through the door Angie unchained the minibar. She's good at prioritizing. We each helped ourselves. Scotch for her, a Gordons for me. She took a belt and looked at me head on.

'Is this for real?'

I shrugged. 'I've got to find out what this bloke has to offer.'

She said, 'But we paid Maureen Frew, what, eighty thousand?'

If her office were any bigger she would have got

up and paced to and fro. Instead she had to make do with clicking her ballpoint button up and down.

She said, 'Have you even stopped to think what this might mean?'

'That Mo might be wrapped up in a triple murder?'

Angie wasn't concerned with such trifles. She wailed, 'The Editor's going to blow a fuse. It was his idea to pay her.'

Oh dearie me.

She said, 'I don't think you realize how serious this is. If we run this we'll make the Editor look stupid.'

Personally I feel he doesn't need any help from us on that score. I swigged my gin and watched Angie's crisis control in action.

'Oh, *God!* What are we going to do?'

I was soothing. 'Don't fret. There might be nothing in it.'

'But what if there is?' She was off again in free-fall. I let her go on for a minute or two because that's what she wanted. She treated herself to another stiff one, but she didn't share it around. It was time to get out.

I said, 'Point one: the only info we've got comes from some low-life. Point two: let's just imagine he's telling the truth for the first time in his career.'

Angie imagined and glugged neat scotch.

I said, 'If that's the case, we sue Mo's lawyer, Tullamy, for misrepresentation and we get our eighty thousand back.'

'I hadn't thought of that.'

Well, she can't think of everything, can she?

I said, 'And point three, the Editor emerges as a man who cannot be fooled.'

She leaned over the desk towards me. 'Do you believe that? Do you honestly think that's the way it would come out?'

Yeh. I also believe in the Loch Ness Monster.

I said, 'Why not? We end up with a great story – and it hasn't cost us a penny.'

She was up and away. 'Yes! And we could carry a line saying we always had suspicions about Maureen Frew and we were determined to expose her as a murderer. It was the Editor's own—'

I halted her in mid-flight. 'You're forgetting one thing.'

'What?'

'The story might be total balls.'

Her eyes said she hoped not. She really, *really* hoped not.

Before I snaked off to the Stone I called by the Monkey Desk and got them to release Frankie into my custody. He was his usual trusting self. 'What do you want?'

I said, 'To buy you drink.'

He's not used to people offering to fill him up. 'Why?'

I said, 'If you want to know, you've got to have that drink first.'

Curiosity or thirst got the better of him. 'Oh, right on, then.'

And off we went with him yattering on about nothing I remember. The sole thought in my head was how I could con him into helping me get Cindy Reilly's pic in the paper. By now this had become a magnificent obsession. I say that to explain my stupidity. For I had just committed a folly of horrendous proportions. I'd broken Chard's Immutable Law on Talking to News Editors.

Put briefly it adds up to this: you never ever tell them about a story that you haven't already got in the bag. If you do, they'll believe every single word of it. Then, when you come back and say, 'Ooops. The story bombed out,' they'll hate you. For in the meantime they'll have hyped the thing up and sold it to the Editor, a man of touching credulity.

All this I know. Yet I'd just gone and blabbed to Angie about a yarn which had all the makings of nothing. That was seriously stupid.

But my idiocy was minor league compared to hers. Even before I'd got the first round ordered in, she was hammering away with both fists on the door of Tony Belker, our rancid Executive Editor.

Fortunately I knew nothing of this so I was in breezy form as I plied Frankie with large pints and listened to his lies. It was just the usual stuff about women. By stealth and guile I steered the conversation around to the various bits of whizz-bang gadgetry they have in the monkeys' enclosure. There is, for example, a grabber which allows them to snatch a pic off TV news and stick it in the paper and pretend it's one of their own. That's pretty low-grade. There are others which let you merge two shots into one so you don't spot the join. Say, for instance, you want a front-pager of Prince Charles meeting the locals in Umbangaland. First you find a snap of HRH with his mouth agape and his eyes a-popping. Then you get another pic of some top-heavy bare-breasted rascal wobbling her charms. Stick them all together in the same shot and, well, you can just picture it, can't you?

Anyways, with all this clobber, I reckoned they could sort out my Cindy Reilly problem. All I needed was a gullible soul. I explained the set-up to Frankie.

'What's in it for me?' he demanded.

'Two pints so far.'

Frankie hung on a wolfish grin to let me know he was not the type who could be bought that cheap.

I said, 'And if you're a good little monkey, there's several more where that came from.'

Just to prove that was no idle threat, I laid on another. He was doing his best to think quietly. He packed away two inches of lager. Then, 'And what do you get out of it?'

'Me? Nothing. I told you it's just a joke.'

Frankie wasn't having that. A dim flicker of inspiration lit his beady eyes. 'It's a bet, isn't it? How much – a ton?'

I came clean. 'There's twenty quid riding on it.'

'Balls. You wouldn't go to all this bother for just a score.'

I said, 'I would for fifty.'

'But it's not fifty. It's a ton.'

What the hell, it was worth it. I surrendered. 'Yes. A hundred quid.'

You're not going to believe this, but he wanted it cut eighty-twenty in his favour. The way he argued it, his was the tough part. First he had to find a suitable pic, then he had to do all sorts of button-pushing to change it round. That took time.

How long?

'I could knock it out in about twenty minutes.'

He said that without thinking. I smiled. 'And you expect eighty quid for that? Maybe I'd better find another monkey.'

He swallowed his pride and the rest of his pint. 'All right. Fifty-fifty.'

We shook on it, but first I made him wipe the spit off his hand.

Now I'd got Cindy sorted, for the time being anyway, I turned to item two on the agenda: the bloke who called himself Charlie. My watch told me we were already on the wrong side of nine. I looked around. The only guzzlers in the vicinity were the usual shifty-eyed bunch of subs. No Charlie. So much for his great story. I didn't intend hanging around any longer, especially as Frankie was acting thirsty again.

I said, 'I'm off. I've got to see a couple of people.'

'You getting a taxi? You can give me a lift to Blackfriars.'

I lied. 'No, I'm going south.'

Frankie said, 'That's all right. Just drop me at London Bridge.'

He wears you down in the end.

I said, 'I'll take you as far as Blackfriars.'

We rolled out into the dark and drizzly night. We headed down Winslett Street, round the corner into Taffeta Lane. I was sunk in my own innocent reveries so I didn't see the bloke until I almost bumped into him. He was tall, not in Frankie's class, but tall enough. He said, 'I've been waiting for you.'

Frankie said, 'Me? Who're you?'

Before the tall bloke could answer, another figure loomed out of the shadows. He looked like he might be called Maltese Micky or somesuch.

I said to the tall one, 'I suppose you're Charlie? You've left it a bit late, haven't you?'

Frankie swung his bony nose to and fro. 'Wot's going on, then?'

Over to the tall bloke. 'Yeh, I'm Charlie. But this is none of your business. It's just between me and Mister Chard.'

I said, 'And Maltese Micky.'

The Charlie character stared at me strangely. He'd been in a few scraps in his time. Mostly with double-decker buses, by the look of it. I didn't like the way things were shaping up. I felt I already knew the script. Any second now one of them would say, 'Just get in the bloody car.'

I said, 'This is my special mate Frankie. Anything you want to say to me, you can say in front of him.'

My courageous monkey chipped in, 'Max. I'd better be off. Be seeing you.'

No way. I said quickly, 'Frankie and I were on the Maureen Frew job together.'

'Aah.' Charlie discovered a new-found interest in Frankie. 'Well, maybe you'd like to talk to us and all.'

Maltese Micky muscled six inches forward. I said, 'It's lucky for you that Frankie only hits people his own size.'

Charlie looked baffled. 'Who said anything about hitting? We just want to exchange a little bit of information, like I want to know—'

'—Where Mo Frew is hiding out.'

'That's it. That's all.'

Frankie and I both spoke at once, only he said Gibraltar and I said Pissouri.

Charlie crumpled his brow to match the rest of his face. 'Which one is it?'

I said, 'Before I go into it, might I ask you a question?'

'Ask away.'

Maybe it was the gin, but I wasn't feeling as twitchy as I should have been. I said, 'What are you expecting me to say that I didn't say last time?'

They didn't understand the question. I made it easier for them. 'Last month a bunch of your mates took me out to Westferry, asked me the same questions and then duffed me up.'

Charlie said slowly, 'What mates are you talking about?'

'One was called Harry. The driver had black curly hair, and the other geezer had an eye like this.' I pulled my left eyelid down.

Now they were really fazed. Charlie looked at Maltese Micky and Maltese Micky looked at him. Charlie said, 'They weren't us. Straight up.'

I knew that. 'No they were different blokes, but they must have been mates of yours.'

'Are you making this up?'

I said, 'If you like I'll introduce you to the copper I reported it to.'

No. They'd take my word on that one.

I was growing bolder. 'So why are you giving me a bad time again?'

Charlie said, 'What bad time? This is on the level.'

Maltese Micky gave voice. 'Yeh.'

I laughed. 'Come on, are you trying to tell me there are *two* gangs chasing me for news of Maureen and Stan?'

Charlie took a noisy breath. 'Mister Chard, I don't know who them other ones were; they've got nothing to do with us. And we're not into violence.'

And they weren't into growing roses either.

I said, 'Let's just imagine you're telling the truth, do you mind explaining what you want with her?'

'She did a naughty on some of our friends, okay? She narked on them. Now where'd you say she was?'

I said, 'And what about that other lot? Why did they want her?'

'Search me. Look, if you don't want to talk to us, all right. We walk away and nobody takes the hump. No harm done.'

There was not the faintest trace of menace in there. It was like he was asking me for a favour. I said, 'I'll tell you precisely what I told the other three.'

Charlie cocked a bashed-up ear and listened as I trotted out the Pissouri line again, adding that it was on the sun-kissed island of Cyprus. I also threw in my previous fable about the four armed minders and the yellow bush at the door and all that.

Charlie said, 'And it's definitely Cyprus.'

'Absolutely definitely.'

Frankie was narked. 'You told me to say Gibraltar.' But nobody was paying him much attention.

I went back to my own list of questions. 'Why did you say Mo was mixed up in the three murders?'

'What three murders?'

Whatever else he might have been, Charlie was not a criminal mastermind. I said, 'The job in Coldharbour Lane – when Belly Sloman and the others got shot.'

Charlie laughed. 'No, I wasn't talking about them. I was talking about Barry Frew.'

Barry Frew!

I took a breath. 'He's been murdered?'

'Well, let's put it this way. No one's seen him around for a long while.'

Frankly, if I was sitting on five million of somebody else's money, you wouldn't see me for an even longer while.

I said, 'That's the only reason?'

Yep. That was all.

I said, 'What about Stan Defoe; was he involved in the murder?'

'Might have been. But it's just her we want a word with on account of what she told the police.'

I said, 'You hinted this morning that Mo had all the money.'

'No I didn't. I just reckon she's got her share put away someplace.'

I remembered her talking that last night in Cyprus. 'She told me her cut *would* have been a million, but Barry nicked it.'

Charlie disagreed. 'From what I know she got paid. Not like a lot of people. Anyway, I want to put a little proposition your way, Max. You could do yourself a favour and earn a few bob.'

Frankie was right there. 'How?'

The gist of it was that if I got to hear any update

on Mo's movements, Charlie would pay top money for it.

'How much?' Frankie again.

Five big ones. I said that would do nicely, and just in case I did find out something, where could I reach him.

Charlie smiled. 'Don't worry. I'll give you a bell from time to time.'

And with that, he and Maltese Micky swung about and disappeared back to where they came from.

Chapter Fourteen

This time I waited till morning before ringing Tom at the Yard. He was out beating up suspects. So I chugged off to the office without even the faintest glimmer of what I was letting myself in for. Show me an ambush and I walk straight into it every time.

The first inkling came when Jools tottered over to my desk. Jools is Tony Belker's much inflated secretary, and generally a welcome sight around the place. Not today. 'Max, Tony wants a word.'

I do not know a single sentence more calculated to shrivel the soul.

I said, 'I'll be there in a couple of minutes.' Anything to keep the Beast at bay.

I rang the Yard again, but Tom was still playing hide-and-seek. I gathered my bones together, took a deep breath and set off down the corridor signposted 'TRANSYLVANIA THIS WAY'. Meanwhile I was mentally flicking through my most recent misdeeds. No, nothing there to warrant a Belkering. I still felt queasy.

Belker, I'd best explain, is a sociopath, specifically hired by the Editor to inflict hideous sufferings on us hacks. He likes his job. Belker regards getting pissed as a hanging offence. Expenses fiddling is a mite more serious. For some reason he reserves a particular hatred for me. Thus our frequent contretemps are not the sort of thing you'd like to see broadcast before the nine p.m. watershed.

His office door was half open. There he was fat and hulking behind his desk, wearing something grey from Man at Millet's. Perhaps I haven't mentioned, but in his off-duty hours Belker masquerades as an urban sprawl.

His sneaky little eyes picked me up. 'Get in here.'

The words 'please' and 'thank you' do not figure high in his vocabulary.

I hadn't even got the door closed behind me before he was off. 'What the bloody hell do you think you're doing? Are you mad or what?'

I settled for the 'what'.

He dragged himself upright and the whole office went dark. 'You're a bloody disgrace. You think you can do what you like and get away with it. But this time you've really screwed up.'

This time? Which particular this time did he have in mind? I gave him an encouraging smile because that always blows his circuitry. Never fails.

'You . . . you . . .!' He swivelled away, banged a fist against the filing cabinet, turned back and rattled out every rude word he could think of. The mildest was bastard.

I just stood there in my navy Ozwald Boateng two-piece smiling away in the fond hope he'd have a cardiac. Maybe he sussed my subtle ploy because he began calming down. So far I hadn't said a thing.

Belker planted his great clumsy paws on the desk

and leaned over at me. By God, he should do something about those teeth. There was a long pause, broken only by him snorting air up his hooter. The outline of a twisted little smile warped one corner of his mouth. I didn't like the look of that.

He let the smile spread. 'But now I've got you, Chard.'

I said politely, 'And what exactly have you got, Tony?'

'Haw! Don't pull the bloody innocent with me. You know what I'm talking about.'

Talking? He called that talking?

I measured out a cool frown. 'I wouldn't even attempt to guess.'

Oh dear, there he went again, his pasty jowls turning an encouraging purple tint. I stood there working out what I'd do if he collapsed. How long should I leave it before I called an ambulance? I settled on two days minimum.

He wound himself down to just under a roar. 'So far I've kept this from the Editor.'

I said, 'So far you've kept it from me too.'

For one ecstatic moment I thought I had him. But the quivering blob caught himself just in time. More effing and blinding and general gibberish.

I said, 'If you have nothing intelligent on your mind, I'm off.'

That was the wrong thing to say, for back came the sickly smirk. 'Oh yes, you're off all right. You're out of here. No one is going to make a fool of the Editor. Especially not you.'

Ah. The Editor. A clue to what this was all about. I

joined it up. So Angie had gone and told him about Mo Frew.

I said, 'If I were you I would be very careful here, Tony.'

That made him blink.

'Because,' I added, smooth as silk, 'there is a very grave danger *you* might make him look foolish. Alternatively, if what you say is right – that I've got the heave-ho – there is an equal danger that some other paper might make a fool of him.'

He sucked that in through his teeth. 'Are you threatening me?'

I echoed, 'Are you threatening *me*?'

He heaved and blew for a minute or two. Then: 'Sit down.'

'I'd rather stand.'

Belker turned away and looked out the window. Over his shoulder he said, 'If you want to keep your job you'd better explain.'

Round one to me. I said, 'The rumour is Maureen Frew topped her old man. Sooner or later the police will hear the same rumour. If it stands up, she'll be done for murder. Then the Editor will look foolish. Unless we get in first.'

'That's not how Angela Whipple told it.'

I said, 'Angie forgets things.'

He kept looking out the window. I had an unrestricted view of his vast hindquarters. It's hard to tell which end of Belker is worse.

He said, 'Are you trying to tell me you're investigating this rumour just to see whether it *might* embarrass the Editor? You expect me to believe *that*?'

'Why not?'

He wobbled his head. 'I know you: you're a make-it-up merchant. This is just another one of your lies.'

I said, 'Think of it this way: *if* Mo is a killer, the Editor will need damage limitation. But if you'd prefer, I'll forget the whole story and stop asking questions. Then when it all comes out, you can explain it to him.'

Oh boy. More fireworks. But somewhere in the midst of them Belker began to think about his own fat hide. And a teensy doubt stirred in his brain.

He still couldn't let go. 'At the very least you have been grossly irresponsible. You should have told me as soon as you heard this rumour. In future you tell me and nobody else, not Angela, not anybody.'

He lurched back round. 'I will not forget your unprofessionalism, or your impertinence. Now get out of here before I change my mind.'

He plopped down into his chair.

I said, 'Does this mean I still have a job?'

It really hurt him to grunt in the affirmative.

Back at my desk there was a voice-mail sizzling: CALL ME PRONTO, MAC.

I phoned his mobile. 'Hello, Pronto.'

'Oh very comic, Max. Listen, I've no time for jokes, there's a funny murder just happened in Hadley Wood.'

'How funny?'

Mac said, 'It's *not* being handled by the local nick. But Criminal Intelligence and all the high-falutin' fellas are involved.'

'Anti-terrorist?'

'No. Not that I've heard. There's no facts coming out yet. Not even if it's a man or a woman. I don't know what this is, but it's a big one.'

I said, 'What's your guess?'

He hesitated. 'It might be a spying job. Maybe it's an undercover guy. For pity's sake, give us a chance. But I'm deadly earnest. It's something out of the X-Files. All I've got is the address.'

14 Sweetavon Drive.

I put down the phone and lit up a Bensons. Mac has flogged me many tip-offs, some of them small beer, some the full pint. But he has never once pitched me a no-no. I rang ambulance control. 'Have you had an incident in Hadley Wood, a DOA?'

The bloke on the other end didn't even run down the incident list. 'No.'

I looked up the *A–Z*. The nearest hospital was Barnet. I got through to the administrator there. Another straight no. Barnet police were as helpful as feared. Some twerp of an inspector said, 'If you require any information on *any* incident, the proper course is to contact Press Bureau.'

But he hadn't said no.

Next I clicked on to the library machine and did a search for Sweetavon Drive. It had precisely fourteen houses in it. The owner of No. 14 was listed as a G. Flint. I gave it a try.

A man barked, 'Yes?'

'Mister Flint?'

'Who's calling?'

I said, 'Is that Mister Flint?'

'Who's calling?'

I said, 'This is Trevor from the Jaguar agency. He asked me to ring him.'

'I'll tell him you called.'

He put the phone down. The library directory gave a D. Dornystall at No. 12. A woman this time.

I said, 'Good morning, sorry to bother you, but can you tell me if there's been some sort of incident in your road?'

She said, 'I'm not supposed to say anything. You've got to ask the police.' And that was the end of her.

I tried the rest. Half were out. The other half weren't talking. Damn. I'd have to go all the way out there. I needed a driver.

I zipped across to News Desk and sprung the tidings. Angie said, 'You'd better get there fast.'

Really?

Monkey Desk had all their top men scouring the country for half-naked women. But they let me have Merv, a freelance chimp. He owned a Fiat Punto which he loved dearly. He drove it like he had just passed his test, and judging by his youth, that might well have been the case.

Some days later we wound up in Hadley Wood, a huge tract of land where executive homes peeked out from behind trees. Finding Sweetavon Drive took another good half-hour out of my life. We had to park round the corner because Plod had been playing cat's cradle with cordon tapes. On the front line were two uniforms and a couple of blokes in civvies.

I flashed my Press pass. 'Who's the victim?'

One of the civvies said, 'Phone Press Bureau.'

I said, 'I already have: they know nothing.' Well, it was half true.

The road was a cul-de-sac and there was a log-jam of cars down the far end. Merv began lining up a street shot. The civvy said, 'No photographs.'

Merv wasn't as dim as he looked. He started popping.

The civvy got stroppy. 'Are you deaf? I said no photographs.'

I said, 'He's entitled to take snaps in a public place and there's sod all you can do about it. Look it up. Who's in charge here?'

The civvy said, 'We'll see about that.' He wheeled round and stomped off down the street.

I lit a Bensons and tried to sweet-talk the other civvy. I must be losing the gift for he told me to eff off. I took in the surroundings instead. Two of the cars were police jobs. The rest were plain-clothes. A couple were parked skewy, as if the drivers had raced to the scene and jumped out. All the locals were tucked up behind their trees.

The absent civvy reappeared among a clutch of similarly ill-dressed bods. At the back of the bunch was a skinny type in a musty brown suit. He was lighting a cigarette and his hands were cupped up round it. Then he took his hands away and I saw his face.

'Clovis!' I yelled.

The group froze, all of them looking my way. Clovis was first to move. He began coming towards me. I could see his eyes, hard and black. They told me I was about as welcome as a bring-a-bottle party in the Betty Ford Clinic.

As he got near, I said, 'Who was it? Anyone we know?'

'How did you find out about this?'

'News Desk took an anonymous tip-off. Who's the victim?'

Merv hoisted his camera and snapped him full on. Clovis said, 'Right. That's it. You're nicked.'

It was as if the two uniforms had been waiting all their lives for this very moment. They were on top of Merv before he could say, 'Urk.' Another mob of woodentops came running to join the game.

'Him too,' said Clovis, pointing his skinny cigarette my way.

I said, 'Touch me and you're looking at assault, false arrest and general stupidity.'

They liked the sound of that. Merv and I were bundled through the tapes with our arms stuck halfway up our backs. They'd already collared his cameras. Clovis was still playing the MC. 'Take their phones and hold them in the car. Stay with them.'

He made sure they did the job properly and then he cleared off. Now we were in the back of a panda car with a couple of smug young Plods for company. I wasn't particularly bothered. I knew the rules of this game. Sooner or later they'd wheel us off to Barnet nick where we would be formally charged with obstruction, resisting arrest and assaulting a police officer. Then I would get to phone Royce, our legal bald eagle, and he'd spring us. After that, Royce would launch a counter-action against the Met and some months down the line, both sides would call it quits.

In the meantime I had a job to do. The police jam-jar was parked outside No. 14. It was a big drum with white stucco upstairs and an earthy brown roof. Matching blue curtains screened off all the bedroom windows. I can't say what the downstairs looked like, largely because there was a whacking great hedge in the way. But I could see the mouth of the driveway and the various Plods coming and going.

I began running through what this was all about. Clovis was a minder. Murder was not his territory. Unless the victim was one of his charges. Or one of his team. So it was either a cop or a grass. What did that give me?

ARMED police swooped on a posh suburb yesterday after an undercover operation went disastrously wrong.

A man – believed to be a top criminal supergrass – was gunned down in a palatial safe house.

Now Scotland Yard fears its witness protection scheme has been infiltrated by gang bosses.

Undercover detectives who shielded Zeller Maine informant Maureen Frew were said to have been guarding yesterday's victim.

No. Too many guesses there. I was still chewing the story over when my door popped open and a voice said, 'You stupid bugger. What are you doing here?'

I said, 'Hello, Tom. I'm doing my job. What about you?'

He turned to the slightly less thick-looking woodentop. 'Let him out. Just him.'

It grieved the lad, but he uncuffed me. I got out and lit a cigarette, offering one to Tom. He took it without a thank you. He led me off to the side. 'Now, you tell me what you know about this.'

I said, 'I know that either a supergrass or one of your protection boys has been killed.'

Tom had forgotten that we used to sup drink together. 'Where're you getting information?'

So far he hadn't denied anything.

I said, 'Somebody tipped us off there was a lot of police activity up here. I'm sent out and the first person I see is Clovis. Unless Clovis has been busted down to traffic division, I'm guessing he was minding someone here.'

Tom smoked and said nothing.

I had another bright idea. 'And the victim was either Mo or one of yours.'

He forgot about smoking. He just glared at me.

I said, 'And why do I think that? Because you're here, that's why. People of your rank just never turn up at a murder, unless it's something really tasty, and Mo was the highest-profile grass you've had in years.'

He said, 'You're wasting your time.'

'Who then? Stan? A minder?'

'You're not getting anything. What's your Editor called?'

I said, 'I can't remember.'

'For Christ's sake, we're not fooling around here. We'll slap a ban on this story.'

'Why?'

He came right up close. 'We don't need to give reasons. You're going back in the car. I'll finish with you later.'

I said, 'Give us a break. Look, whoever did the killing knows just who he killed. So the only people not allowed to know are the innocent newspaper-reading public. Does that sound reasonable to you?'

He muttered something about my jeopardizing ongoing police investigations. He stepped back and started squeezing his lips in and out. That must have meant he was thinking. Over his shoulder I could just see the entrance to the driveway. Two coppers appeared in it. They were both wearing body armour, they were both cradling guns. They looked up the street and then they started walking to one of the unmarked cars. Just behind them came Clovis and a clump of forensic types.

Tom stopped thinking and started talking. 'I'll tell you one thing for nothing: it wasn't an informer, and it wasn't a police officer.'

I jerked a glance at the guys with the guns. 'It wasn't somebody nicking a video recorder either.'

He said, 'I'll make a deal with you. I'll tell you what I can only on two conditions.'

I cocked a listening ear. Tom said, 'One. You do *not* mention Maureen or Stan, and two, you do not mention police protection officers. And you don't even hint at an informer.'

That's three conditions, but you don't expect A-level maths from the Old Bill. I nodded a yes.

Tom said, 'The owner of the house was found murdered this morning.'

I said, 'That's a Mister G. Flint?'

'No. He bought the house off Flint six months ago.'

'So what's the new one called?'

Tom shook his big squared-off head at me. 'Come

on, Max, you know we can't give that out until next of kin have been informed. Give me a day or so.'

A day? By then the story would be history.

I said, 'All right, what did he do? How old was he? Was he alone?'

Tom just stood there smiling sadly. There are times when you want to bop them on the beezer.

I said, 'You can't tell me, but you can give me off-the-record guidance. I'll tell you what I plan to write and you let me know if it's a million miles wrong.'

He didn't say anything.

I recited it as if I was on to Copy: 'Armed police swooped on a posh suburb yesterday after a mystery businessman was gunned down in his million-pound mansion.

'The middle-aged victim was slain in a cold-blooded contract killing.

'Now police are hunting the hitman – and the gang boss who ordered his execution.

'Neighbours in the leafy street were tending their gardens when the killer forced his way into the house and opened fire.

'Last night they were too shocked by the horror on their doorstep to talk about the incident.

'But one revealed: "He had just moved here about six months ago and he kept himself to himself. He seemed a respectable businessman, though none of us knew what he did."'

I paused. 'How am I doing?'

Tom said, 'You just made all of that up. I never said anything about a contract killing.'

And this man is supposed to be a senior detective.

I heaved a sigh. 'You've got an armed response unit here. You don't do that unless it's a bit hairy. You don't call in National Criminal Intelligence people for a one-off killing. That means it's linked with something else. Like what? Well, you say I can't mention Mo or police protection officers. Therefore it's a gangland hit. That all adds up to a contract killing.'

He said, 'And then you said the house cost a million. It's nowhere near that.'

'Who's going to complain? The neighbours just love it when we jack up the price of the property.'

He was still picking holes. 'Who says he was middle-aged?'

I said, 'Only somebody middle-aged or over could afford a place like this, unless he's a rock singer or a footballer, which I'm betting he wasn't. And he wasn't elderly either because villains don't put out contracts on old geezers. They leave that up to God.'

Tom grumbled. 'And you quoted the neighbours and you haven't even talked to them.'

I looked shocked. 'I've rung every single one of them before I came out here. But tell me, was the story off the wall?'

Tom said, 'There's a lot you don't have and some things are wrong.'

'Such as?'

'Don't chance your arm. I've given you plenty already.'

I stared at him solidly. I ran over it again in my head. Where was I wrong? I said softly, 'It wasn't just one hitman.'

He didn't disagree. He turfed the cigarette stub

away. Then without looking at me he said, 'And it wasn't the quick in-and-out bang-bang job that you make out.'

It wasn't?

I squeezed on that for about five seconds before it popped.

I said, 'They *tortured* him first?'

Tom swung around. 'Come on, that's your bloody lot. Now clear off, and if I catch you hanging round and pestering the neighbours, I'll nick you for sure.'

That suited me fine. I was getting thirsty anyway. Tom stumped off to tell his underlings to unchain monkey Merv and I ambled back up the street towards the cordon. I was passing number eight or ten when a woman with scrambled-up hair stuck her bean over the hedge. She must have been blind or something for she mistook me for a copper.

She said, 'What's happened at Mister Tullamy's?'

Tullamy! She said Tullamy.

I had to tell the truth. 'We shot him because he hadn't paid his car tax.'

For once I behaved myself and did what the Law told me. I got well offside, found a boozer of sorts, and had a single pint in the course of which I knocked up a meaty holding story on top brief Tullamy with underworld links getting himself tied up, pistol-whipped and finally put out of his misery.

I shot it down the line and buzzed Angie. She wanted to know where I was. I said I was sniffing around suburbia for more of the same. That's the first time Hamptons has ever found itself in suburbia. She told me to stay put and I didn't object. None of the usual cronies was on hand so I nursed a glass and did a spot of logical reasoning. I knew what had happened, but I was a bit miffed that I hadn't been able to file it. Barry Frew and/or Dave Stretch were hunting for Mo. They probably knew that Tullamy was her brief, therefore Tullamy had access to her. He might even know where Mo was now hiding herself. So Frew sent round a couple of the boys to ask Tullamy politely. But he, I imagine, said something on the lines of: 'Kindly vacate these premises forthwith, or I shall be obliged to contact the appropriate authorities and seek their assistance in having you ejected on your arses.' The villains took umbrage, so they tied him up, tickled his toes with a feather duster, and, when that didn't work, started knocking him about a bit. Then a bit more. And after such simple pleasures lost their spice, they popped him. The only question on Plod's mind was: did Tullamy tell them where to find Mo? I'll bet the only answer they could come up with was yes. No doubt that's why Tom and Clovis & Co were a shade fractious.

So now Mo and Stan, wherever they might have been before, would be on the move again. And with yet another fresh set of identities. I sighed. It was a neat little story but I was not allowed to write it. Maybe tomorrow . . .

'Hi, Max.'

'Oh hi, Susannah.'

Does that girl never do any work? It seems the only times I see her, she's in a bar.

She fetched herself up on an adjoining stool and scratched her curls while she pondered what to slosh back today. In the end she plumped for a spritzer, for Susannah likes to build up gradually.

She sipped away in silence, and I wasn't feeling all that talkative either. Then she said, 'I've been thinking about how to kill Cindy.'

'And?'

'Well, she's got to have some sort of violent death, the bloodier the better. I mean, it would be great if she was murdered.'

Ever since *Thelma and Louise*, girls have never been the same. They're all filled with this blood-lust thing.

I ran down the options. 'Murder is too messy. It involves the Old Bill. The same goes for suicide. And if she dies in an accident, you still need a body.'

Susannah said, 'That depends.' She spoke in a faraway voice.

I woke up. 'You've already got something worked out?'

'Just wait and see.'

Uh oh. 'Just how long do I have to wait?'

She went kittenish. 'Maybe this weekend . . . who knows?'

The weekend? That gave me only a couple of days to get my own humdinger Cindy story in. But I just smiled and said nothing. We gassed away for an hour before Susannah hied herself off to the ladies. I watched her out of sight before I got on the mobile and called Frankie.

'It's Max.'

'You owe me fifty quid.'

I was delighted to hear it. 'You've got the snap done? What's she like?'

Frankie was full of it. 'It's a real scorcher. And I've done it just the way you wanted. It's worth a lot more than fifty.'

Tough. That's all he was getting. I said, 'Where did you get the original pic?'

'It's a bird I used to know.'

'Jesus, Frankie – it's one of your girlfriends? This Cindy is supposed to be tasty.'

He was hurt. 'Wot? Are you saying my babes are all dogs?'

No, only the better ones. But I speedily backpedalled. 'I just want to make sure this one actually looks like a woman.'

'Well, she bleeding well does. And she's well stacked and everything, but I've done the changes. Now where's my fifty?'

Susannah came tripping back into view. I said down the phone, 'Meet me in the Stone about seven, okay?'

By now Hamptons was sucking in its afternoon tide of Fleet Street flotsam, and seeing as how I wasn't my usual perky self, Susannah found herself more stimulating company. I got busy with the mobile again, this time ringing Mac.

He had only a few smatterings to add to his early tip-off. Guns and knives were both involved in the killing of E. Tullamy. Though Mac didn't have his name. I didn't feel like telling him either, because Mac sometimes talks too much. What he did have was the victim was in his forties and a bachelor. The body was discovered by the cleaning lady.

I got off the phone, strung together another four paragraphs and filed them through before talking to News Desk.

Angie said, 'You'd better come back. Belker's looking for you.'

This is the one big thing I've got against villains. They always kill the wrong bloke. They'd do their public image no end of good if they popped Belker instead. I grumbled but I said I'd be there as soon as poss. This meant I had to hang on drinking in Hamptons for another hour, because if I showed up immediately Angie would know I had not been whiling away the day in suburbia. I guess she already suspected as much, but they don't like having their noses rubbed in it.

I got back to the funny farm around six, marched straight through the newsroom to Belker's lair and gave his door a hearty blam. Back came the customary welcoming snarl.

I swung open the door, smiled winsomely and said, 'Tony, I need to talk to you.'

This was not quite the start he had in mind. He tried to wrest back the upper hand. 'No, *I* need to talk to *you*. What's this story about Tullamy?'

I didn't answer at first. I closed the door carefully behind me and then pointed at a chair. 'May I?'

I think he'd have preferred me on my knees but he let it go. I sat myself down, straightened my trouser crease, and began. 'Tullamy is – or was – Maureen Frew's lawyer.'

Belker curled a rubbery lip. I pretended not to notice. I said, 'But I deliberately left that out of the story because we both know how sensitive this is.'

His piggy little eyes had all but vanished. I don't think he's ever regarded me as the sensitive sort.

I trickled on smoothly. 'Before you ask, no other paper has Tullamy's name yet. They don't even know about the killing. When I did the Mo Frew series, I never mentioned Tullamy, so the odds are no one else will make the link for several days.'

He didn't say anything.

I flipped a hand. 'If you want, I'll put the Mo connection in the story. But if we do that, then everyone else will start snooping around and I don't think the Editor would like that.'

Belker whirled to and fro in his swivel. This was all getting away from him. I could sense his evil little brain creeping round the dark and empty rooms inside his skull, looking for a cudgel to blat me with. He got all the way up to the attic before he found it.

He stopped swivelling and poked his big pasty face at me. 'Just what gives you the right to decide what to cut out of a story?'

I said, 'Possibly you don't remember this, but I was in here with you earlier today.'

He remembered all right.

'And,' I added, 'you told me I must not mention Mo Frew to anyone but you.'

Belker felt the cudgel fall from his flabby fingers.

I said, 'So let's just imagine how you would have reacted if I'd linked Mo to Tullamy in the story. It would have been all over the newsroom in ten minutes, and five minutes after that the *Sun*, the *Star*, the whole pack would have been on to it.'

He leaned both hammy elbows on the desk so his head sank into his shoulders. 'But you made the decision this afternoon without reference to me.'

That was a puny swing, even for him. I smiled to let him know it. I said, 'No, *you* made the decision for me. But if you've changed your mind since this morning . . .'

He hadn't.

I said, 'Fine. Now, I've got to see a special contact about the murder. That is unless you require me for anything else.'

No, that was it. The monstering was over. The monster retreated into its folds and sulked. Me? I just went whistling on my way.

There is a rule about meeting Frankie Frost in a pub: you have to get there first. Otherwise he faces the distressing prospect of having to buy his own drink. Therefore it was a good twenty mins after seven before he deemed it safe enough to stick his nose through the doors of the Stone dive bar. He had a big brown envelope in his talons.

'A pint?' I offered.

His Adam's apple bobbed out a yes. 'Now, where's the money?'

I refused to be rushed. 'Let's see the snaps.'

The fool was all set for whisking them out in front of the entire bar. I got in the beer and propelled him to an empty corner. He began wolfing as I inspected his handiwork. There were two big colour pix, both featuring the same rascal. She was blonde, or blondish, and contrary to general expectations, she had a face that wouldn't frighten small children. Though the chin looked like it had just starred in a Punch and Judy show. She was sporting a soppy uneven smirk. I think she thought it was sexy. So much for the face. Not exactly the Cindy Reilly of our dreams, but it would do. Now, let's have a look at the rest of her. What can I say? All right, first of all she was topless. Her left breast, the one nearer the camera, was I'd guess something like a 36B. But its sister . . . well, you'd have to walk around the thing for a couple of days to absorb its true dimensions.

I said, 'Wow!'

Frankie stopped drinking long enough to demand his fifty quid. I paid up without a quibble.

He said, 'Is that what you wanted?'

'It's more than I ever imagined.'

I stared at it raptly.

Frankie said, 'She's a honey, isn't she?'

A sudden doubt assailed me. 'Tell the truth Frankie. Do you have a girlfriend who looks like this?'

'Naw, more's the pity. The face is a mixture of two different babes and the ordinary boob comes from Fern, you know, the one that used to work in accounts?'

'What about the extraordinary boob?'

He put on his sly-boots face. 'That's a bit of technological wizardry. Same for the hair.'

I wanted to be absolutely sure. 'So there is no

woman in the world who can stick her finger on this picture and say, "That's me"?'

'Are you serious?'

No. I suppose not. I put the snaps back in their envelope and tucked it inside my jacket.

Frankie said, 'Wait a minute. You don't need both of them. I want one too.'

I didn't have the nerve to ask why.

Rosie took one gander at the pic and collapsed in a heap. I poured myself a fresh one and waited for her to stop chortling. I had to wait a while.

She came up for air and said, 'You'll never get away with it. No one will believe it's a real woman.'

Rosie never even glances at newspapers so she has no idea what readers are prepared to swallow. I said, 'Once they've read the story they'll believe it all right.'

So she wanted to know what the story was. But I was still working on that. I was also working on how I could get both pic and caption into our paper without them being traced back to me. For if the Cindy spoof ever became public knowledge and if my dabs were found on the story, then Belker would drop his nice-guy role and fire me through the door strapped to a rocket.

But I had an idea. The name of this idea was Dinger Bell. Dinger is a flaky freelance who flogs even flakier stories, and more times than enough the tabloids buy the things. His territory is the nether world of would-be celebs. They don't mind the tosh that he makes up about them because they'd do anything to get their faces splattered across the paper. Sometimes they even pay him to invent it.

Dinger lives and drinks in various unholy dens around the darker edges of Fulham. I didn't fancy a long night's trawl through his patch so I bleeped him. He came back on when Rosie and I were disentangling a bowl of tagliatelle apiece.

'Hiya Max. I've got a nice little story for you.'

I stopped him right there. 'No, Dinger, I've got a nice one for you.'

That threw him. He wanted to know what, but you've got to admit it wasn't the sort of thing you could explain on the phone. So I arranged to meet him around ten in General Dogsbody's, one of those holes I mentioned earlier.

Rosie came too, just to hold my hand and make sure I didn't fall into the clutches of bad women. And Dogsbody's had plenty of those on tap. We found Dinger easily enough. He was propped against the bar yattering to a couple of pieces of naughtiness who looked vaguely familiar. I tipped him a wink and he shook himself free to join us. He took a swift dekko at Rosie and asked, 'Is this the story you were on about?'

Strangely she didn't cleave his skull with the ashtray. I put that down to the way Dinger looks. He's got a wide open face with a smile to match and eyes that are bright and innocent. He might even have freckles. I've never met a farm boy from Nebraska, but I imagine he looks like one of them.

I pulled out the snap of Cindy. 'No, *this* is the story.'

Dinger said something you wouldn't expect a farm boy from Nebraska to say.

I told the whole saga, right from the moment of Cindy's conception to her present impending doom. His eyes got wider and wider. I ended, 'So you've got to get this placed in our paper within the next few days.'

Dinger was silent for a long while, looking first at one half of the snap, then the other. He said, 'I could get it in the *Sunday Sport*.'

Too easy. Anyway, the Cindy Reilly Assorted Pals had a bye-law ruling that stories in the *Sport* didn't count.

I said, 'It has to be ours.'

'But it's a complete fiction.'

I looked at him sternly. He didn't even have the grace to blush. 'Say what you like, Max, but at least my stuff involves real people.'

'Yeh. It's just the facts you make up.'

He studied the picture some more. I knew sooner or later he'd come round. Dinger never lets facts get between him and the money. I filled in the gap rustling up Blue Label vodka for him and Gordons for the rest of us.

He said, 'How much is this Cindy thing worth?'

Rosie jumped in. 'I'm the one who should be getting paid. It was my idea.'

Dinger dropped the pic and stared at her in awe. As well he might. I said, 'Our paper pays you for the story *and* the snap. You'll lift a good couple of hundred.'

'Yeh, but come on, Max. They'll never fall for it. What if I'm just wasting my time? I mean, I'll still be putting in all the effort.'

'They'll buy it okay, but just in case something goes wrong, I'll bung you twenty quid for your time.'

A sardonic snort. 'Would you write a story for a score?'

I said, 'I'll write it for free. Then all you have to do is drop it into our office and act like it's legit.'

Dinger plonked a finger on the more outstanding boob and said, 'So what's the story?'

I made him get out his ballpoint first. Then I lit a Bensons, took back a noggin and dictated. He wrote it all down on the back of Frankie's envelope. And this is what he wrote.

CABARET starlet Cindy Reilly took one look at her new breast implant last night and squealed: 'Someone's made a BOOB!'

The curvy blonde found herself with a real knocker shocker after her big-top op went disastrously wrong.

Singer Cindy said: 'I'm a natural 36B but I've always wanted to boost my assets.

'Now I'm still a 36 on one side, but I'm about 54XX on the other. I can't even find a bra to fit.'

And she points the finger of blame at a former bosom pal who suggested she have silicone implants in a cut-price Russian clinic.

London-born Cindy fumed: 'Silicone? It turned out to be a SILLY CON instead.

'The doctor didn't speak a word of English and he must have been blind as well.

'The op cost me £500. Now all I can say is "Thanks for the BEEPING mammary!" '

There was about another five or six pars of this including the 'biggest one I ever saw' line, but you've read enough. The pun-laden style, incidentally, is not my own. That's the way Dinger writes.

When I was finished he read it all through out loud. He liked it. You could tell that by the way his grin spread out to his ears. He put down the envelope and raised his glass at me.

'Do you know, Max? I can taste that money already.'

Chapter Fifteen

I suppose I was feeling reasonably happy with my little lot when dawn paid its customary call on Battersea next morning. I had a nice exclusive in the paper, I had Cindy Reilly destined for stardom. I also had Rosie whuffling away on the adjoining pillow.

This simple contentment lasted all the way through the early morning until I ran into the following yarn folded away inside the *Mirror*:

Police are probing reports that Zeller Maine mastermind Dave Stretch has been sighted on the Costa del Crime.

The fugitive gangster was said to have been spotted in a bar frequented by other underworld figures in Marbella earlier this week.

Now Robbery Squad detectives are flying to Spain to determine whether Stretch and his partner, Barry Frew, have found sanctuary in the crooks' colony . . .

There were about eight or nine paragraphs tacked on, mostly about well-known villains similarly soaking up sunshine and sangria, safe beyond the clutches of Plod. But the only other line of note was that Stretch was seen in the company of two unnamed Brits who were also strangers in those parts.

This required thinking about, preferably over a steaming cup of tea. In most homes in the land this would pose no problem. You boil the water, dangle the tea bag and wheek the milk out of the fridge. Not in Rosie's gaff. The only milk on hand was of the soya variety. Here is my tip for the day: Darjeeling and soya milk do not like each other. Keep them apart.

I sipped anyway and rang my mate Clive on the *Mirror.* 'Not guilty,' said he. His betting was the story originated from a freelancer on the Costa. But he'd let me know. Meanwhile Rosie had surfaced and was floating around the place like a fizzy-haired ghost. Her misty blue eyes were far away and she was humming a tune that sounded like she'd just made it up. I recognized the signs. She was thinking about drawing more lizards and gekkos. That meant she didn't want me anywhere around the place. I left before she chucked me out.

My desk phone was tinkling away to itself when I got to work.

'Why the hell did you mention Tullamy? I thought I warned you to say nothing about Maureen Frew.'

'And the sunniest of days to you too, Tom. If you have another look at my story, you'll find that the words Maureen and Frew are singularly lacking.'

Tom grizzled. 'But you named Tullamy. That's just as bad.'

Swift switch to hurt innocence on my part. 'But you never said anything about Tullamy. If I'd known I wouldn't have used the line.'

'Haw!'

I said, 'Have you seen the *Mirror* tale about Stretch and pals in Marbella?'

'The embargo is still on. I don't want you linking Tullamy's death to anything to do with Maureen Frew.'

'For how long?'

He was baffled.

I said patiently, 'How long do I have to go on pretending there isn't a connection?'

'Until I say so.'

Thank you for confirming the link.

I said, 'Fair do's. And seeing as how we are filled with the spirit of friendly co-operation, what's the score on this Marbella thing?'

'Friendly my backside. I'm making the rules.'

Of course you are.

I said, 'All right then, what are the rules on the Marbella story?'

He went silent. I imagine he was doing that thing with his lips again.

He said, 'As long as we understand each other, yeh, it sounds like Stretch all right.'

I asked, 'And Barry Frew?'

'Looks that way.'

Big deal. So far all I'd got was the same as the guff in the *Mirror*. I said, 'But if they're out in Spain, who's doing all this business in London?'

'What business?'

They have a different memory span, these coppers.

I said, 'Three blokes duffed me up down Westferry, wanting to know where Mo was. Then the other night two different blokes come along and ask the same questions.'

'What blokes?'

So I explained about Charlie & Chum. Not that he sounded interested.

And I asked, 'Who are all these geezers? And which lot topped Tullamy?'

'You leave Tullamy out of it.'

All right. For the time being.

I said, 'So who are the two mobs?'

Tom said, 'You work it out.'

I think that meant he couldn't. I gave it a shot anyway. 'These two guys the other night – Charlie and the other one – they said Mo had grassed on their mates. They also reckoned Mo and Stan had knocked off her old man.'

A snort from the far end. 'Well she didn't do a good job of it if he's living it up in Spain.'

I said, 'But who were the first blokes who put the frighteners on me?'

'Friends of some others she put inside. Remember, she put seven of them away. Anyway, I've got other things on my plate.'

He was all set to dunk the phone down but I got in just in time. 'Tom, isn't it possible that Dave Stretch is still running his gang from Spain?'

'Eh?'

I said, 'Some of the Zeller Maine lot got away. Just say they're still working for him.'

'What are you getting at?'

He knew damn well what I was getting at. I was offhand. 'It was just a thought.'

'Leave the thinking to us. Just you keep Maureen's name out of it.'

And off he went, satisfied with a job well done.

Oh, but it wasn't. There was nothing to stop me writing a story about runaway tearaway Dave Stretch having his boys murder shyster lawyer E. Tullamy for reasons unspecified. I dragged the keyboard six inches closer and began pecking away.

I was thus happily engaged when out of the corner of my left eye I espied a solemn little procession tracking across the newsroom. All day long we have people racing, pacing, sneaking, creeping, bumbling, stumbling and just plain staggering through the neighbourhood. But this little lot were doing none of the above. They were marching. I suppose that's what paused me in my labours.

In the van was Royce, our cyclopsical lawyer, his nose aiming straight towards the Editor's suite. Nipped in tight behind him was Huddersley, his deputy. Legend has it the two pursued a common interest in their days at Sodtheboys Hall. After Huddersley there was a little gap and then an oil slick which goes by the name of Corton Powell, our widely despised Diary editor. Powell, pronounced Pole, or Prat, depending on your point of view, was sporting his standard smarmy smirk and invisible cravat. And tripping along at his heels was an underchinned character called Toby Hyphen-Something. I know as little as possible about Toby, seeing as how he's a junior scamboli merchant on Powell's People, our squalid saga of what the glamourati get up to when nobody's looking.

Toby had his head down but you could see he was less than happy with his lot. My fellow hacks had also stopped hacking so that they could enjoy the drama.

None of us said a thing, but we were all thinking the same: LIBEL. And the villain of the day was clearly Toby.

Just as the parade reached the Editor's suite, the door beside it burst open and Belker blobbed out. 'Urrrgh!' he growled, his eyes battened on Toby. Then all five rolled into the Editor's den, taking care to shut us out behind the fake mahogany doors.

We started speculating. Dinesh reckoned the alleged libel concerned an item on a Tory MP and a lapdancer. Lucy sniffed, pointing out that the Tories need all the publicity they can get. Sid Weatherall guessed Toby had blown it in a piece on Arsenal's latest pretty boy, whose name happily escapes me. I disagreed anyway, for the legal definition of a libel is something which lowers one's standing in the eyes of one's fellow man. But if you're already an Arsenal player, you can't get any lower, therefore no libel. So the argument rolled on. The general consensus was a three-paragraph filler in Thursday's Diary about the bedtime habits of an MCC selector. What swung it his way was the fact that the said dirty dog was known to be a pal of our revered publisher, the celebrated leather fetishist.

Next we got down to the question of Toby's future, or lack of it. Now it is true to say that all honest hacks, such as us, have a deep and justified loathing of the fiction artists in the Diary column. But libel changes things. Instantly we forget that the bloke with his head in the noose is a pseud, a toady and a habitué of Stringfellow's. Before you know it, the berk's a saint and a martyr in the cause of crusading journalism.

What makes the difference is we know that the so-called libel victim is guilty of far, far worse things than the Diary guy has even hinted at. Besides, if our paper is forced to pay out half a million to some lying git, we know that somewhere down the line the money will come out of our pockets. So, as you can imagine, we were now starting to root for Toby.

But things looked bad. Libel lawyers sling half a dozen writs at us every week. What usually happens is Royce & Partners then threaten to spill even greater libels unless their clients stop mucking about. That normally does the trick. All of this chicanery goes on without us knowing about it until a week or so later. But today's procession was right out there in the open and it had all the feel of a lynch mob. Toby was for the high jump.

In any civilized business, the boss would simply call you in, hand you your P45 and say, 'On yer bike, matey.' But in newspapers they've got to kick your backside round the Editor's office for an hour before they remember their manners. And that's the way it happened with Toby. The double doors eventually opened up and there he was looking a shade crimson about the ears. Royce, Huddersley and Corton Prat were a couple of yards in arrears and trying to pretend they hadn't enjoyed themselves. Toby got halfway into the newsroom before a bawl from Belker halted him in his tracks. He stopped dead. Belker shouted, 'Stay there.'

Royce and the rest drifted back to their holes without once glancing at him. He was almost abreast of my desk. I said, 'How much was it, Tobe?'

He spoke like a zombie who'd lost the will. 'Just three months' money.'

Not your redundo, you cretin, how much was the libel?

Lucy hissed, 'Who did you libel?'

But Toby had used up all his words. He stood there in the centre of the newsroom slowly turning grey. There was utter silence. Even the phones had gone schtum. Then from the far end we saw an approaching black mountain. Dan-Dan the Security Man. He beefed up to Toby and touched him lightly on the shoulder. Toby looked up at him but I don't think he saw him. Dan turned the lad through ninety degrees and gently led him over to his desk on the outskirts of the Diary patch. This was where I suppose we should have averted our eyes and got on with making up a paper. But we're not called ghouls for nothing. So we watched.

Dan produced a big grey bag from his lower slopes. Toby didn't appear capable of anything more strenuous than breathing and Dan had to do it all. One after another he opened Toby's desk drawers and emptied them into the sack. He scuffed around the desk top for any other mortal remains. I saw a half-empty bottle of Perrier plop into the grey folds. Dan turned back to Toby and said something. No response. He tried again. This time it got through. Ever so slowly Toby reached into his pocket and produced his security pass. He looked at it for a long moment and then he handed it over. Dan trousered it. I think it was about here it dawned on the ex-Diary scribbler that this was for real. At any rate he breathed in and tried to act like one of those minor aristos in the French Revolution.

He wasn't fooling anybody. Dan spoke to him again. Toby nodded. Side by side they tooled off down the newsroom, Dan with the grey sack over his shoulder. We watched them all the way to the lifts. If you listened hard enough you imagined you could hear the Dead March in Saul. The lift bell pinged and the door shushed open. And that was it. Exit Toby. Never ever to darken our expenses sheets again.

The silence lasted ten, maybe fifteen seconds. Then came a sound which chilled the bones. It came from the hidden depths of the Editor's suite. It was Belker. And he was laughing.

After that I could have done with some cheering up, but I still hadn't topped and tailed the Tullamy story. I rang Ed O'Neill, our Costa stringer, to see if he was sitting on anything other than a sun lounger.

'No,' reported he, 'nothing's changed since the stuff I filed two days back.'

What stuff?

The long tranche of copy he had zapped through to us on Monday night. Ed asked, 'What sort of show did it get in the paper?'

No show. Not a word.

He was aghast, for Ed is an old Fleet Street hand and he nurtures the fond illusion that papers are as slick and professional as they were when he was banging on doors. I mean, he still thinks that we have a Night Foreign Editor, a deputy, an assistant and God knows what else. We don't. After darkness falls our tinpot Desk operation is entirely in the butterfingered hands of Vic, the so-called Night News Editor. It is his onerous duty to scroll through all the copy – home and foreign – which pours in. Vic has never been abroad in his puff, so anything beyond Dover he ignores. He also ignores about ninety per cent of the stuff that happens in England, but that's just out of sheer stupidity.

I promised Ed I would mark him down for a credit and he returned to his rotgut brandy. I called up the FNEWS file on my console and did a word search for Marbella. Up it popped.

From Edward O'Neill, Marbella, Monday

THE international hunt for Britain's two most-wanted men focused on Marbella last night after they were seen drinking in a notorious night spot.

Violent gangster Dave Stretch and his partner Barry Frew have been on the run since the £5 million Zeller Maine safe deposit robbery 15 months ago.

Early reports suggested the pair were living under assumed names in South America.

But police sources in the Spanish jet-set resort now confirm that Stretch celebrated a champagne night out at Bad Habits – a club owned by Teddy Bockham, another fugitive.

His lavishly decorated club, near the Playa D'Oro, is a well-known haunt for British criminals on the Costa del Crime.

According to one drinker there, Stretch and a companion, believed to be Frew, along with a heavily built bodyguard, were in the company of two leggy blondes.

He added: 'Stretch pulled out a wad of £50 notes and

ordered drinks all round. He was acting like he owned the place.

'After he'd been boozing for some time he got up on the stage to join in the karaoke music. But his companion just spent the evening cuddling a shapely blonde.

'The two stayed in the club until the early hours and when they left Stretch was so drunk he had to be helped to a waiting Mercedes.'

Spanish police suspect the men may now be hidden behind the 15ft-high walls of a Costa villa with its own high-tech security system and patrolling guard dogs.

But there is also the possibility they have moved on to Tenerife where Stretch's younger brother, Allan, is known to have widespread property interests.

That was a new one on me. I read through the rest of the yarn but it petered out in general fluffing and padding. I lit a Bensons and asked myself whether I'd like a jaunt to Marbella. The quick answer was yes. Next I asked myself whether Belker would agree to such an iffy trip. I sighed and forgot all about it.

I consoled myself with a long cold one in the Stone. I would have preferred elsewhere but I wanted to hear the inside track on why Toby Thingy got the bullet. Diary people don't talk to rough boys like us, but Jacqui does. She's Powell's secretary bird but she's also a member of the human race. So a couple of us laced her glass with dry white and got her going. No, she said, it wasn't the Tory MP, nor even the cricket selector. The libel sprung from a boring, snippety interview with an airhead Hollywood star presently in London and making a fool of herself in the West End. For the purposes of the argument I will call her Doris

Dumb, for she is a litigious old trout. Toby had been dispatched to grab a few quotes from the ageing lush after rehearsals but when he got to the theatre Doris was already skiffed out of her tree and in no condition to talk. Toby did the next best thing. He imagined what she might have said had she not been lying under a table.

So far no problem. Unfortunately he took for his launch pad a recent fiction from the *National Enquirer* about the said doxy buying her boobs off the shelf from a Los Angeles plastic surgeon. Toby quoted Doris extensively on the joys of plastic. For those unfamiliar with it, the *Enquirer* is America's answer to the *Sunday Sport*, only minus the *Sport's* proud tradition for accuracy. This may or may not have something to do with the American Constitution, which basically allows you to write any old libels you fancy about anybody without having to worry about lawyers and suchlike. This is called freedom of speech. It does not exist in England. What we have instead is a bunch of money-grubbing briefs who scan the tabloids to see if we've recycled any stories from the *Enquirer.* One of their fell number spotted Toby's bilge and phoned Doris. She sobered up sharpish when she heard she could actually sue a newspaper. She stuck her chest out and declaimed, 'This is all Mother Nature's handiwork. I'll screw that sonofabitch.' Her first idea was to whack us with a fifty-million-dollar lawsuit, but the brief persuaded her that a hundred grand might be a shade more realistic. For he didn't want the thing going anywhere near the High Court. And indeed it was all settled out of court, probably for about half that, plus we threw in a front-page pic story 'Doris Bares All' in which she paid a touching tribute to her Creator for her Bristols. There was also a full-page feature in the showbiz section about what a wonderfully witty, sexy, talented screen goddess she was. I vaguely remembered seeing it in the paper and thinking, 'That's odd.'

Anyway, Doris and her brief got what they wanted, and Toby got slung out. As Jacqui spilled out the story I thought of my own upcoming yarn about Cindy Reilly's amazing frontage and I allowed myself an inward smile. For say what you like about her, Cindy was not the sort of girl to land a decent hack in it.

And talking of Cindy, that night the Assorted Pals were in their usual slots in Hamptons and sampling the Montenegrin Beaujolais Vieux because it was marginally cheaper than aftershave. Susannah, as is the way with her lot, was having second thoughts. That is to say she was getting wobbly over the plan to kill Cindy off.

'We could keep her going for ages,' she wailed.

'Why?' from Tommy.

'Well . . . I don't know. It just seems such a shame.'

Rebecca, fellow freelance, fellow desperado, said, 'It's a bit late now. I've already sketched out a great way to kill her.'

Seeing as how Becky had never done a thing for Cindy in life, this did not go down too well with Susannah. She bristled. 'Why? How?'

Becky tackled the why bit first. An idiot reporter on the *Sunday Mirror* had gone and grassed about Cindy to somebody on their News Desk. Pretty soon every Desk on the Street would get to hear of it, therefore Cindy must die.

Susannah was still in there fighting. 'Couldn't she just disappear for a while? I mean, we could bring her back to life after Christmas, say.'

No. Too risky. There was always the chance that some Desk exec. might remember. Stranger things have happened.

Susannah wouldn't give up. 'All that's wrong is her name. If we changed her name, they'd never know. Cindy disappears but somebody else takes her place.'

I said, 'Let it rest for a couple of months. Then we can think it over. Anyways, Becky, what sort of death are you plotting?'

A fairly fast one. The way she painted it, it went thus:

Cindy goes for a holiday in Australia.

Tommy broke in, 'I get it. She gets eaten by a dingo.'

Nooo. This was one death you couldn't pin on a dingo. What happens is she goes swimming, off the Great Barrier Reef to be geographically spot on. And while she's butterflying away out there on the wide and blue ocean, whom should she bump into but the local killer shark on his lunch break. After this things get a bit messy. Thrash, thrash, thrash, go Cindy and her watermelons. Gnash, gnash, gnash goes the shark and his incisors. Gash, gash, gash goes Cindy and the rest of her.

Wind it on a couple of days and Cindy's bodyless head rolls ashore on some hitherto unheard-of beach. But here's the jolly bit. Around what's left of Cindy's neck is a thin golden chain, with a little heart-shaped locket tagged on the end. And when you pop the catch on that, it opens to reveal a mystery man, dark, handsome and tall. Well, you have to guess the tall part.

Susannah, who had listened to all the above with squeezed up lips and flared eyelashes, suddenly pealed out a laugh to rattle the glasses.

'And his name is . . .?'

Becky said, 'His name is Joshua.'

As I recall, she was once more than heavily involved with a City sub called Josh.

Susannah said, 'Oh yes, I like that. And we could make *him* a . . .?'

Becky offered, 'How about a male stripper?'

Olly butted in. 'We could make *him* a her. It's more fun writing about busty blondes.'

Becky froze him dead. 'You're just a sexist pig.'

I switched off for I was thinking my own thoughts. They were many and various and they all ended with a question mark. I will mention only one of the lesser queries rattling around my head: when was that lazy git Dinger Bell going to sneak Cindy's pic into the paper?

I need not have feared. Next morning I was rustling through our mighty journal when I ran up against the headline WHAT A BOOB!, over a badly-cropped snap of Cindy, and under her lopsided frontage there was a five-paragraph caption. The copy had been butchered by one of our more villainous subs, but the story was still intact. Also, it was tucked away on a London late change page which meant that only those readers in the inner metropolis could feast their eyes on her. It didn't bother me. I'd got a publication and that's what counted. Now all I had to do was await the begrudged plaudits of the Assorted Pals. Tra-la-la.

I was still humming when I rambled into the newsroom. All the hacks in the locality were standing in a clump in front of the reporters' notice board. Not the most fascinating spot in town. Its usual attractions are the duty roster, the holiday list and the occasional stupid memo from the Editor. I was ambling by when I heard Sid Weatherall say, 'Belker's bloody certifiable.'

Belker? That stopped me. I pushed my way through the thicket of reporters. 'What's he done now?'

Lucy just rolled her eyes at a memo tacked onto the board. Somebody must have typed it out for Belker because it was largely in English. It read:

Owing to a recent piece of shoddy journalism, the paper has been obliged to pay a considerable sum in legal costs.

The reporter responsible for the wholly inaccurate and defamatory article has been summarily dismissed.

The Editor is anxious to maintain our standards of accuracy and good journalistic practise. (sic) *He wishes to put behind us this unfortunate and damaging episode, and he is confident that the staff will support him fully in maintaining the high criteria required of them.*

However, should any journalist fabricate quotes or otherwise fall below the professional standards demanded of him or her, that journalist shall be deemed to be in breach of contract and the requisite steps shall be taken.

I shall be monitoring copy carefully to ensure that our journalistic integrity is not jeopardized.

T. Belker, Executive Editor.

In other words, screw up and you get the tin-tack. These have always been the rules so why bother spelling them out? Even so, I felt a momentary twinge at the thought of my Cindy yarn. If Belker ever found out the truth, the slimeball wouldn't just fire me, he'd call in the Fraud Squad, for on my lost crystal ball story I'd fiddled 25 quid in exes. Still, what's the point of worrying about ifs? I shook the thought away and got down to ringing round my mates. Mac was getting to the punchline of a particularly grisly joke when I saw Jools bouncing my way. I said, 'Hold it a sec, Mac.'

Jools turned her fist into a pretend gun and pulled the trigger. 'Bang,' she said.

She's sick, that woman.

I said, 'Bigfoot wants to see me?'

'How did you guess?'

I got rid of Mac, but not before he finished his joke. It wasn't worth waiting for, but he laughed anyway. Right. Deep breaths. I straightened my tie and trotted off to meet the monster. I banged on Belker's door and gave it a push. There he was, more hideous than remembered, force-feeding himself with a Mars Bar.

'Mmmwargh,' he said.

So I sat down. He golloped for a while, keeping his nasty little eyes on me. I looked away because there was a smearing of Mars Bar round the hole in the middle of his face. My idle glance took in the desk and came to an abrupt halt. Right in front of him was the morning's paper. The late London edition. I knew that because the paper was open at the Cindy Reilly story. Gulp.

He finished munching, drew a paw across his maw and said, 'Well?'

I don't think he was enquiring after my general welfare but I couldn't resist it. 'Fine thanks. And you?'

Glower, glower. He said, 'You don't seem to appreciate the seriousness of this.'

One fist was plonked on Cindy's turbo boob, but he was still looking at me. My gaze was serene and blue and if my pulse was a shade shaky, you would never have sussed it.

Belker opened on a lively note. 'When I tell you I want to be kept informed about a story, that means you come to me and tell me. I don't expect to have to *send* for you every time I want an update.'

So the subject before us was Maureen Frew.

I said, 'If and when I have something, you'll be the first to know.'

'And when will that be?'

I measured out a cool frown. 'I was on the phone to a senior police contact asking him about Mo when your secretary said you wanted to see me immediately. So I had to cut him off.'

In other words, Mister Sodding Blobby, let me get on with my job.

'Well you'd better get back on to him then.'

I said, 'Providing he still has time to talk to me. He's a busy man.'

'*I'm* busy too. But you seem to think I've got all the time in the world. We need this Frew thing sorted out now. What are you doing about it?'

Maybe his hearing was up the spout. 'Like I said, I'm getting on to police contacts.'

'And what else?'

What else? I'm consulting a ouija board and praying a lot. I said, 'I've been talking to Ed O'Neill in Malaga.'

His eyes flickered out. 'Eh?'

I explained, 'Dave Stretch has been seen on the piss in Marbella.'

He wasn't following this. I started again. 'Stretch and Barry Frew planned the Zeller Maine job together. Ed says the two of them are on the run down his patch.'

Sometimes I talk too much for my own good. Belker slapped a hand on the desk. 'And you said nothing was happening? For Christ's sake, why wasn't I told?'

'Because it's not confirmed. At the moment it's no stronger than a rumour. But if you like, I'll keep you up to date with every whisper, every false sighting.'

He went quiet. Well quieter anyway. Belker breathes through his blow hole. Then his eyes fizzed into life. 'You say Frew and this other man were seen together?'

'*Reportedly* seen.'

Belker had on his evil smirk now. 'But if Frew's on the run in Marbella, his wife couldn't have killed him. So this whole story of yours about her being a murderer is just another one of your flyers.'

I said, 'I told you from the start, the murder line was something that came down the grapevine. I am investigating it to see whether there is any truth in it.'

'Balls. You used this false alarm to start a major panic. I can't trust a single word you say.'

Well at least that's something we have in common.

I said, 'If we want to check out this Marbella line, the only way to do it is by going there. But it seems a long way to go on the off chance.'

Snarl. 'I get it. You're just trying to line yourself up a junket in Marbella.'

Me? Good grief, whatever gave him that idea?

Belker tried to look foxy, a neat trick for a whale. 'Well, let me tell you right now you haven't a hope. You stay glued to this office until you find out what's really going on.'

I said, 'Suits me. I already anticipated you would say no, so I've told Ed to have a quiet poke around. I'd rather be here.'

Belker grunted. For a fraction of a second I could hear him debating whether to pack me off on the next Iberia flight. Then he sobered up.

'Too bloody right. You get back on that phone to your police contact and let me know *exactly* what he's told you.'

'Sure.' I stood up. 'I'll better try for him now. That is, providing you're finished.'

He was finished. Apart from grumbles and growls. I gently closed the door on them.

Meanwhile my phone had been having a hectic time without me. One after another Cindy Reilly's Assorted Pals had been buzzing with congrats for the oddjob boob-job yarn. Susannah rang just as I got back. 'You're an absolute bugger, Max. That was a brilliant wheeze.'

I suppose I should have said it was all down to Rosie. But I thought of the grand prize – free nosh at Hamptons. Frankly I've got too much respect for

Rosie's innards to subject her to that. So I smiled modestly and said thank you.

I spent a huge whack of the next hour fielding tributes and plaudits before I started thinking about work. In the absence of anything useful from the Old Bill, I had just one slender line to go on: Tullamy. And he was dead. But not yet buried.

I flicked through my contact book for his number and punched it out. 'Good afternoon,' said his hyper-efficient secretary. It was all of fifteen seconds past noon.

I let my voice drop five fathoms and added a dollop of syrup. 'Hello, my name is Mortimer Sillitoe. First of all, may I say how deeply sorry I am over the death of Ernest.'

She said, 'That's very kind of you, Mister Sillitoe. We are all still shocked by the tragedy. May I ask how you knew Mister Tullamy?'

'Ernest? I haven't seen him for a few years I'm afraid, because I've been practising in Hong Kong. But at one time we were close acquaintances. We sat our bar exams together, you know.'

The secretary swallowed it. 'We have had a great many of his colleagues calling to express their condolences.'

I cut to the important bit. 'Yes, he was a most congenial fellow. Naturally I would wish to send a wreath, and indeed, to attend the funeral. Can you tell me when that is occurring?'

No, she couldn't. Mainly because the pathologist was still playing jigsaws with Tullamy's bits.

'However,' she said, 'there is a memorial service

tomorrow afternoon. We realize it is unconventional to have the service before the funeral has taken place, but we have no way of knowing when Mister Tullamy's body might be released for interment.'

'And where,' droned I, 'is the memorial service to be held?'

'At St Godfrey's in Newbury Heath. It's at two o'clock.'

I repeated it slowly as if I was writing it down. 'Newbury Heath. I'm not familiar with that area. I take it that's in Berkshire?'

A light sprinkling of laughter. 'No, you're thinking of Newbury. Newbury Heath is in Essex.'

And might I know where the hell in Essex? I certainly might. I even got directions. Basically it was up the M11 and turn right. She tailed off with a lie, only she didn't know it. 'I shall enjoy meeting you tomorrow.'

I borrowed Lucy's *A–Z* and looked up Newbury Heath. It didn't exist. Bugger. That meant it was somewhere way out in hillbilly land. The library pinned it down as a teensy hamlet in the bit of Essex that looks like a normal county. I'd need transport. That meant a monkey. And I didn't need one of them. My vague plan was to mingle with Tullamy's fan club and see what came up. I was also hoping there might be some heavy-duty Plods who might slip me a morsel. There might even be a decent pub.

Chapter Sixteen

There is in our newsroom a hack called Ned the Nerd. He's called this for three good reasons. His name is Ned, he's a nerd and nobody likes him. How he even got a job on the paper is a lasting mystery, though the popular line is his old man and our Woman's Editor used to share a jacuzzi. If you saw the state of our Woman's Editor you'd get the feeling that Ned senior must have more than his rightful share of nerdishness too.

Like most everybody else, I keep a good stretch of clear blue water between myself and Ned. He's a big lumpish type with all the subtlety of a water buffalo. We each have our own reasons for shunning him. What narks me most is a situation where, say, I'm down in the dive bar and regaling the horde with the tale of some horrendous drunken mishap. Just as I get to the gut-wrenching climax I hear this phwuff-phwuff-phwuff from behind. I look around and there's Ned with a nerdish grin wrapped round his face, holding a half pint of lager top (which he's bought himself).

Lucy calls him the Gollum, who apparently is some character in a book she once read. I don't know anything about the book, but I get the impression the

Gollum character is somebody who creeps up on you and earwigs what you're saying. I suppose this is the whole thing about Ned: he's not one of us but he thinks he is. He tries to copy the way we operate, even the way we talk. But it's like his drinking habits: he never even gets close to the real thing.

None of us ever risks saying anything dangerous in front of him because we don't trust him to keep it to himself. His own conversation is enough to clear the bar. Ned loves toys. Bugs, mobile phone scanners, directional mikes, night vision binoculars, the lot. He's even got a mini videocam squirrelled away in his briefcase with its little beady lens poking out from under the handle. I'm not making this up, but there are times in the newsroom when one or other of us accidentally-on-purpose kicks his briefcase under the desk. Just to be on the safe side.

He's also red hot on conspiracy theories, going back to Julius Caesar and beyond, and if you're not careful, he'll tell you everything he thinks he knows. According to him, MI5 spends its days wiretapping our every word, taking only the occasional break to bump off a Princess or such.

Fortunately none of this bilge ever gets in the paper. Even more fortunately, Ned is rostered for a lot of night shifts so we don't run up against each other much. But when he is around, you're constantly aware of this lurking presence, listening to everything you say. Maybe he works for MI5.

I try not to think about Ned, for pretty obvious reasons. And on this particular evening Rosie and I were happily putting away a sundowner or three so he was even further than usual from my mind. We were in my flat for a change, mainly because if we were in her place she'd be getting set to dish up something green and ghastly for dinner and I had my heart set on proper grub. Then the phone went. Night Desk.

'Max?'

'Vic.'

'Are you doing anything right now?'

I'm answering the phone, you blethering idiot.

'Nothing important.'

Vic said, 'I just got a call from Ed O'Neill in Malaga and he'd like you to give him a ring. You got his number?'

That's what contact books are for. But I was feeling bloody.

'No.'

'Oh, God, hang on a minute.'

Vic moves with all the speed of primeval ooze in a built-up area. I laid the phone aside, lit a cigarette, topped up my glass and counted to five million. Vic came back. 'Here it is.'

I made him read it out twice just to hack him off.

I said, 'What's this about? Any idea?'

'It's just a tip. He says those Maine Zeller people that the police are looking for have shown up in Tenerife. I've got one of the night staff knocking a story together but Ed said you'd want to know.'

I said, 'Just make sure whoever writes the story gets the words the right way round. It's Zeller Maine.'

'Yeh. That's what I said.'

What's the use? I let him go and rang Spain. Ed snapped up the phone. 'O'Neill, Malaga.'

I used up all the Spanish words I know: *'Arriba! Arriba! Donde este el bar?'*

'Oh, hello Max. You heard the latest then?'

Dave Stretch and three or four other blokes had flown into Tenerife from Marrakesh the day before. They were on a Gulfstream or some sort of exec jet. An unidentified man in a Lexus had picked them up from the airport, after which they vanished.

I said, 'No women?'

Not unless some of Stretch's fellow passengers were into transvestism in a big way.

'Who made the sighting?'

A local hack with a mate in the control tower.

I asked, 'Much baggage?'

Ed said, 'He didn't say. I filed what I had but I've since heard that the plane belongs to Jimmy Guffin, so the car's probably his too.'

Guffin. Alleged triple killer, alleged drugs-runner, alleged porn merchant, and anything else you care to allege.

I said, 'What about Frew? Was he on the plane?'

Nothing there. The pilot had filed a manifest for seven passengers. None of them was called Stretch or Frew. You can't get away with this sort of japery down Heathrow, but Tenerife has its own quaint customs.

I said, 'What have you on the brother, Allan Stretch?'

A lot of nasty little stories, beginning with time-share sharking and dodgy clubs. The main thing against him was the company he kept, such as Jimmy Guffin. And that, basically, was all Ed had.

I plopped the phone back in its thingy and lit a

cigarette. Rosie said, 'I'm getting hungry. Shall we go and eat?'

I promised her a veritable banquet, but first I needed ten minutes to rattle off the story. The way I saw it, Stretch and Frew had got themselves linked up with extra-heavy hitters. And . . . just pushing it a little bit from there, the Zeller Maine loot was now being used to flood Britain with coke, heroin, the whole heap. And . . . stepping back a second, the money had been laundered through flaky timeshare deals in Tenerife. Well, it made sense to me anyway. I called Copy and fired off ten or twelve paragraphs.

By this time Rosie was getting fractious. You've got to keep that girl's blood sugar topped up or she turns strange. Or even stranger. We took ourselves off to the nearest feeding trough, *Bizbaboom!*, an overpriced burger joint sometimes frequented by rock bands on the way up, or mostly on the way down. The walls are stapled with Americana tat and the hired hands compete ferociously with each other for the Rude Git of the Month award. The only plus I can think of is you never see Michael Winner there. But Rosie's got a soft spot for this hellhole because there's a salad bar that stretches from here to Slough and they give you whopping great plates. I contented myself with the Rock Island Special, more commonly known as cheeseburger and chips. Ever calorie-conscious, Rosie staggered back carting half a ton of salads and dips and dressings.

I finished first and, because I'm devoted to my calling, I rang Night Desk on the mobile.

'What do *you* want?' growled Vic.

A Night News Editor with brains would help.

I said, 'Any queries on my Zeller Maine story?'

'No.'

'What are you doing with it?'

'I don't know, do I?'

No, I suppose you don't.

Vic said, 'One of the Night reporters had it nearly finished before you filed.'

I said, 'The Jimmy Guffin line is new. We've got it to ourselves.'

'Who's Jimmy Guffin?'

He hadn't even read the sodding copy. I said, 'Forget it.'

In the bleak and lonely cavern of his mind something went, 'Forget what?' But I'd already rung off.

Rosie, who usually displays a magnificent disdain for newspapers and things connected with, forked back a shovel of coleslaw and said, 'What's the story?'

Touched by this sudden interest I told her.

She asked, 'But is it true?'

I shrugged a shoulder. 'Maybe. I don't know.'

There were, and are, many things I don't know. Like I didn't know who Vic's Night reporters were. Nor did I know that Vic considered one of this sorry bunch the coming thing in hard-nosed hackery. Nor could I imagine that this very man might be Ned the Nerd.

I would know soon enough.

The story made the paper all right. It was hived off in a single column on Seven. Below the header was my very own dear by-line. *By Senior Crime Correspondent*

Max Chard. Stuff like that is always good for the soul. It gets you every time. *Bizz*-ing! Maybe I'm coming across here as a crazed egomaniac. It's not just me. I've known hacks twice as old as God's dog – people with awards and herograms by the bucket – and the first thing they do of a morn is go flickety-flick-flick through the paper until they find their by-line. Only then do they allow a smile to rumple their terrapin chops. They murmur happily, 'Yep. That's me.' But if some foul quirk of fate, or more likely, some even fouler sub, has robbed them of a by-line on their story, there is woe and wrath in the land.

Perhaps other professions share the same trauma. Sometimes as I whizz about this capital of ours my ranging eye picks up the FOR SALE placards growing out of people's hedges. And I wonder, does grizzled estate agent FRED FUNTERFACE roll down these same avenues and gaze upon his sign and say to himself, 'Yep. That's me'?

No. Maybe not.

Anyway, after that first heady zap of adrenalin I read the story just to see what bits they got wrong. The subs must have had a busy night for they'd left it relatively unscarred. And then I read the final three paragraphs.

Travel consultant Cindy Reilly was waiting to fly out of Las Palmas airport in Gran Canaria just as Stretch and his cronies landed.

The 34-year-old blonde Londoner said: 'It was definitely him. I've met him several times before.

'But he and Barry Frew walked right past me with their noses in the air.'

I must have roared or something, for Rosie called from the bathroom, 'What's up with you?'

Up? *Up?*

She padded into the bedroom with a towel where her clothes ought to be. The rest of her was covered in morning dew. I refused to be distracted.

'What's up is some dork has stuck Cindy's name in a story.'

Rosie squeezed up her eyes at me. 'Isn't that what you're supposed to do?'

Honest to God. Do women never understand men's games?

I snorted air. Lots of it. 'No. The whole bloody thing depends on the quote. You've got to have the quote.'

Rosie turned her back and started bashing her hair about with *my* hairbrush.

'What quote?'

'It was the biggest one I've ever seen.'

She said, 'What was?'

Maybe she should go on News Desk.

I got myself under control. 'That is the signature quote. If it's not in the story it doesn't count.'

Brush, brush, brush. 'Well then, it doesn't count.'

I said, 'And whoever wrote this crap left out her boobs.'

Rosie just got on with batting her hair out of shape. I flumped the duvet with both fists.There was something I was trying to get across here but I couldn't nail it. Then I had it.

'Don't you see, some herbert has gone and put Cindy's name in *my* story.'

She swung round and there was a clinical cant to

her eyes. 'It's only a joke. Cindy's not even real. Why are you getting so upset?'

I think I said Rrrrgh or something. Rosie finished with the dressage routine and came and sat on my foot. She said, 'So he left out her boobs and what she was supposed to say. What are you going to do – shoot him?'

'When I find out who did it, he'll sing falsetto for the rest of his natural.'

There was this funny look on her face. It might have been a mix of love and care and adoration. It might have been something altogether different.

She said, 'Life's too short. It's nothing to worry about, Max.'

And like the fool I am, I believed her.

My first port of call when I reached the office was Belker's pit. If the oaf insisted on being kept abreast of every minuscule detail of the Mo Frew story, he'd get it in spades. His door was closed so I thumped it a couple of times. No answer.

From behind me I heard the warble of Jools. 'He's not here.'

Perhaps he'd died in the night.

Jools said, 'He's having a few days off to take his kids to Euro Disney.'

Kids? The Beast had spawned? This is the sort of thing you need broken to you gently. I conjured up an image of twenty or so little Belkers all harpooning each other in the back. It was too awful to think about. I nodded dumbly at Jools and trudged off to the tea machine. It stole my first 20p, spat out the second, but eventually delivered a half-full plastic cup of gloop just as I was running out of silly money. The machine had short-changed me on the sugar. I once hit the beef soup button by mistake, and, do you know, it tasted just like the tea. Only it had sugar in it.

I retired to my corner and tried to cheer myself up. Belker was out of town, I had a merry little memorial service on the day's agenda. So why wasn't I smiling? Then I remembered. Cindy Reilly.

I prowled over to the reporters' notice board and looked up last night's duty hacks. Anjou, Clement and Ned the Nerd. I should have known. I saw he was scheduled down for this evening's 5.30 slot. Among his many, many failings is a slavish punctuality. So back to my keyboard, where I hammered out a timed message which would greet the moron when he switched on at 5.30 sharp.

Dear Plonker,

Next time you feel like taking Cindy Reilly's name in vain, please specify which particular window you'd like me to kick your fat arse through.

Signed: A Friend.

There, that made me feel better. Not for long. Angela Whipple, floating by on her way to morning conference, got a couple of yards past me, stopped, wheeled back and looked at me. Her eyes were clouded with pain or thought or both.

'Max.'

Desk people need every encouragement, no matter how small.

I beamed, 'You got it.'

She was holding the usual sheaf of lies which makes up our news schedule and she was patting herself on the chin with it. She was trying to remember something. It all came out in a burst.

'Zeller Maine. Somebody's been on from the Yard this morning about your story. They want you to ring them.'

'Any particular them?'

'I can't remember. It was Ay Cee somebody or other.'

An assistant commissioner. I didn't like the sound of that.

I said, 'How did this bod come across? Griping?'

Angie corrugated her brow. 'No. Seemed okay. But the Yard said you had some information you'd want to talk to them about.'

Oh no, I bloody well didn't.

'So,' said Angie, 'be a darling and give them a ring to keep them off our backs.'

She smiled sweetly and wandered off to join the other execs in their daily game of snowing the Editor. Unbeknownst to me, Angie had left out a small but hugely significant detail.

I sipped tea and pondered. A.C. Who? And what exactly did he want to squeeze out of me? Off to my right the phone went. I let Dinesh answer it. He listened briefly, turned to me and said, 'Are you here, Max?' I've trained that boy well.

I was ultra cautious. 'Who is it?'

'A woman.'

I eased up. 'Any name?'

'Corduroy or something like that. She didn't say what it's about.'

It was probably American Express again, whistling for their money. I sighed and said, 'Okay, I'll take it.'

'Mister Chard?' A brisk all-mates-together voice. 'We've never met.'

I didn't know whether that was a good thing or a bad 'un. I just said, 'But?'

'My name is Irene Cordray.'

A silent howl from my end. Irene God-help-us Cordray, the only woman in the Met allowed to wear scrambled egg on her lapels.

She said, 'I am an Assistant Commissioner with the Met . . .'

I wasn't listening. I was devising a dozen different ways of killing Angela Whipple. They were all too merciful.

A.C. Cordray was saying, ' . . . and we would like to interview this woman as soon as possible.'

'Woman?'

An impatient click. 'This Miss Reilly you quoted.'

Not me, guv. That bugger Ned. For one shameful split second I thought about tossing him to the wolves. All I had to say was, 'He made her up.' No. I couldn't do it, not even to the Nerd. Grassing up a fellow hack is the great unforgivable sin. For generations to come, people would point me out to their children: 'See that lonely old geezer? That's Max the Knife. The Man Who Sneaked.'

So I fudged it. 'I didn't actually speak to her myself. I believe the quotes were filed by a freelance in Las Palmas.'

'Who?'

Can you not take a hint, love?

I said, 'We have several stringers who file stories on Spain, Majorca, Tenerife and so on. I spoke only to Ed O'Neill in Malaga and I know the quotes didn't come from him.'

Irene Cordray turned the chill control to max. 'I should have thought you could easily establish which correspondent interviewed her.'

I said, 'Miss Cordray, there are two things you should know: I was not in the office yesterday evening. And secondly, every night our Desk handles upwards of two hundred stories. We're talking about half a million words of copy. Tracking down a particular quote is not quite as easy as you might imagine.'

Old Irene hadn't earned her gold embroidery by making kootchie-koo eyes. She said in steel-tipped tones, 'Correct me if I'm wrong, all these stories are on a computerized system?'

She wasn't wrong so I didn't correct her.

'Therefore I presume you have some form of search facility on your system which would enable you to find a particular story?'

Oh yes, we've got that all right.

'So,' she wound up, 'it should not require an unduly arduous effort on your part to locate the article and to determine who spoke to Miss Reilly.'

I said, 'Leave it with me and I'll see what I can dig up.'

'And how long will that be?'

I acted like I was consulting my watch. 'Unfortunately I've got to go out now on a story. I hope to be back this afternoon and I could start going through the copy files then.'

She unbent half a degree. 'This is of course merely a request, Mister Chard. As you are well aware, we are still pursuing our inquiries into the Zeller Maine case, and we would imagine your Editor would be willing to grant us his fullest co-operation. However, because you are the author of the article, I felt this matter might be expedited by contacting you in the first instance.'

There's only one thing worse than a Big Chief Plod and that's a Big Chief Plod with a Ph.D. from the Open University.

I said, 'I'll sort it as soon as I can.'

'Good. I look forward to hearing from you.'

Clang. She banged the receiver down. I sat there listening to the dialling tone and thinking thoughts that would never make it past the censors. I lowered the phone. Dinesh puttered up with a fresh round of tea. He stuck a cup into my nerveless fingers. I swigged deeply. There was sugar in it. How does he *do* that?

Dinesh asked, 'Bad news?'

'Worse than that.'

'How so?'

I shook my head to and fro like a caged bear. After a while I said, 'You know Ned the Nerd? Well, I'm putting out a thousand pound-contract on his miserable life.'

Dinesh digested this slowly. He said, 'All right, I'll pay a thousand to kill him.'

I was deeply moved, but even topping the berk didn't solve things. I was still left with a great big hole to climb out of, a hole dug by Ned the Nerd.

I called up my brain's escape committee. They looked at it this way and that and shook their beans sadly. There was no way out. Well . . . actually . . . there was just one . . . all I had to do was pin it on Ned. No! Get thee hence, foul hounds of hell. The escape committee shrugged their shoulders and mooched off muttering among themselves.

But I refused to give up hope. Many's a time I've landed myself in a ten-foot heap of manure without a shovel for miles. There was that time in Naples, for example . . . Yet always some genie in my head has popped up with a solution. It's never failed me yet. So I posted an urgent telegram to the genie and got on with my day's work.

Right. Now for the memorial festivities for Ernest Tullamy. I lassoed Angie Whipple as she was cruising back from morning conf.

'There's a job I want to do today, but it mightn't produce.'

She wasn't listening. She said, 'Did you get on to the Yard?'

'Yeh. Why didn't you tell me it was a woman Ay Cee?'

Angie tried her best to think back. 'Was it? Oh yes, so it was. What's this job you're talking about?'

I told her. She puckered her lips. 'Forget it. I've already got you slated for a couple of early stories.'

No chance. So I whispered in her little pink ear the words 'Belker', 'Mo Frew', 'Editor', and a few other words besides.

She folded. 'All right, then. But I need you back here afterwards.'

Onwards to Picture Desk. 'Let me have Frankie Frost for a couple of hours. I promise I won't bust him.'

They were strangely reluctant to part with their prize exhibit, and he just plain refused to come down his tree. I had to murmur 'free drink' three times before he bit. Even then he was wary. 'What's the story?'

I said, 'Remember Mo and Stan in Cyprus?'

'You mean Gibraltar?'

Oh all right then. I said, 'Their brief got murdered and there's a memorial service for him. I want to see if Clovis shows.'

Frankie's little forehead wrinkled itself up. I was going too fast for him. In the end I had to lure him down to the Stone and explain the whole thing ever so slowly over a pint.

He was still having difficulty with it. 'I don't get it. Where's the picture in this story?'

I suppose I could have told the truth and admitted there wasn't any pic. All I wanted was a driver. But somehow I fancied he'd throw a moody.

I said, 'Just look at it this way: if you don't get a snap, you do at least get out of the office, and I pour drink down your gullet until you stop griping.'

Oh, if I put it like that . . .

A pint later and we were on our way. Frankie learned to drive at the Ben Hur School of Motoring where they operate an elaborate points system. One point for busting a red light, two for thumping a biker, three for scaring the hell out of an old lady, four if she's on a zebra crossing, and so on. By the time we reached the M11, I reckoned he'd chalked up about 270 points. Sounds high, but that blind bloke must have been worth at least 50.

We racketed on, changing lanes every five seconds, and leaving in our slipstream a whole army of drivers sticking their fingers in the air. I distracted myself by inspecting the inside of Frankie's jam jar. I have seen cleaner bin lorries in my day. The floor is three inches deep in ripped-up film cartons, bits of old pizza and things that belong in a biological warfare lab. The back seats are scarred and battered, bearing eloquent testimony to Frankie's crazed attempts to cross-breed with a human. I turned my attention back to the road.

We slewed off the M11 at junction five and promptly got ourselves lost. Maybe somewhere under all that untreated sewage was a map, but I didn't feel like digging for it. So we roared around until we found a pub.

'Let's stop here,' said he.

Sometimes you've got to be downright callous. 'Okay, but you stay in the car. I'll go and get directions.'

He hung his tongue out and popped his monkey eyes at me. It didn't work. I clambered out of the debris and went in search of a guide. The boozer was full of them, and every punter knew a different short cut to Newbury Heath. I consulted the guv'nor, as he was the only half-sober soul in the place. Back to the bin lorry.

It was pushing on for two when we ripped round a corner into a sleepy villagey place. Directly ahead lay a fussy little pub with flower tubs, hanging baskets and all sorts of embellishments.

'Aha!' said Frankie. 'There it is.'

'Later. I'm going to church first.'

'You? What about me?'

I said, 'I'll tell you when you've got this heap parked.'

Fifty yards beyond the pub was a squat grey church, crouched among a forest of tall dark trees. Out front were about twenty cars, all of them new or newish, and some with hefty price tags. I made Frankie tuck his motor way at the end of the line.

I said, 'You stay here and keep an eye out for Clovis. Or maybe even Kay might show. Snap them with the long tom because I don't want them to know they've been snapped.'

Frankie bickered. 'I could always wait at the pub.'

'What – and buy your own drink?'

'Ah.' He hadn't thought of that.

I stayed with him until he had rooted out his Canon and the telephoto. 'Okay, Frankie, now whatever you do, don't get out of the car.'

He grumbled but stayed put. I buttoned my jacket and set off through a stretch of graveyard for the church. It was a tawny golden afternoon with chippy little birds perched on the headstones, piping, 'Piss off, piss off' at me as I passed. After the sunshine, the inner porch of St Godfrey's was blindingly dark. A bass voice in the blackness intoned, 'Good afternoon. So glad you could come,' and stuck a book in my hand.

I edged through to the main event. It was a fraction lighter in here. Sunlight spilled through the stained-glass windows and painted the faces of Tullamy's old chums crimson and blue and yellow. I'd have a job recognizing anybody in here. But then there was not much chance they'd spot me either.

I took up position at the back and counted heads. This was harder than it sounds, for St Godfrey's housed a right collection of floor-to-ceiling columns, each about five foot across. I'd counted to about nineteen blokes and six women when an unseen organ wheezed into life and started pumping out something that sounded like it had been written for the bagpipes. Everybody stood up and began howling. I just mimed. One of the women up in the ringside seats had on a big stiff straw hat with a black band wrapped around it. She looked about the same general shape as Kay, but that didn't mean anything. So, with the hymn book covering half my face, I searched the ranks for Clovis. The problem was all I could see were people's pin-striped backs, and that wasn't much to go on. Just as we were all sitting down again I glimpsed a skinny type in a shapeless suit. His face turned a quarter towards me. Ha! Got him.

Two seats along from Clovis was a woman with a feathery job glued to her head. Kay? Possibly. Between them was a heavy geezer with purple hair and indigo nose, courtesy of the stained-glass windows. Here's a useful tip for would-be acid trippers: save your money. Just go to church and you get the same effect for free.

Up in the pulpit a man with a Santa Claus beard and a weirdly squeaky voice began recounting the myriad virtues of Ernest Tullamy. I switched on my tape recorder. There followed another dirge or two, interspersed with guest appearances by various suits saying much the same as the vicar only in proper voices. I learned many things I had never suspected of the late brief. He was a great public benefactor, a man of considerable erudition, a true friend, a lawyer whose diligence and probity were renowned. I watched the faces of the speakers closely as they rattled out this tosh, but they didn't look like they were taking the mick.

The vic. returned to his box and led us in a rousing chorus of something which might have been all right if the composer had stuck a tune in there.

As the befrocked one was wrapping up the Benediction I stepped back into the darkest shadow I could find. There was a chunky stone thing covered in hieroglyphics. I'm guessing it was a War memorial to the fallen sons of Newbury Heath. I developed an all-consuming interest in this as one by one the Glee Club filed out. I had them in profile. Clovis steamed into view looking mournful, but that's the way he always looked. Then several fat-faced bods, then the feathery-headed woman. Kay? Curses. It was only Tullamy's sniffy secretary. I turned smartly back to the War memorial tablet. After a while the footsteps and the hubble-bubble of voices ceased. I gave it half a minute and then I followed them, keeping a tree or two behind. The congregation had split itself up into small bunches. Clovis was twenty yards off with two other blokes. The taller one was Tom, the geezer who had set up the Mo interview, and when last seen was tearing me off outside Tullamy's. The third party was a new one. He had silky blond hair and steel-framed polychromatics. He was solid but he didn't look like Old Bill. I heard Tom say, 'We passed one down the road. We might as well leave the car here and walk it.'

I held back and worked out the next move. If I

strolled up to them here, they'd stamp and storm and scoot off in their car. But . . . if I gave them enough time to sink a pint, they might just mellow. So I watched them go: Clovis loping along on the left, Tom marching on the right and the silvery-blond bod tucked in between them. It was his walk that threw me. I'd seen that walk before. The puffed-up chest, the arms sticking out from the shoulders as if he was about to lift a car by the bumper.

Stan bleeding Defoe.

An alarm bell clanged in my brain. Right now Frankie was squeezing off shots of a bloke on the witness protection scheme. If Tom clocked him, both monkey and hack would be buried side by side in this very churchyard in the next five minutes, or sooner. The trio had reached the knee-high gate leading out onto the road. Defoe turned and looked back. I took one step towards cover. Too late.

I heard him yell out, 'Max!'

Clovis swivelled hard round. Tom's mouth fell open. I think I had on a crinkly smile. But Defoe was grinning like a loon. He began coming towards me. Clovis jumped right in front of him and pushed a hand in his chest. Stan pushed it out of the way and began an argy-bargy with his minder. Meanwhile Tom had got himself in gear and was pumping my way. He was not chuffed to see me.

'Do you never know when to stop, Chard?'

I said, 'Who's your friend? He seems to know me, but I can't place him.'

'Stop playing silly buggers. You know bloody well who it is.'

Over his shoulder I could see Clovis and Defoe having a right go at each other. Defoe was using words you don't normally hear in a quiet country churchyard. The general gist was: 'I'll do what I effing well like and there's eff all you can do about it. And you effing touch me again and I'll knock your effing teeth down your etc.' There was a slight trace of a Yorkshire accent buried in there. That was new.

Clovis spilled open his hands. I guess it meant: 'It's your funeral.'

Defoe came up with both arms open as if he was going to hug me. 'Max, Max. It's good to see you, Max.'

At least he'd remembered the name.

Tom rounded on him. 'Get back in the car. Now.'

Defoe dropped his smile and gave him a blasting, ending on the lively note: 'I'll do what I effing well want.'

Tom bit back. 'You do that. You just bloody do that. But don't expect me to keep mollycoddling you and your precious girlfriend. All right?'

I've got to admit, I was enjoying all this. Mainly because they'd forgotten M. Chard. Not for long.

Tom squared up to me. 'And as for you, just wait till I get on to your Editor.'

I said, 'You'll have to wait a while. He's on a month's sabbatical in Katmandu.'

That slowed him down. It also gave Defoe the chance to talk. He was holding my right hand in both of his and squeezing a bit more than was comfortable. 'Ah, Max, you did us proud with those articles. You've just *got* to come back and see Maureen. She'd *love* to see you again. How's Frankie? Still misbehaving himself?'

You wouldn't believe it.

My voice was a shade mechanical. It gets that way when I'm trying to juggle too many things at once, one of which was that any second now Frankie might come lurching through the trees with a long tom dangling round his neck. I said, 'He's fine, Stan. You're looking fit yourself. How's Maureen?'

Tom returned to the fray. 'Just get the hell out of here, Chard.'

'Why?' That was Stan, not me.

'Because I bloody said so.'

I dropped out of the game for a couple of minutes while Defoe and Tom slugged it out. Defoe won on a technical KO.

'It's my life: it's *our* lives. If Maureen and me want to see our friends, we see them. We're effed off being your prisoners.'

Tom rolled his eyes at the church spire. I said, 'What are you so miffed about? This isn't going to appear in the paper. It happened, you can't make it unhappen.'

Clovis who had been floating round the edges said, 'Where's your cameraman?'

I've got to hand it to Clovis, he covered all the angles.

'My monkey? He's down the local pub waiting for me.'

Clovis said, 'But he's taken photographs?'

I was puzzled. 'What of? And even if he had taken

snaps, and *even* if they were in focus, and *even* if he shot Stan, the pix will never appear.'

Tom bounced back. 'I want his film.'

I said, 'Fine. If he's used one. Now, why don't we all go to the pub and sort this out sensibly?'

Stan Defoe was up for it. Tom was wavering. Clovis was moving his head from side to side. There's always one. I switched my innocent blue eyes to him. 'And have *you* seen much of Maureen lately?'

His teeth framed a warped smile. But he stopped shaking his head.

I turned back to Tom. 'I hereby promise not to ask any questions. I hereby promise not to write a word. I hereby promise to buy strong drink. How's about it?'

He was not happy, but he couldn't think of anything better. We moved off pubwards with only Defoe doing any talking. It was mostly about the magnificent series I'd penned, and the panchromatic artistry of Frankie. I wasn't really listening. All I was thinking was: is that imbecile Frankie still out there popping pix?

Sometimes I malign the lad. We found him in the otherwise deserted saloon bar of the Woolsack, caressing the mortal remains of a half pint of cooking lager. There was maybe a bubble left. Frankie had folded himself in half because the Woolsack is one of those pubs that likes to have a nicotine-stained ceiling suspended on the bonces of the boozers. There was not a camera in sight.

Frankie stared hard at Clovis and said, 'I met you in Gibraltar, right?'

Yeh. Right.

Frankie took very good care not to look at Stan. He must have sussed him. Snappers are good on faces. I was feeling expansive so I waved a twenty-quid note in the face of the barkeep and said, 'Whatever these gentlemen want.'

We waited until the drinks were in, then Defoe started.

'There's no good reason why you shouldn't come out and have a drink with me and Maureen.'

Frankie played an absolute blinder. 'Who's Maureen? Who're you?'

I flashed a quizzical look at Tom. He said, 'This is just bloody stupid. You're talking about a major police operation just to get you there.'

You can take only so much negativity. I said, 'For God's sake, Tom, the stuff I did before was just what you wanted. This time I'm not even writing. We're talking about a couple of old mates having a drink. Just like we're doing now. What's the problem?'

Clovis said, 'Where's his film?'

Frankie licked lager off his nose. 'What film?'

Tom pushed a hand at him, 'Give me your bloody camera.'

The boy deserved an Oscar. He blinked, he boggled, he gawped. 'What for?'

I said, 'This is a man called Simon. Remember Simon and Meg? And Mister Clovis thinks you've been taking pretty pix of him. Give them the camera.'

With reluctant fingers Frankie dipped in a pocket and pulled out his Sureshot. Clovis snatched it off him and thumbed it open. Inside was a half-exposed roll.

'And the rest,' Clovis ordered.

I sat back and savoured Gordons while Frankie hoked through his warren of pockets. I took the time to have a proper gander at Stan Defoe. The silvery locks were not a wig. They must have pushed his head in a bucket of peroxide. The face was fatter than I remembered. His gestures, the way he talked were faster.

Frankie unearthed nothing that I'd care to mention. Clovis was still foxy but Tom began to uncoil.

Defoe said, 'How're you fixed for Friday, lads? We could do it then.'

Tom said, 'Let's just have this drink and then we'll all clear off. It's better that way.'

'Better for who?' Defoe was back in pitbull form with his teeth locked on Tom. 'Either you set up a little get-together for us or we'll do it ourselves and you can't stop us.'

Clovis said, 'It's a needless risk. You—'

I got up and bought in another round. Behind me the battle raged, with Frankie acting like he was watching the Ladies' Final at Wimbledon. I deemed it smarter to stay out of the action. So I stood at the bar and smoked and watched it all in the mirror. Stan Defoe was no longer the self-complacent berk we'd met in Cyprus. Maybe Doc Coadwell had given him one of those personality transplants he'd bragged about.

Things went quiet. I weighed in with the drinks. Defoe was the only one to speak. 'Happy days, Max.'

'Happy days.'

Tom swung his big ponderous head at me. 'All right.

This is a one-off. You don't write anything about it and you—' a jab at Frankie '—no cameras.'

I said, 'When?'

Seven o'clock Friday. Clovis would pick us up from the office. And when it was all over, we would not breathe a word to *anyone*. He didn't actually say 'or else', but it was there all right.

So we stayed on for another round, which Stan, heroic man, insisted on buying. The conversation was commonplace stuff. I had a whole stack of questions lurking, but they could wait.

Tom sank his pint and said, 'Right. We'd better get moving.'

Stan went without protest. I followed them out to the door and got Tom off to the side. 'What's the line on this sighting of Barry Frew and Dave Stretch in Tenerife?'

He looked at me sourly. I said, 'Don't tell me that's classified too.'

Grunt. Then. 'It looks kosher. There's a witness.'

I said, 'Oh?'

'Yeh. Some bird called Reilly.'

I watched them lumber off and I shot back into the bar. Suddenly I needed a stiff drink.

Frankie said, 'In case you're wondering, the real film is in my sock.'

Chapter Seventeen

On the dodgem ride back to the office I called Susannah's loopy friend, Rebecca. Her trills told me she was glad to hear from me. She soon changed her mind.

'Becky? You know that death you've got set up for Cindy? You'd better forget it.'

'Why should I?'

I spent ten miles of M-way mayhem explaining it, starting with Ned the Nerd's imbecility and finishing off with the Assistant Commissioner on the rampage.

Becky said, 'So we just kill her as planned.'

No.

'No?'

I took a deep breath and joined it all up for her. 'Your story won't appear until Sunday – and that's only providing you manage to sneak it in.'

'So?'

So in the meantime A.C. Cordray had four whole days in which to rant and rave and apply thumbscrews.

'Just pretend you're out of town on a story.'

I ground my teeth. 'If I'm not around, Cordray will go straight to the Editor. Think about that.'

'But he doesn't know anything.'

True. But that wasn't the point.

I said, 'He damn well will know if he gets one of his lackeys to start sifting through the system. He'll also find about a dozen other Cindy Reilly stories on file. Then he'll start asking Serious Questions. And the last one of those will be, "Do I call in the police, or do you clear your desk, now, Chard?" Are you following this?'

'Shit!'

She was following all right.

'Therefore,' I said, 'Cindy has to die faster than planned, and in a common-or-garden death. No sharks. No heart-shaped locket.'

'Aaah.'

'I know, Becky. It was a great idea. Blame that moron Ned for screwing it up.'

She said some suitably unpleasant things about the Nerd and then she popped the question I was trying to keep locked in an airtight box in the darkest corner of my brain.

'Just say the Yard keep asking questions. Just say they want to look through your library files.'

'I'm working on that.' It was an arrant lie, but it made me feel better.

Becky said, 'If only there was some way of purging her out of the system . . . as if she had never existed.'

'What?'

She said it again, but I don't think I heard her. For at that very moment my genie sat up and went, 'BING!'

There was a five-second gap while I let it echo round my head. I said, 'Becky, I love you. I want to pick flowers for you, I want to write songs about you, I want to be your little puppy and fetch your slippers.'

She said, 'You could always just buy me a drink instead.'

Whatever happened to romance?

'Anyway,' she asked, 'why this sudden devotion?'

'Because, sweet-brown-eyed beauty, you have just given me an idea.'

Becky said, 'It must have been a great one. I can't wait to tell Rosie what you said.'

I didn't care. My genie could sort out a trifle like that in two seconds flat.

Angela Whipple grabbed me before I could murder Ned the Nerd. 'You've been on the skive all day. It's time you did some work.'

I was in no mood for distractions. 'I have *not* been skiving. I've been fulfilling Belker's secret mission. You'd better ask him.'

Seeing as how Belker is a good nine yards further up the greasy pole than she is, she clamped her mouth shut. I relented.

'Can we have a word in your office?'

Sure. She was getting thirsty anyway.

So we looted the minibar. Angie swung a leg my way. 'Care to tell me what's going on here? I know I'm *only* the News Editor. But sometimes it would be nice if *my* reporters told me what was happening in *my* newsroom.'

I gave her the severely watered-down version. I'd arranged a secret meet with Mo Frew to find out if she was as scarlet as she'd been daubed.

'And how are you going to find that out?'

Why couldn't she have asked me something simple like the Secret of Life?

I smiled a grim one and said, 'There are bits and pieces that don't fit in her story. I want to iron those out. Maybe she was lying. I'll know on Friday.'

'Is that when this clandestine meeting is?'

No, Angie, that's the night I wash my hair.

I said, 'Belker warned me not to tell you anything about what I was doing. So if you let it slip, I'm for the chop.'

She put her hand on mine. 'Don't worry, Max. And thanks for telling me.'

There are times Angie is more fanciable than your average News Editor. Much more. Still, I had things to do.

I chucked back my gin and said, 'I've got to make a few calls.'

'Okay. Catch you later.'

I was on my way out the door when she called, 'By the way, that Courtney woman was on for you again.'

'Cordray. What did you tell her?'

'I told her she'd get you about now.'

They just can't help themselves.

Ned the Nerd was crouched behind his console with his tongue poking out his teeth. I biffed straight up to him. 'You stupid berk. You've really gone and screwed it.'

'Hello, Max.'

He has the sort of face you find at the front end of educationally subnormal cows. Likewise with the smile.

I leaned over him and fixed him with a murderous glare. 'You went and put Cindy's name in *my* story.'

'Yeh.' The smile broadened.

The cretin was PROUD of it.

In the absence of a stiletto I stabbed him with my right index. 'Listen, you moron, the Yard want to talk to her. And there's an Ay Cee dumping on me.'

The Nerd looked foggy. 'Why?'

'Because Cindy positively identified Barry Frew and Dave Stretch. You made her a sodding witness in a major investigation.'

'Oh?'

'*Oh?* Is that *it?*'

His mouth opened and shut a few times.

I said, 'So now I have a problem. My name is on that story, which is why the Yard are giving me a bad time. All I have to do to get rid of them is to say, "It wasn't me: it was that stupid git Ned Madagan." How does that sound?'

It didn't sound too clever.

I poked him again because it looked like he'd died. 'And that is precisely what I'm going to do.'

The Nerd sat up and swallowed hard. 'You wouldn't?'

'Wanna bet? Any second now Ay Cee Cordray is going to come on screaming for me and I'll put her straight on to you.'

He was breathing in little puffy breaths. 'But what do I tell her?'

I unplugged my finger and perched myself on the edge of his desk. 'This is exactly what you say. You don't change a word of it. Okay?'

He might have nodded. It was hard to tell.

I made him get out a notebook and write it down. I put it as flat as possible, so he couldn't balls it up. Here's the script:

'Last night whilst I, Ned the Nerd, was writing up Ed O'Neill's tip-off from Malaga, a woman came on the phone.

'She gave her name as Cindy Reilly and said she was a travel consultant and she was ringing from Las Palmas airport. She told me she was about to leave Tenerife for Spain and then she was flying on to New York.'

Ned butted in, 'New York?'

'Just write. Don't speak.'

He got busy with the Biro again.

'Miss Reilly said while she was waiting for her flight she saw two men who she thought were Stretch and Frew. But they walked past ignoring her.'

I said, 'And that's the lot.'

The Nerd said, 'That's all?'

'Every single word of it. If Cordray asks any other question, you don't know.'

He repeated, 'I don't know.'

I stood up. 'And,' I said, 'if ever you mess with a story of mine again, I'm going to rip your stupid fat head off.'

It was only then I noticed that everything had gone quiet. All the other hacks were listening in.

I fired one last awful glare at the Nerd and stomped off to my corner.

Dinesh said, 'You won't rip his stupid head off.'

'I won't?'

'There's a queue. You've got to take your place like everybody else.'

I had cooled down to something just above a simmer when Petra stole up beside me and laid her dainty fingers on my shoulder.

'Max.'

I've got a lot of time for Petra. Not only is she blonde and beautiful and built entirely out of curvy bits, she has a laugh that would stampede half of Kansas and some shocking jokes to go with it. But there is one little tiny flaw in her make-up. She's the Editor's trophy secretary.

I said, 'Have I been summoned to the presence?'

She melted a smile. 'It's your lucky day.'

Oh no, it wasn't.

I asked, 'What does the buffoon want?'

'Didn't say. But he wants it now.'

Just this once I wasn't edgy. I'd already worked out why the Forrest Gump of tabloid newspapers urgently desired words with me. I also had an ace plan stuffed in my pocket, providing the Nerd didn't screw up. So I tripped along on Petra's heels, simply admiring the view.

She pitty-patted on the Editor's door. Silence. Then 'Ummh.' I entered. He was flipping through a mock-up of our much threatened new Saturday supplement, the name of which deliberately escapes me. He didn't look up.

After a while he tired of browsing through pictures

of Breakfast TV babes and he spared me a glance. 'Ah,' he said.

It is hard to believe that this man is reputedly fluent in five languages. His mother tongue is Waffle.

I prodded him along. 'You wanted to see me.'

'I did?'

No, I just invented that so I could sneak in and bask in your Wildeian wit.

The Editor thumbed his red and black braces. He thinks they make him look like a hands-on newspaper boss and no one has the heart to tell him otherwise. He ransacked the shambles of his brain.

'Ah yes. It was to tell you not to worry about it.'

I said slowly, 'Worry about what?'

By way of answer he started raking through the general debris on his desk. I filled in the time admiring the walls and their framed famous front pages of our paper, all created before we were landed with the present fool.

He found what he was looking for, a scrappy sheet of paper with crabby writing on it. Another delay until he found his bifocals which were hiked up on his fuzzy little head. He read haltingly from the sheet.

'Miss Cordray . . . yes, Scotland Yard . . . she wanted you to . . . she wanted information on your story.' An accusing glint my way. 'But apparently you were too busy to help the police.'

Cheeky old trout.

I said, 'I told her I would start working on it as soon as I could.'

'Yes. Well, there's no need. I have given one of her officers access to our system.'

The room tilted, turned dark and started playing the theme tune from *Jaws*.

My voice went wavery. 'You have?'

'Yes. So there's no need for you to worry. I thought you'd like to know so that you are not duplicating her officer's efforts.'

I swallowed. 'Is he here now?'

'No. Tomorrow morning. I have arranged for him to see the Systems Manager.'

Tomorrow! By this time tomorrow Cindy Reilly and I would be exposed as rogues and charlatans. No probs for her, but I was really in it.

Someone more sensible than I might have flung himself on his knees, grabbed the Editor by the braces and wept bitter tears of remorse into his stripy shirt.

I lied. 'Good. This saves me a lot of bother.'

The dolt said, 'Yes, well I didn't want you er . . .'

Right now I didn't have time to hang around waiting for him to find words.

I said, 'Thanks. I'd better be getting back. I have a story to finish.'

The specs were up on top of his head again. He'd already forgotten me.

I got out and stumped straight back to Ned the Nerd. He flinched at my coming. I said, 'You get rid of this bloody woman *now*. And make it good.'

I grabbed up his phone and began banging in the number.

'Scotland Yard.'

'May I speak to Ay Cee Cordray please?'

I pushed the phone at Ned. He took it from me with shaky fingers. I sat on the edge of his desk like the Angel of Sudden and Nasty Retribution. Nothing happened. Gradually a tiny glow illumined his bovine eyes. He said, 'There's no answer. She must have gone for the day.'

I refused to give up. For the next ten minutes I made the Nerd ring just about any other Yard department I could think of. Nope. Not a single soul worth talking to. The big clock in the centre of the newsroom ticked away the seconds to my doom. I gave it another shot, this time calling Mac and getting him to reel off all the names of Cordray's yes men. Back on to the Yard. Each and every one of them had done a runner.

Ned put down the phone. He was trying not to let his relief show. I don't think he ever realized how close he came to a horrible death at that precise moment. But I could enjoy myself later. I had some dirty business to attend to first.

I raced towards the lifts and jammed my thumb on the arrow pointing up. God knows how long I held it there. Every lift in the building was rocketing south, filled with the Gadarene swine from accounts, admin, advertising and so forth. At length a mightily reluctant lift hove up. The doors looked at me blankly for a moment and then remembered why they were here. They slid open. The lift was empty of human life. I shot inside and thumped the button for the eighth floor. Hiss, clunk, thump, groan. The lift began to rise at about the speed of grass growing. I raised my hollow eyes to the yellow display panel and willed the bugger upwards. And what was I going to do when I finally got to eight? Please, oh *please*. Ding. There went three. I leaned my forehead against the cool brushed aluminium walls. 'Re-laaax,' they whispered, 'there's no hurry.' Ding. That was four. And even if the man I wanted was up there, would he go for it? In my entire career I must have said fewer than fifty words to him, yet here I was counting on him to save my life. Ding. Five. Honestly, people have scaled the North Face of the Eiger a damn sight nippier.

By the time eight arrived I was hanging off the ceiling. I took a deep, deep breath and set off down the hushed corridors. It is always cool and quiet up here, but for the eternal background susurration of five zillion megawatts of air conditioning. Sterile signs pointed the way. I already knew it. And then I was there, outside a glassy-eyed door with SYSTEMS MANAGEMENT stencilled across it. I knocked once and went in. Two bods I've never seen before glanced up from their labours and froze. I think my eyes were not their usual sparkling selves.

I spoke in a voice from beyond the grave. 'Cyrille?'

One jabbed a finger to the west. Maybe they weren't allowed to talk.

I trekked over to a glass-walled office the size of a phone box. Cyrille was squashed up inside. He has the face of a man who has seen many things in his time and hasn't let them bother him. He looked upon my jaggedy eyes and frayed limbs and said nothing.

I said through the door, 'Cyrille. Have you got time to pop out for a swiftie?'

Never in the history of newspapers has a hack gone up to the Systems Manager and offered to shower drink on him. Cyrille merely looked at his watch, did a spot of thinking and then shrugged an okay. I almost hugged him. But I hadn't even got close to the hairy bit yet.

I watched as he forced his way into his jacket, patted his pockets, picked up his ID tag and generally drove me round the twist. Next he rolled across to his underlings and had a dekko at what they were up to. Speed and Cyrille are strangers. If he kept on like this it would be chucking-out time before we reached the pub. But somehow he managed to tear himself away from his playthings. Back up the dead and endless corridors.

The slowest lift in the world hadn't budged an inch. I wasn't surprised. We got in and I tapped R for reception. On the long, long journey down I said just two words to Cyrille. 'Stone okay?'

He was more economical. 'Dusty's.'

Dusty's it was. A pub I usually do my best to stay out of. The drink is fine, but the place is chocked up with flashing, shrieking, chittering fruit machines and dumb games consoles. Personally I'd have thought that if you spent your eight working hours pressing buttons you'd want to give your fingers a break. Apparently not.

It was too early for the regulars and there was plenty of space to moor Cyrille against the dark end of the bar. 'What do you fancy?'

'Pint of Guinness.'

I should have guessed.

The barman was one of those sorts who believe it takes twenty minutes to pour a Guinness properly. The ice in my gin had turned to neat water before he got the head right.

Now. How was I going to handle this?

Cyrille raised his glass in wordless salutation. I said, 'Cheers.'

So far he had not shown the faintest interest in what this was all about. I held back and studied him. Cyrille, as previously described, is a big bloke with acres of padding. He hails from Martinique or someplace where the sun shines bright. He might be fifty, he might be thirty-five. He's got round, soft eyes. He doesn't look the type to turn down a plea for help.

I said, 'I need a favour.'

Cyrille slupped Guinness.

I said, 'A *big* favour.'

No answer. For one fearful moment I contemplated what might happen if I blurted out the story and he promptly scurried back to the Editor. No. Cyrille was not a natural-born scurrier.

I began with the tale of a heavy night oh so long ago when out of devilment and drink we had conceived of a woman called Cindy Reilly. I got as far as her first appearance before his Guinness ran out. Back to the barman.

Off I went again. Once I thought I saw Cyrille's shoulders shaking. I forged on with the saga. I spared nothing. The superboob pic, the mad axeman, even that foul libel when some berk wrote her off as the mother of *two* Arsenal fans.

Cyrille spoke. 'Why're you telling me?'

I sucked up gin. This was it. I said, 'Because tomorrow morning a police officer is going to come in and sniff through your computer system.'

Sometimes for a very good reason, sometimes for

no reason at all, some black people don't go a bundle on the police. I suppose I was hoping Cyrille was among the many.

He said, 'Do you know a Dee Cee Durrant?'

I didn't. 'Why?'

Cyrille said, 'He's my son.'

Arrrgh.

I forced myself back on track. 'One reporter recently stuck Cindy's name into a crime story. Now the police want to find out what we have on her. When they see what's been written . . .'

Cyrille turned on a big slow smile. 'You're in bad trouble.'

Correction. I'm dead.

I said, 'So, I was wondering . . .'

'If I would wipe the files?'

'Yes.'

Cyrille gazed lovingly at his Guinness. I waited. He lifted the glass, held it up, rocked it gently and sipped. Still I waited.

He said, 'The police have already seen the story. It can't be wiped.'

I spoke in a rush. 'No. That story has to stay in. It's all the rest of them I'm worried about.'

He wasn't. He said, 'How're you going to explain *that* story?'

'The reporter who cocked it up, he's got an explanation.'

Cyrille turned ponderously to face me. 'My wife always says you shouldn't believe what you read in the papers.'

Smart wife. I said, 'Can it be done?'

'Oh, sure.'

Let's rephrase that. '*Would* you do it?'

He acted like he hadn't heard me.

I said, 'Naturally, whatever it costs . . .'

He said, 'Don't even think about it.'

I shut up and stared him in the eyes. He must be a terrific poker player.

He said, 'Destroying computer records is wrong. Taking bribes is a crime. I'm no criminal.'

'So the answer's no?'

He let me dangle there. When he finally opened up I didn't interrupt. 'You bought me a couple of drinks, that's all. I'm going to forget everything you said about this Cindy Reilly. And I won't remember you asking me to interfere with the system.'

He polished off his Guinness and stood up. I think my head slumped on my chest. He walked behind me, stopped and placed a giant hand on my shoulder.

'Nobody knows, okay?'

I said, 'Nobody knows what?'

A rumbly chuckle from him. 'Nobody knows I've got to go back and wipe a few files.'

Berr-dinng! My heart went bungee jumping. I swivelled round. There were probably pitiful tears of gratitude welling up in the blue. Cyrille never saw them. He was already ambling off to purge Cindy.

I ordered myself a tall one and stayed on. I didn't need a mirror to tell me I had a big cheesy grin chasing itself all over my face. And I let it have its moment. But there was a part of me still on the case. So far I'd given Ned the Nerd a way out, *and* I'd wiped the slate clean on Cindy. Now all I had to do was kill her in a quietish sort of way.

I'd already worked out her demise, even where it would happen. That's why I made the Nerd say she was flying ex-Tenerife, via Spain to New York.

New York has many things going for it. The best from my present point of view is that it's not one place, but two. There's the great teeming city of that name. And there's also the state, sprawling from Lake Ontario to the Long Island Sound, from the St Lawrence down to Poughkeepsie. I simply had to top Cindy in New York without specifying city or state and no one, not even Irene Tightknickers Cordray, would know where to begin looking. I started writing it in my head. It didn't take long.

This sounds hard to credit, but when I'd done, I felt a sudden shaft of sadness. I'd given Cindy a reasonably painless death. One minute she was bubbling and bouncing. The next she was brown bread. She didn't even have time to rip out a scream. Inwardly I was glad Cindy hadn't been mangled to bits by some hooligan shark. The girl had been good to us and she deserved a merciful exit. Even so, I was still a touch downcast. It was like losing a mate. Never again would she frisk and frolic through our pages, bringing joy into the sad lives of her many and assorted pals. This was it. End of story.

Nearly. But not quite. I still had the painful duty of slipping her death notice into the paper. Hold it a moment. Why me? I'd just gone and killed her, *and* wiped her history. Someone else could be the undertaker. But who? Ned the Nerd. That's who.

I yelled for more gin and worked out the details. First the timing. Friday night was best. For on Fridays, Vic, the colossus of our Night Desk, is even more comatose than usual. From time to time he snores himself awake and takes a gander at the latest PA headlines. But he never once dips into the incoming Foreigns. A couple of toadying minor hacks are happy to do that for him. Sooo . . . how could I get Cindy's tragic death to pop up on screen?

A single word leapt to mind. *Dhopa.* That's a rude Russian word for bum, they tell me. It is also the secret sign-on of Norbert, our geographically-challenged Foreign Editor. So, let's say the Nerd switches on his screen and taps in *Dhopa.* He's now in Norbert's system. He goes straight to the Foreign Reporters file, creates a story and types out the Cindy paragraph with a phoney by-line. Vic slumbers on.

'Oi,' says the Nerd, 'here's a home story that's just come up on Foreign.'

Vic rubs the grot out of his eyes, doesn't even read it, but says, 'Bang it across,' and goes back to sleep. For he trusts Ned's news judgement.

Half a split second later, up it bobs in front of the late copy sifter on Back Bench. He slaps a two-word header on top and scoots it down the line. Next morning, deep amid the page five fillers, there's the death notice. No more Cindy. No more awkward questions from the Old Bill. Much relief for me.

Yet I still felt a pang. Maybe all first-time killers feel the same. Or maybe they have the good sense to stay out of crappy boozers afterwards. A couple of yards off to my right some dork was whacking the buttons on a whizz-bang game called *Homicide Highway*, an entertainment which appears to be based entirely on the way Frankie drives.

I drank up and got out.

Chapter Eighteen

Even by the time morning rolled around I was still way below my sunniest. Though I suppose there's nothing new there. I had stopped fretting and pining over Cindy, but another woman was causing me grief. Mo Frew. Tonight was the grand reunion and I was nowhere near ready for it.

I had the day off. The usual pattern of such days is I laze in my pit until gone nine. Then I shake off the duvet, scramble together a breakfast of sorts and plod through the morning's crop of newsprint. And when all that's out of the way, I mooch down to the Cat's Whiskers and whistle up a pint of Fosters.

But here I was at 15 minutes short of eight, rubbing my stubble and moping. I booted aimlessly around the flat without even the radio on to keep me company. I spared a stray thought for Cindy. At least I could get that settled right now.

I unhooked the wall phone and rang Ned the Nerd. It cheered me to think that he'd finished his shift only five short hours ago and would still be snoozing away, teddy bear in hand.

'Hullo. Ned Madagan,' he said in a fuggy voice.

I didn't waste time on chit-chat. I just laid out his

day's agenda in a couple of tight sentences. At 8.30 he was to call A.C. Cordray and tell her how Cindy came to wind up in his story. If Cordray was still putting on her jackboots, he was to ring every half hour until he'd got her. And then this evening he was to smuggle the death yarn into the paper.

He still sounded not quite together so I made him repeat every instruction until he had it set in concrete.

'And don't go back to sleep,' I warned by way of a farewell.

Back to Mo. I keep all my old notebooks for at least a year. That way if some lout accuses me of misquoting him I have the evidence to fend off the lawyers. I went to the stack and dug out the notes for the trial and for the Cyprus stuff. I thumbed through page after squiggly page. I wasn't even reading. Time for a tea break.

That didn't help. I started on the mechanical things instead. I picked out a charcoal two-piece from the gallery and rifled through my shirts until I unearthed a soft blue cotton button-down. Now the tie. That took longer. I finally settled on one with chrome yellow lizards cartwheeling on a dusty blue field. It's Rosie's favourite. But seeing as how she made the thing, she's probably biased. Then charcoal socks and black loafers. I draped all the clothes on the bed and wandered back to the living room for my brain had begun to buzz. I had another go at the notes. There was nothing there. Not a single line I could put my finger on, and yet I knew, I knew for certain I had something.

Just before noon I slouched down to the pub and treated myself to a pint. Dermott behind the bar was hopping to dish out his regular crazed soccer punditry. After a while it dawned on him he didn't have my 100 per cent attention and off he roamed to bore some other punter rigid.

I sat with the lager before me, hardly drinking, but thinking at max torque. Piece by tiny piece things came to me. A throwaway remark. A name used when it shouldn't have been. A direct lie here, an evasion there. I put it all together. It added up to one hell of a lot. I raised my glass and silently said, 'Thank you, Cindy.'

For she had pointed the way.

By half six I was in the Stone, having a sharpener with Frankie. He was a chippy little monkey, mainly because a night's free drinking was on the cards. I had to talk him down.

'Take a camera, Frankie.'

He said, 'Clovis said—'

'Forget Clovis. There might just be a terrific snap in this tonight.'

'He'll frisk me.'

I said, 'No one, absolutely *no* one, would dare to look in your socks. Stick the little Olympus in there. You mightn't need it, but . . .'

'It's already down my right sock.'

As I say, sometimes I forget Frankie is a proper monkey.

I bought another pint and while he slurped on it I told him the honest-to-God truth about my plans for the night. By the time I was through his chin was hanging half a yard lower than normal.

I warned, 'But remember, play it dead straight.'

Frankie got his chin back in working order and we went to meet our driver for the evening. He was waiting out there on the double yellows in front of the office.

I said, 'And how are you this fine and balmy eve?'

Clovis said, 'No cameras, no notebooks.'

Frankie and I looked at each other, shocked at the very suggestion. And off we rolled. It was a long and tedious trek, made all the more boring by Clovis refusing to answer any of my questions, least of all the polite inquiry as to how Mo's bum was feeling these days.

We eddied through the traffic, out onto Marylebone and then towards the foothills of north London. We left Hampstead way behind and ventured further and deeper into the empty acres of suburbia. And still we journeyed on.

A sudden fear assailed me. 'You're driving us back afterwards?'

'You'll get transport.'

We were clear of London and steaming towards Watford when Clovis took a right off the main drag into a road which called itself Cherrywood Gardens. Hard at the top of that he branched left, then left again. Fifty yards on he stopped outside a blocky detached house and switched off the engine. We all piled out.

There was a creaky gate with one of those archway things over it. Then a short path through a modest garden, ending up at a solid wooden door. There was a spyhole dead centre and a burglar alarm the size of a tea chest glued up on the wall.

Clovis pushed the bell. I whiled away the seconds betting on who would open it. Kay was the hot favourite, with Stan some distance behind and Mo way back of the field. Wrong.

'Hello, *hello!*' gushed Ralph Coadwell. 'Do come in.'

Well, yes Ralph, that was the whole idea.

We made it two steps into the hall before the rest of the party mobbed us. Stan Defoe whacked me on the shoulders with both paws. Mo, glass in hand was right there with him.

'Max! Oh, it's lovely you could make it. And *Frankie!*' There was that south-western tinge in her voice again.

Kay, standing with her back against the living-room door, was silent and chill. She looked different out of her bikini. I tossed her a bright-eyed 'Hi!' No response.

Stan pummelled us into the room amid a firestorm of unanswerable questions. 'What have you been doing with yourselves?', 'How's life treating you?', and so on. Mo skipped straight on to the important question: 'What do you want to drink?'

She fussed over a bus queue of bottles on the dresser and I took in the room. It didn't suit her. Green walls spaced with bobbly gold bracket lamps. Black-beamed fireplace with a phoney fire flickering below and a gilt mirror strung above. Fat lumpy green sofas. Lashings of dark wood. Patterned plates lined up on the dresser like ducks in a shooting gallery. A low table cluttered with glasses and bowls of things. Over in the corner a TV buried in a wooden cabinet. It was all pretty grim. No photographs. Nothing to tell you this was a real room.

I settled in a chair out on its own because that's the way I felt. Stan pulled up another right alongside. 'I bet you can't wait to hear what we've been up to since Cyprus?' He bit the ends of his words, northern fashion.

Actually I could. Mo clinked in with a fully loaded tumbler. Gin all right, but Bombay gin. I gave her a candid going over. They'd done things to her hair. It was cut in little choppy slices, some bits blonde, the others a blondish-grey. It looked good on her, but I still missed the glorious rusty red bell. She was in lilac or mauve or one of those colours. Her mouth seemed different somehow, fuller and not as wide.

I told the truth. 'You're looking terrific, Maureen.'

She smiled from way deep down in her eyes. 'And you too, Max. Cheers.'

Clink clunk went the glasses. Clovis wasn't drinking and Kay was out of vision behind me. Coadwell, sprawled, legs apart, on the sofa to my left, hoisted a tankard of beer. Stan was topping up on brandy. He had arrayed himself in a golf sweater and slacks. He was also wearing white trainers. But then Stan never was much of a fashion icon.

Mo pushed Coadwell further along the settee so that now she was close on my left. She put her hand on mine and said, 'We thought about you a lot. I suppose you've been much too busy to think about us.'

I said, 'You're never off my mind.'

Coadwell gave a ripe laugh. He was easy to amuse.

Maureen waved a hand at the room. 'Hideous, isn't

it? But it's just temporary. They're moving us again, you know, after what happened.'

'Tullamy?'

A slight shadow. 'Yes. The police were worried that Ernie might have said something.'

I said, 'What happened to your accent?'

Coadwell lowered his beer. 'A brief course in elocution, Max.'

'So how's she going to speak next time – Geordie?'

Mo said, 'You'll know. I'll call you.'

A dry cough stage right. That was Clovis saying 'bollocks' without having to waste words.

Mo gave him a tight sharp glance. When she turned back to me again her eyes were warm. She said, 'Thanks to Ralph, we've already made it through one change. We can do it again.'

I was looking into my glass. 'Only one change?'

It went past her. She squeezed my hand. 'But what about *you*? I'm sure you've been doing all sorts of interesting stories since us.'

I said, 'Just one.'

She had very light eyebrows. The left one arched a fraction higher than its sister. 'Is that all? And what was that about?'

I took my time lighting a Bensons. 'It was about a girl called Cindy Reilly.'

The name meant nothing. It didn't mean much to me any more, except for this moment.

I said, 'The interesting thing about Cindy is she doesn't exist.'

Ralph Coadwell sat up and tuned in. Maureen

etched a frown and Stan just swished his brandy around.

I said, 'We invented Cindy for a joke and we wrote stories about her and those stories got in the papers.'

Mo chimed out a laugh, a real one. 'You *didn't*!'

'We did. We got her name in maybe twenty times.'

Maureen said, 'You're making this up. You couldn't get away with it.'

Stan asked, 'Why did you want to make somebody up anyway?'

This time I turned to him. 'For money.'

On the sofa Coadwell was chortling away to himself. 'I think that's *won*derful. You actually pretended she was a real person.'

I rattled the ice cubes and fired a smile at him. 'That's right, Doc. Just the way you do.'

Coadwell served up a clever-clogs smirk. 'Ah, but I do it only with a real person.'

I jumped on it. 'Real? Who's real here? Is Coadwell your true name? Is Kay honestly called Kay? Is anybody in the world actually called Clovis? What about Meg and Simon or Maureen and Stan or whatever they call themselves now?'

He threw out a palm. 'When I say real, I mean in terms of real existence: someone who is actually living. Not like your . . .'

'Cindy,' I filled in.

Maureen uncurled herself from the sofa. 'Time for a top-up?'

I held out my glass. I glanced across at Clovis. He was rolling one of those miserable little cigarettes but he was locked onto me. From somewhere over my shoulder Mo asked, 'How was the last drink? Enough tonic?'

'Yeh. The tonic was fine, but the gin was a shade thin.'

That Coadwell bloke mustn't get out much, for off he went chuckling again.

Mo returned. 'Taste that.'

I looked up into her eyes. In Cyprus there had always been a distance between us, except for that last moment of that last night. It was close to that now.

I said, 'Perfect.'

We were both talking about something else. Maureen sat down again. She'd also treated herself to a refill. She said, 'And this woman, Cindy, what is she supposed to do?'

I looked at my watch. 'In about five minutes from now she'll be dead.'

Stan flashed his specs my way. 'What?'

I said, 'I have arranged to kill her. Just like somebody arranged to kill Tullamy. And for the same reason.'

Mo had her glass half up to her lips. She lowered it slowly to the table. 'Ernie was an old and dear friend. What happened to him – well, we don't make jokes about it.'

I walked away from it. I said, 'In our paper we have a whole raft of people with twenty-syllable titles and fat wallets. Every morning they come in and tear the paper to shreds. That headline's wrong. Why have we not got the Fergie picture? Where's the Cabinet revolt story?'

Nobody else was talking so I just kept going. 'They

read the paper cover to cover. Time after time they've read about Cindy, yet not one of them ever spotted it because they were not looking for her.'

Coadwell intoned, 'Perhaps that is because she would be below the parapet of their perceptions.'

I ignored him. 'But one day Cindy got herself in trouble with the police. Somebody twenty floors up in the Yard started asking embarrassing questions. So I had to kill her.'

Stan bumped me with his elbow. 'You lads get yourselves into some right scrapes, don't you?'

Mo hushed him. 'What did you mean, Max? You said she died for the same reason as Ernie.'

I leaned forward and I was so close I could smell her perfume. 'Cindy knew too much.'

Maureen's grey gaze held me. She said softly, 'And what *did* she know?'

'She knew where Dave Stretch and your husband, Barry Frew, were hiding.'

Stan sat up so fast he slopped brandy over the sides. 'How did she know that?'

I killed my cigarette and reached for another. I was in that sort of mood. I said, 'You're not listening. Cindy was an invention. The only words she could say were the words we put in her pretend mouth.'

Stan again: 'So—'

'So some stupid reporter was stupid enough to quote her identifying Stretch and Frew at Las Palmas airport.'

Kay drifted into range, cupping her boobs under one arm, a glass in her spare hand. She had a mean little smile toying at the corners. 'And the police want to interview her?'

I said, 'That's it, Kay. But I wouldn't want any of this getting back, because if it does I might tell some senior Plod other things. Are you on message here?'

Clovis said, 'She understands.'

Kay's smile wobbled for a second and then faded away.

Stan pushed his jaw out. 'But this story about Stretch and Frew at the airport, was that all made up too?'

I shook my head. Not quite.

I switched everything back on to Mo. 'There are things you don't know. After I interviewed you, when I got back to London, I was shanghaied one night by three blokes.'

'Shanghaied?'

'All right, then. Kidnapped. Abducted. Grabbed by the shirt and banged into a car. They thumped me when I refused to tell them where you were.'

She crooked her hand back over mine.

I said, 'Then not long afterwards two different blokes offered me five grand for info on you.'

Clovis said, 'She doesn't need to know this.'

There were too many oars in the water. I stared levelly at him. One of us had to shut up.

Mo said, 'What did you tell them?'

I was still fixed on Clovis. He knew I was up to something and he wanted to know what. He gave the faintest of nods. I said, 'The point is what they told me. And both of them said you took a slice of the Zeller Maine money.'

Her hand gripped mine. It was one way of saying no.

I said, 'So I started chasing the money. And the first place I went was to a mate of mine who knows about this sort of game. He told me a couple of things which didn't make any sense at the time. Like I never knew you need a really bent brief to help you launder money.'

Maureen's voice was tight. 'If you're suggesting that Ernie was in some way involved . . .'

'I'm not. I'm saying he was in *every* way involved. Which is why he's dead.'

Stan waggled his glass. 'Hold on a minute, I just refuse to believe that.'

I ignored Defoe. I said, 'The other thing this mate of mine told me was the perfect way to launder money was to pretend it never existed.'

Stan wrinkled up his nose. 'What?'

My glass had dried up again. Kay spotted it first. She reached over my shoulder and took it from me. I waited for its return before I got back on stream.

I said, 'Let's play a just-suppose game. Just suppose your gang robs a safe-deposit bank. And just suppose you lift ten million quid. But then one of you turns Queen's Evidence and says the real haul was only five million.'

I let it hang there a moment, then I said, 'In under a minute you've laundered the other five million. The police don't even know it exists. Now that is really clever.'

Maureen's voice came right off the Siberian permafrost. 'Are you implying that I lied?'

I looked at her sadly. 'Mo, this is a just-suppose game.'

She said, 'I don't like it.'

You weren't meant to.

I went on as if she hadn't spoken. 'All the time I was chasing the money. And then Cindy got herself in trouble.'

Stan was listening. 'Cindy?'

Yes, Stan, the wonderful buxom, blonde Cindy Reilly. R.I.P.

I said, 'That's when I finally learned how to play the game.'

Ralph Coadwell blinked at me. He was reaching for it but he was a long way off.

I said, 'You don't launder the money; you launder the person. Cindy, as of now, has ceased to exist. I've even wiped her files, her photograph, her entire being.'

Maureen sat back on the sofa as if to put space between us.

I still had a bit to go. I said, 'Laundering people is just the same as washing money. There's a million ways to do it. Cindy might have vanished off the face of the earth. Or she might have her own Ralph Coadwell to turn her into somebody different.'

Nobody said anything.

I prodded Defoe. 'What do you think, Stan?'

His eyes were placid and amiable. 'About what?'

'About changing your identity.'

He was still smiling. 'Don't ask me. Ask Ralph.'

I said, 'If I were you, I would switch from gardening to accountancy.'

'What, me?' chesty laugh.

'Yeh. For a start you know sod all about gardening. That shrub outside your drum in Cyprus is not "a yellow thing", as you so eloquently put it; it's a bougainvillaea. Any gardener could tell you that.'

Stan said, 'I know. I knew that all along.'

I said, 'No you didn't. A pro gardener would reel off the Latin name first, the common or garden name next, and then tell you how to take cuttings. The smart ones can sometimes tell you the colour. That comes last.'

He squared his shoulder. 'I just didn't mention. I suppose I thought you knew what it was.'

I said, 'Okay, a simple question for our resident gardener. My girlfriend has a tippihendren in a tub in her yard. It's started to wilt. Why?'

Stan said, 'It needs a lot of watering. They're delicate, they are.'

I said, 'Any pretend gardener could come up with that. But what a genuine professional gardener couldn't do is convert one hundred and eighty Cypriot pounds into two hundred and twenty-four pounds sterling in a blink, or centigrade into fahrenheit just as fast. You got too flash there.'

He waggled his head. 'Ask Maureen. I just have this thing with figures.'

Clovis was sitting on the lip of the sofa, watching.

I said, 'And then there was the late Ernest Tullamy who told me he had never met Barry Frew, yet three seconds later he said he had handled the purchase of Maureen and Barry's house.'

Stan was still shaking his head. 'I don't know anything about that.'

Maureen was utterly quiet and locked into herself. Frankie's hand was hovering over his right sock.

I said, 'And if we go back a bit further, there was that moment in Cyprus when I said you were lucky you weren't involved in Zeller Maine, and you said, quote, "Too right. Look what's happened to those three guys who got topped." Remember that one?'

Stan was dug deep in his chair. 'So?'

I looked across at Mo. Her eyes were wide and wondering.

I said, 'Yet Ralph here said the first thing he does with people like you is he isolates them. No TV, no newspapers, no incoming calls. So how come you knew of the murders in Coldharbour Lane? Maureen didn't.'

No answer. I said, 'But if you *ordered* the hit by phone from Cyprus, you would know all about it. Unless you can think of some other way you got to hear of the killings.'

This time he was slower. 'I don't know. Somebody must have let something slip.'

'Yeh, there have been a lot of slips. Like both you and Mo playing hanky-panky with your minders. For a long while I couldn't square that. It might have made sense if you were a jaded old married couple looking for fresh kicks.'

Maureen opened her mouth but didn't say anything.

I said, 'But that wasn't the story you were putting about, was it, Stan? Your line was you'd stuck your life on a limb just so as you could be with your darlin' Mo. Yet here you were having a right old time of it with Kay. And Mo was up to likewise with Clovis. So why were you both still playing this lovey-dovey lark? What did you have in common? It took me a while to work out what held you together – the Zeller Maine millions.'

I was throwing everything I had yet he was sitting tight as a mollusc. I pulled my seat back so I could get him in full profile. Without even glancing round I held out my glass to Kay. She took it.

I said, 'Two different mobs said they were after you. The first lot knew you were both in Cyprus. Did somebody let something slip there too, Stan?'

He shrugged, but he refused to look at me.

I said, 'The second lot were only interested in Maureen, because she narked up their mates. But the first ones laid it on thick that they wanted to top you too. And just so I'd remember that, they beat it into me. The whole idea was to fool me into thinking Stan Defoe existed. There is no Stan Defoe. There's only Barry Frew.

'And Barry Frew pulled a brilliant stunt. He conned us into laundering him into Stan Defoe. He even got eighty grand for it.'

I was trying to read his eyes but he had his head down. I said, 'And that stuff about Frew being on the run in Spain was a no-no. *Stretch* was spotted, all right. But if you read the stories carefully they all say the bloke with him was *believed* to be Frew. The only positive sighting of Frew came from Cindy Reilly, and we all know about her.'

He still wasn't talking. I had just one shot left.

I spoke slowly and carefully. 'So you arranged for the killings of Belly Sloman and his mates. They could connect you. You arranged for Tullamy to be murdered.

Same reason. And Maureen knew nothing about the killings. I bet she doesn't even know you had Tullamy tortured first, just to make it looked like someone was trying to get to her.'

Out of the corner of my eye I saw her knuckles grip the cushion.

But Stan was stone still. I waited. Kay came up with the gin. I lit a cigarette. I drew on it and blew smoke up towards the ceiling. I watched it eddy and curl around the lampshade. I did not look at her. I said softly, 'Tell me, Stan, how long before you kill Maureen too?'

For a frozen moment nothing happened and then Mo was off the sofa and flaying at him. 'You bastard! You murdered Ernie.'

Clovis and Kay were sharp out of the blocks. But not as fast as Frankie. He popped his first shot before they even grabbed her. And he kept on popping as Clovis pinned Barry Frew.

Me? I just sat and smoked. I'd done enough damage for one night.

Some time later Maureen and Barry Frew were carted off in different police cars. Clovis laid on a local uniform to drive us back. Kay kept well out of the frame but Clovis walked with us back up the crooked path to the gate.

We got to the car without talking. Then as I opened the door he said, 'That plant your girlfriend has. What was it again?'

I said, 'A tippihendren.'

'Never heard of it.'

I said, 'Did you ever see *The Birds*, you know, the Hitchcock movie?'

He had.

I said, 'Well, Tippi Hendren was the sexy blonde.'

Rosie woke me with a kiss and a cuppa. No milk. She wedged the late London edition in my one visible hand. I sat up faster than I should.

My name was spelt out in big letters over the page-one story on the nicking of Barry and Mo. I ignored that and zipped straight through to page five. There at the bottom of the shorts was a single blob paragraph:

* *THE body of a tourist killed in a New York car crash was identified last night as that of 34-year-old London travel consultant Cindy Reilly.*

I raised my cup and drank to her memory. In neat Darjeeling.

She deserved something better. A lot better.